PRINCESS AUROLLA GOES ABROAD

Sarah Jane Arcwyk

First Printing: Sept 2018

CONTENTS

A WELCOMING IN THE COURTYARD

Thelwyn stood in the warm spring sunshine, clutching Princess Aurolla's colourful cloak. She was a fair distance from where the Princess was slightly anxiously awaiting the first guests that she had the sole duty of welcoming to the castle. Thelwyn wasn't concerned about the Princess's safety because of all of the precautions that had been made; she was at a distance for a couple of reasons. One, she was the third maid and it would have been somewhat unusual for her to be in the welcoming party and two, she couldn't get too near the visitor's horses without frightening them. Thelwyn didn't want the visitors or anyone in the castle to remark that horses tended to shy away from her and begin to wonder why that was. So she was standing a distance away from the Princess with Annilee by her side; the young girl was holding both Bettinka's and Dezadillia's bright cloaks. The three women were unsure of what the weather would bring so they had made sure to have at hand their best cloaks. Fortunately, the weather was calm and sunny so cloaks weren't being worn as they awaited the arrival of the group. Thelwyn could see that Lady Ashmont was standing at the ready, slightly in front of where the Princess and her two maids were awaiting the arrival and she thought back to the meeting that had occurred the day after the assassination attempt on the pretty Princess.

Princess Aurolla, her three maids, Gwendaleir and Annilee had arrived at the meeting room before the King and Queen did; there was only Hargold, Lady Windlington and Lagalaise waiting for them. The Sorceress and Hargold were talking in low tones to one another while Lagalaise was attending to bringing some wine over to her mother. They glanced up, smiled and waved a welcome to the group; Hargold gestured for them to find seats while they waited for the appearance of the rest of the people who would be attending. Lagalaise came over to inquire if they all wanted some wine and they did so Annilee hastened to help the small blonde girl. When they all had their wine in their hands, Lady Windlington asked Thelwyn if she still wanted to maintain her disguise or if she would rather go back to her original appearance. The Sorceress felt that there was no need to maintain the fiction that Thelwyn was still laid up in bed due to her supposed injuries. Thelwyn thought about it for a moment and then decided that the Sorceress was probably right in the matter. Besides if they determined during the meeting that she should remain disguised, Lagalaise could easily re-establish it for her. She stated that to the older woman who nodded in agreement and Lagalaise dropped the spell that she'd put on Thelwyn. Princess Aurolla and the other two maids just nodded in acknowledgement as Thewlyn's true features reappeared but Annilee had never seen Thelwyn in her true form before and was quite startled by the new appearance. She gaped at Thelwyn for a while, trying to come to terms with Thelwyn's plainer features and the fact that she was still the same physical size; she'd assumed that the disguise spell had made the fierce fighter appear smaller and less impressive so that she could take advantage of her opponent. Annilee had assumed that the true Thelwyn was larger, given her strength but she soon decided that she could accept Thelwyn as she was and chose not to remark on anything to the wolf girl. Thelwyn could see her thoughts flit across her face but decided not to comment on anything if Annilee didn't bother to ask about it.

The Queen arrived to the meeting and left her bodyguards outside of the meeting chamber and then the King also arrived; he brought Lady Ashmont into the meeting with him but left the rest of his bodyguards outside as well. Everyone was soon seated and wine was poured for all of them. Thelwyn could see Annilee looking around the room with some consternation. Annilee realized that she was the only serving person in the room with all of these dignitaries and she was feeling totally out of place; she started to glance around the room to find a place to hide herself away from the noble's sight so she wouldn't offend them by her base appearance. While Thelwyn was determining if she should go over to support the young girl, Bettinka beckoned the small girl over and sat her on her knee so that she could put comforting arms around her. Annilee realized that the older woman was indicating to her that she wasn't just included as an oversight and had a purpose in this meeting so she settled her nerves and relaxed a bit. Thelwyn gave the first maid a nod of respect and approval for how she had handled the matter and Bettinka returned the gesture which gave Thelwyn a warm feeling.

The Queen cleared her throat slightly to indicate that she wished to speak and the low hubbub of noise ceased as the group paid attention. She addressed Hargold saying "I think that we are all assembled now. Perhaps you can tell us what you have found out about the assassination attempt on the Princess's life." Hargold nodded and began to lay out the information that he'd found out; it wasn't very much more than the group of assassins truly did appear to be from Hellsford but he wasn't convinced that the royal family in that duchy was behind the attempt. He thought that the group might have been misled or even enchanted in order to make the attempt. The Queen questioned his reasoning and he stated that if those people had been behind the attempt, why have their soldiers wear such recognizable armour. Neither the King or Queen were convinced by his statements, feeling that he was being too devious in his thinking but were willing to entertain that he might just be correct. Thelwyn had heard Hargold's arguments previously and had been convinced that he probably was correct in the matter; Lady Ashmont had reserved judgement about the argument but had not been able to put forward any conflicting evidence. Hargold explained how the group had managed to infiltrate the kingdom but not how they had been allowed to enter the castle. He did not think that the group of followers of Herasius that Thelwyn had been tracking at the time of the assassination attempt were connected with the incident but his people were still investigating all possible leads. The Queen asked Thelwyn her feelings on the connection and Thelwyn agreed that the soldiers did not seem to be linked to the group she'd been tracking. Thugular could come up with no one who acknowledged seeing anyone from the two groups being in contact with each other and the assassins had only been in the kingdom for less than three days before they struck. The Queen expressed her dissatisfaction with the information but she acknowledged that it was hard to find out the total truth in any matter; especially when all of the assassins had been killed before they could be questioned.

The Queen frowned at Hargold and then said "I want the three of you to continue to follow up on this. We need to know who was responsible for this attempt so that we can make sure that it never happens again." She turned and addressed Thelwyn. "I want you to find out all you can about the Herasius followers and what they are up to. Capture one of them if you must and deliver them to the questioners so that we can get some information about their deeds." Thelwyn frowned slightly in disagreement. She felt that it would tip off their interest in the group if they made it too obvious that they were investigating them too hard. She decided that she would only follow those instructions if it looked like she could create another reason for the person she grabbed going missing. She was careful not to let the Queen know her true feelings in the matter because she did understand the reason behind the Queen wanting action to be done. She knew the Queen was quite upset about the threat to her daughter and was willing to do anything to ensure that it ended. The Queen looked carefully at Thelwyn, recognizing a hint of reluctance and she sighed; she did not begrudge Thelwyn her thoughts and feelings and knew that the young girl would do as much as she could to protect Aurolla. But the Queen felt that she had to do something that might upset Thelwyn in order to guarantee her daughter's safety.

The Queen carefully looked Thelwyn in the eyes and stated softly "I know that you were the one totally responsible for saving Aurolla from the assassins." Thelwyn grimaced and shook her head in disagreement. Bettinka and Annilee had been instrumental in giving her time to foil the attempt and even Dezadillia had shown her willingness to lay down her life to save the Princess. The Queen ignored Thelwyn's facial expressions and continued on "However, because of the role we have asked you to play, we cannot let the matter be known and have had to let the credit for the foiling of the attempt go the the young man playing the bodyguard that was killed. I feel that leaves Aurolla vulnerable to further plotting of attempts and I am not happy about that fact. Therefore I would like to ask Lady Ashmont to act as Aurolla's bodyguard."

Thelwyn felt a spark of shock; was she being dismissed, then? Princess Aurolla gasped in dismay and faced her mother with a furious look on her face. "Mother, you can't do that to Thelwyn. She should be rewarded for what she did for me, not replaced. She is the reason that I am still alive and I refuse to accept what you are proposing."

The Queen held up her hands in a placating gesture, trying to calm her outraged daughter even as she continued to keep contact with Thelwyn's eyes. "I am not replacing Thelwyn. She will continue to be your bodyguard and spymaster for you. But she has no public standing as such and therefore you look more vulnerable than you actually are. Lady Ashmont has a public reputation as a vicious swordswoman and that might discourage people from tangling with her. I want Lady Ashmont to be your public bodyguard and Thelwyn to be your hidden one." She shifted her gaze over to her daughter and said lovingly "That way I can be quite sure that they will be successful in protecting you."

Princess Aurolla looked at her mother with a puzzled and slightly rebellious set to her face; she understood what her mother was saying but couldn't help but feel that it was disloyal to Thelwyn. She was about to say so when Thelwyn interrupted her by saying quietly "It is an excellent idea, Princess." She glanced over to see that Thelwyn had a calm and thoughtful demeanor so she swallowed her protest. Thelwyn faced the Queen and asked "Do I take orders from Lady Ashmont then as far as protecting the Princess?"

Lady Ashmont stepped up and stated quietly but firmly "No, Thelwyn. I only agreed to this proposal if you were the one who was in charge. I can't be seen taking orders from you in public but we will have plenty of opportunity for you to tell me what you want away from the eyes of others. I trust that you will believe enough in my abilities to allow me to take charge if there is a serious crisis and I don't have the time to consult with you." She kept her gaze steady on the younger woman and Thelwyn felt a rush of warmth as she recognized how much confidence the blonde swordswoman was putting in her.

She paused slightly to think about the matter and then said calmly to Lady Ashmont "I will need your experience and knowledge in this matter so can we just agree that we will both co-lead the effort?" The blonde woman was about to protest the offer but then paused to think about it. She recognized that Thelwyn was trying to offer what would be best for the Princess and she thought that the two of them could work difficulties out between the two of them. She gave Thelwyn a bright smile and a nod of affirmation. The Princess gaped slightly in surprise at the two of them while the Queen beamed at their cooperation. The Queen was surprised but very happy that they were going to work together to ensure her daughter's safety. Thelwyn then turned and gave the Queen a slightly cool look before stating "But I didn't foil the assassination by myself. There were others who were instrumental in delaying the attackers so that I had time to act. Some of them lost their lives in the process and they all deserve to be acknowledged for their efforts."

The Queen nodded calmly and said "We had always planned on acknowledging their efforts but I still maintain that you are the main reason for Aurolla's survival." She smiled a little wistfully and continued "Would you at least accept that for my sake?" Thelwyn flushed and then nodded somewhat curtly as the Queen smiled at her acceptance of the compliment. Then the Queen looked over to Lady Windlington to see if she had the gifts ready and the Sorceress motioned towards a small bundle on the table before her. Lagalaise took the bundle over to the Queen and she called out "Annilee, please step forward." The young girl looked at her in shock and refused to move; Bettinka pushed her gently but firmly from behind so that she moved towards the Queen. The Queen took two small necklaces from the bundle and held them forth towards the young girl who was still looking nervous and ready to bolt. The Queen held out a gold necklace that had the crest of the kingdom as its pendant. "This gold necklace is a symbol of our appreciation of your efforts and willingness to lay down your own life in order to protect the Princess. We also offer you a position for your future as a servant to a lady in waiting once you are finished with helping Thelwyn with her future tasks. There will be a monetary reward for you and your family and I have arranged for your family to be brought to the castle so that we can find them suitable positions that will guarantee their futures. I recognize that you can't wear the gold necklace in public while you are helping Thelwyn so I have had a cruder copper one made so that you will always have a reminder of our gratitude." The Queen held out both necklaces but Annilee was too shocked and shy to retrieve them. Bettinka came forward and accepted them for Annilee and then led the stunned girl back to the chair she had been sitting in. Annilee just looked around in a daze as she thought about what the Queen had just promised her. It was more than she'd ever dreamed about in her wildest dreams.

The Queen called Bettinka forward and stated "For your brave actions in attempting to fight off that assassin we also have a gold necklace for you, will award your family some more land for them to control, will give you choice of a small estate for your personal use and will allow you to immediately assume the title of Lady." She smiled as Bettinka graciously accepted the gifts and curtsied. Then she summoned Dezadillia and proclaimed "Although you didn't engage the assassins, Princess Aurolla has stated that you were ready to do so. Therefore we have a gold necklace for you and your family will also be granted more land." The second maid nodded her understanding and also curtsied before moving back to her chair. The Queen then relayed to them that the guards families would be taken care of and the young man who played the bodyguard role, who was being recorded as the hero in Thelwyn's stead, would be given an estate for his family who would now be made lesser nobility. Everyone nodded in understanding as to why this was happening; namely so that Thelwyn could continue to remain hidden as the Princess's unknown bodyguard. They understood that it wasn't really fair but it was the best practical thing to be done.

The Queen called Thelwyn forward and proclaimed softly "Thelwyn, we all understand that we can't call attention to your heroic actions because that would expose what you actually are. However, we who are in the know, can give you your due. You will be addressed as Lady Thelwyn and we are creating a large estate for you." Thelwyn bristled at this and was about to protest but the Queen held up a hand silencing her. "No, I have thought this through and will not be dissuaded. Lady Windlington has agreed to hold your estate in her own name for you and has thoughts on a young man and his family to work as your stewards for the land while you are tied up with matters of the court." The Queen looked steadily at the small girl and stated firmly "You will accept these honours. However they will have to be kept secret amongst this group until your duty is finished. When we do this ceremony in public, I will only be giving you a gold necklace for your actions during the assassination attempt. The excuse that we will put forward as to why Annilee is acknowledged as acting as an impediment while you supposedly did nothing is that you were still bedridden by your injuries. Is that acceptable with you?"

Thelwyn stated "I am fine with that excuse but I refuse to be called Lady Thelwyn, even just amongst our group. If you are accustomed to doing that, you might slip in public and have to explain why and I don't want that to happen. Besides, I am not a Lady."

The Queen looked at her for a moment and then decided to give in. "Fine, we will not address you as Lady due to your wishes but you will have the title in our minds." Then she smiled and said "I have one more gift to give. Gwendaleir, would you come forward." The Pixie had hung back as Thelwyn had been called forth but now flitted up beside the wolf girl. She looked at the Queen with curiosity. She hadn't really been involved in foiling the assassination and wasn't expecting to be rewarded. The Queen said softly "You bravely delivered a message to Hargold, summoning him to Thelwyn's aid. Even though she didn't end up needing his help, it was a wonderful thing that you did and we wish to recognize it. No jeweler was confident that they could make a necklace small enough for you to wear comfortably so instead we had them make this small gold shield for you to carry on ceremonious occasions." She held the object out to the Pixie and Thelwyn could tell that it was really just a reshaped ring that the Pixie could use as a shield. Gwendaleir was delighted to accept it even though it was very heavy for her to carry. Thelwyn was grateful that the Queen had decided to honour the Pixie and nodded her thanks to the woman; the Queen smiled her acceptance and nodded back. Both of them recognized that they were grateful and respectful of the other for different reasons and it cheered both of them. The Queen lowered her voice, beckoning Thelwyn a little closer so they could talk privately and stated "Thank you for accepting my reasons for appointing Lady Ashmont as Aurolla's public bodyguard. I hope you don't find her too much trouble to deal with." Thelwyn just gave her a curt nod.

THE TENSE WELCOME

So now Thelwyn was awaiting the arrival of the guests, feeling a trifle warm in the sunshine but otherwise quite content with happenings. She was thinking about what had been going on since the assassination attempt. Hargold, Lady Ashmont and she had been able to dissuade the Queen from trying to question one of Herasius's priestesses to determine what they knew about the conspiracy against her daughter. The conspiracy had warned Malispyre to cease his activities on their part and had seemingly disappeared from view; that seemed to suggest that they were spooked by the assassination attempt and hadn't been involved in it. The three spymasters understood that since they hadn't been able to identify the ringleaders before the group went to ground, that they were unlikely to obtain too much usable information from a random target. Hargold insisted that not all of the followers of the goddess were involved and the other two agreed with him. The minor nobles that had been implicated all found reasons to return to their estates and it would have done the royal family a lot of political damage to root them out. The Queen had thrown things when they'd told her of their opinions since she was so upset; she felt that targeting her daughter for assassination crossed the line and wanted to teach people not to do that. She was somewhat willing to be bloodthirsty to prove her point but the King was instrumental in tamping down that inclination. Nothing much had been going on in the kingdom since Hargold had taken advantage of the assassination attempt on the Princess to destroy some operations that he'd already known about.

Thelwyn let her mind come back to the happenings around her. She could see the horses beginning to enter the castle gate and the stable boys moving up to take them from their owners. She scanned the group carefully but didn't see anything to arouse her suspicions. This group was a young woman just slightly younger than the Princess and her even younger brother as well as their retainers. They were from Barcless where their father owned an estate on the southernmost edge of that kingdom. They had sent a messenger asking for a meeting with the Princess and it had taken them nearly a month to make the journey down once it had been granted. Nothing had been in the message to indicate any reason for the request but no one had seen any harm in letting it happen. There had never been any bad blood between the two kingdoms nor had there been any hostilities because they were too far apart for any disputes to have occurred. Thelwyn knew that there were some kingdoms that relished having all others at odds with each other but Barcless didn't seem to fall in that category. They were more interested in trading and the Queen hoped that they saw something of interest in Darkcloud that could be traded with them. Thelwyn hummed softly to herself as she watched the girl and her brother dismount and approach the Princess with a somewhat older woman. Gwendaleir settled on her shoulder, tired from holding her gold shield; the Pixie couldn't carry it for too long due to its weight but Thelwyn knew better than to suggest that she leave it in the room because the Pixie was immensely proud of what it represented.

Thelwyn was casually watching as the Princess and her maids exchanged greetings with the group. The boy was now exploring the courtyard with his eyes as his older sister continued to discuss matters with the Princess. Thelwyn could see his eyes wandering and sympathized with him, thinking that she was often a little bored at ceremonies while she knew that the Princess and her maids truly enjoyed the pomp and circumstance of the occasion. She could see his eyes flicker over her in a dismissive manner but was shocked when he quickly whipped his head back to look at her more intently. She could feel her inner wolf rise up in a challenge and fought to control her emotions. Why was he creating this disturbance in her, she wondered; he didn't feel like an enemy but her feelings were cautioning her to treat him with some trepidation. Gwendaleir, having rested, took wing again and Thelwyn was shocked to see the boy's eyes follow the Pixie up from her shoulder. The boy could see Pixies, she thought. That meant that he had to have some magical powers. Nothing had been said about these newcomers being magical and Thelwyn began to wonder if that was going to be an issue. Since most visitors carried magical items with them and Gwendaleir had proven to be somewhat unreliable about being able to determine the power and intent of them, she'd stopped the Pixie from alerting her to magic. Gwendaleir had alerted far too often for her to be useful in the castle where there was a lot of magic. It wasn't her fault since she'd grown up in the forest where there was less magic around her. Thelwyn contemplated whether or not she should approach the group to be ready if there was any trouble or not and also made a decision that the Sorceress should be made aware of these people in case she was needed. Thelwyn hissed to Gwendaleir "Go get Lady Windlington and tell her I need her in the courtyard at once. There is something about these newcomers that she may need to deal with." The Pixie flew down and deposited her shield in Thelwyn's open hand and sped off. Thelwyn moved toward the group as the boy rushed up and whispered into his sister's ear.

Princess Aurolla became startled about the activity around her and started to step back from the guests as Lady Ashmont moved to guard her, alerted by the actions of Thelwyn and the boy. The Princess had thought things were going quite well and was concerned about what was happening. She darted her eyes around the courtyard looking to see if there were any other potential dangers lurking. Bettinka and Dezadillia moved in front of their mistress to block her from any dangers and the castle guard started to move cautiously out to contain any problems. The young visitor, Chesmyse, heard what her brother had to say, glanced intently in Thelwyn's direction for a moment and then moved into a more defensive stance. Her small party closed in on her as the Princess's people reacted. Thelwyn arrived as the two groups stood there watching one another, both ready to respond to any provocation.

"Princess" Chesmyse called out in a somewhat shaken voice as she indicated Thelwyn. "Are you aware that this young woman projects magical abilities? My brother tells me that he gets the image of a snarling wolf from her and that she appeared to have a Pixie near her. He says that she radiates violence." She paused briefly before asking "Is any of this a surprise to you?"

Thelwyn threw a glance to the Princess and then to Lady Ashmont as she stated "I've sent Gwendaleir for Lady Windlington and suggest that we wait until she arrives before trying to resolve this matter. She will be able to help us determine what threat these people might be. The boy obviously has some magical abilities and we don't know his intentions or capabilities." She glared menacingly at the newcomers who continued to watch her carefully.

The Princess nodded at Thelwyn's information as she thought matters through; it was a shock that these circumstances had occurred but she'd matured somewhat since the assassination attempt and realized that they shouldn't be discussing such matters in front of this many people. She stepped slightly closer to the visitors but remained behind her protectors and stated in a low voice "I am aware that there are some issues here that require a good deal of discussion but we don't want to do that in public, do we? A person was sent for that should allow us to resolve most of this and I suggest that we wait for her to arrive. Perhaps it would be best for our two groups to move back from one another until she is here. Do you feel comfortable with that?"

Chesmyse pondered that suggestion as she looked around the courtyard. It didn't appear that they had too much of a choice. Their party was too small to fight their way out of the area even though she, her brother and their advisor could all use magic. The fact that Thelwyn had magical abilities and that there had been at least one Pixie could mean that their magical advantage would be very slight and the Princess definitely had the advantage in regards to armed guards. She also didn't like how competent and relaxed this blonde swordswoman standing in front of the Princess appeared to be. She'd heard the rumours about Lady Ashmont and was now inclined to believe them. She bit at her lip in thought and then said quietly "I think that would be a very good idea for the moment, Princess. But I would like to reassure you that we came here with peaceful intentions and mean you no harm. I would like to believe that you feel the same way about us." She quietly gave a command and her group began to move backwards towards the courtyard entrance but not too near it to suggest an attempt to rush through it. The Princess directed her people to move backwards away from their aggressive position.

Lady Windlington entered the courtyard a few minutes later in quite a bustle; Lagalaise followed her mother and Gwendaleir buzzed around the two of them. The Sorceress noted the tension between the two groups as she hurried up to where the Princess was waiting. She glanced over at Thelwyn before addressing the Princess. "Gwendaleir says that Thelwyn needed my help here. What is going on?"

Lagalaise had been examining the visitors and now she hissed slightly "Magic users." The Sorceress frowned and scrutinized the group herself.

Thelwyn grimaced and asked "Magic users, how many? The boy obviously is one because he noticed me and Gwendaleir; that is why I sent for you, Sorceress." She cast her eyes over the visitors to see if she could determine which of them might have magical powers and asked "Which other ones can use magic, how powerful are they and are they dangerous to the Princess?"

Lady Windlington scrunched up her face slightly as she contemplated the question before looking over at her more powerful daughter for her opinion on the matter. Lagalaise shrugged her shoulders slightly and said "I get the feeling that their magic is currently keyed for more of a defensive role than offensive right now. There are three of them that I detect and their power isn't inconsequential but it's not extremely strong." She was of the belief that she could match the three of them by herself but didn't want to state it, being somewhat modest.

Her mother nodded in agreement and said "Yes. The girl, her brother and one of the advisors all have magic but I agree with Lagalaise that it isn't too strong and seems more defensive at the moment. I should go over and talk with them to determine the best plan to proceed." She looked the Princess in the eyes and said softly "I think we need to involve your parents in this right now, don't you?"

Princess Aurolla nodded as she thought about matters; she recognized the sense in what the Sorceress was saying and that she was out of her depth. "Yes, I agree. The girl's name is Chesmyse and her brother is Charlymi. We didn't get too much farther than that before matters developed as they are." She gave Lady Windlington a slight smile but her eyes remained quite worried.

Lady Windlington called over a messenger and gave him instructions to alert Hargold, the King and the Queen to what was happening in the courtyard before she approached the visitors on her own. She wasn't worried for her own wellbeing but was cautious about sparking an incident by provoking the visitors. She noted that the three magic users had linked their hands and stood in a triangle with the girl she assumed as Chesmyse at the point facing her as she approached. She could see the combined power that the three of them projected and was intrigued; she'd never thought of using the combined power of more than one person before. She'd always thought it would be dangerous and unwieldy but these three appeared to be able to handle it quite well. She stopped a respectful distance away and addressed the girl. "Princess Aurolla informs me that your name is Chesmyse. Mine is Lady Windlington. I have asked for the King and Queen to be informed of what is happening here. I think that we should all sit down and discuss matters before anything untoward happens." She saw them examining her and that they recognized that she was a Sorceress. She nodded and stated "Yes, I am also a magic user and so is my daughter. We weren't expecting you to have magic or else we would have been more prepared to greet you." She looked them over coolly and continued "I don't think that we need to have any dispute here. You obviously came here because of a reason and I think that we should talk about it before any decisions are made. The alternative as I see it is for you to just leave and not return. We will make no move to prevent you from doing that if that is what you wish." She let a small smile grace her face as she said "It is your choice. I don't think either of us wants to be a threat to the other."

Chesmyse frowned and asked "What is that girl? We recognize the power that you and your daughter have as similar to ours but my brother says that girl projects what appears as a wolf and radiates tremendous violence about her. And why have you allied yourselves to Pixies?" She looked quite affronted by the matter.

"Thelwyn is definitely something special that you probably haven't come across before, I'd wager. But we should address what that is in a less public forum" she ventured with a smile that turned into a frown. "What is wrong with having Pixies?"

"They're evil little beings that are causing us much trouble" Chesmyse hissed.

The Sorceress nodded thoughtfully and asked "Is that the reason that you asked to see us?"

Chesmyse looked around carefully and stated "They are part of the reason that we asked to meet but there is also more. As you said, we probably shouldn't be discussing it in the open here where there are so many ears."

Lady Windlington could see that Hargold had made his way out into the courtyard and had joined the Princess's party so she assumed that the King and Queen were probably just about ready to meet with these visitors. She said "I will have to discuss matters with some of our people to ensure that the royal family will meet with you but I think that they will. We will have to meet in one of the rooms in the castle and I think that we should try to keep the meeting as small as we can. Perhaps just the three of you and two of your most trusted guards can meet with us. I don't think that the royal family will agree to meet without some of their bodyguards present in the room but I will see what I can do." She once more gave them a slightly reassuring smile as she turned to leave.

Charlymi asked "But the wolf girl and the Pixie will be present?"

The Sorceress turned back and studied him for a brief moment before stating "Yes, I believe that the royal family will insist on Thelwyn being present and her Pixie, Gwendaleir, goes where she goes." She paused to let that information sink in before continuing "As I said previously, we will raise no objections or take any offense if you decide to leave at once." She wanted to stress the fact that they were the ones here to ask for help and that her kingdom had no obligations to provide that help.

Charlymi asked "We couldn't just meet with you and your daughter, Lady? That is really who we came to ask help from." His sister and the advisor turned on him and hissed for him to be quiet; that was not how matters between kingdoms was done. Besides, Chesmyse knew that wasn't exactly true. Charlymi turned a bright shade of red under their rebukes as the Sorceress frowned at his breach of protocol.

Then she decided to grant him the benefit of the doubt since he was young and said softly "I will choose to overlook that suggestion. Are you staying or leaving?" Chesmyse confirmed that they would be happy to meet with the royal family so the Sorceress went over to where the Princess and her entourage were waiting. She asked Hargold "Are the King and Queen ready?" She trusted that Lady Ashmont, the Princess and Thelwyn had filled him in on what had happened.

"Yes" Hargold replied as he kept his eyes fixed on the visitors. "But are you sure that this is a good idea? Can you and Lagalaise contain them if they have malicious intentions? I don't want to put the royal family at risk."

"I don't get that impression from them and I think that we have more magical power than they do. Where are Queen Blossom and the other Pixies?" the Sorceress asked after sparing a glance at her daughter to confirm she held a similar opinion.

"I believe that they are playing tag in the lower rooms of the castle" Hargold replied. "Why?"

"That should keep them occupied for a while and keep them out of our hair. Our visitors appear to have issues with Pixies and I don't want to complicate matters any more than they already are." She looked over at Thelwyn and stated "They also aren't very happy about the vibes that they are getting from you but I told them that they would have to tolerate your presence or leave if they wished." The group shared a look and then Lady Windlington asked "Should we go have this meeting then?"

AN UNEASY MEETING

When the group consisting only of Princess Aurolla, Thelwyn, Lady Windlington, Lagalaise, Gwendaleir, Lady Ashmont and Hargold entered the meeting room, the King and Queen were already seated and waiting, they quickly found chairs for themselves and awaited the visitors. The small visiting group of the three magic users and their two guards was ushered in and clustered near the doorway of the room. The Queen took charge and said "This is not a formal audience so please find yourselves some seats. We would like this meeting to be as cordial as possible." She paused while they also took their seats.

Chesmyse immediately stood up and proclaimed "Forgive me your majesty, I know that you said this isn't a formal audience but I would like to make a formal greeting and apology before we start, if I may." The Queen frowned slightly but nodded her head; it was plain that she felt they could have dispensed with that formality but if the visitors felt inclined to do it, she would suffer through it. "I bring you greetings and well wishes from my parents, Lord Archled and Lady Sylvagia of the kingdom of Barcless. My name is Chesmyse and this is my brother Charlymi. We come to you with a plea for help that our own King is unable to provide to us." She paused for a moment to let her request sink in and the Queen once more frowned at her. She sensed that the Queen was feeling reluctant to involve her own kingdom in the affairs of others and was about to say so, therefore she quickly continued "We regret the incident that happened in the courtyard just now and wish to apologize for it. My brother noticed the wolf girl." She indicated Thelwyn with the wave of her hand. "And it disturbed him. He was also distressed by the presence of her Pixie because Pixies have been one of the main problems that we have been having plague us. He brought these matters to our attention and we reacted poorly to it." She had cast her eyes down as she said her apology but now raised them up to meet the Queen's own. "We know of magic and came here seeking stronger help in that matter but the difference that the wolf girl has to our own magic startled and frightened us into doing something quite foolish. And so I would like to extend my apologies to you, your husband and your daughter. We would appreciate it if you could grant us some time to discuss our plight and whether or not you will help us." She sat back down while keeping her eyes on the Queen.

The Queen looked at the group intently as she thought through her response. She wasn't happy with how the group had approached them or the fact that they were looking for aid from a foreign King and Queen but she recognized that they must be under a great deal of distress to act as they were. She was not so hard hearted to dismiss them without hearing what they had to say and they were from a trading nation that she would like to have further dealings with. She glanced over to the King to assess his feelings and saw him nodding agreement with her decision. She pursed her lips and stated "As I said earlier, this is not a formal audience and therefore I do not have to follow diplomatic protocol. You had requested a visit with the Princess and it was granted to you. My husband and I only became involved in this matter because of the disturbance that occurred." She looked over at Thelwyn before continuing "The person that you refer to as wolf girl has a name and it is Thelwyn. She is a treasured member of my daughter's retinue and has tremendous respect by the King and I. We would appreciate it if you were to address her properly." She glared hard enough that Chesmyse blanched and slumped somewhat. The Queen noted her reaction and softened her approach a bit. "But we recognize that she would have been a surprise to your group, much as the fact that you are magic users came as a surprise to us. And if you have been having problems with Pixies, I can see where Gwendaleir would also cause you some concern." She sat back slightly and twitched her mouth. "Suffice it to say that the greeting in the courtyard did not go as planned. I guess that we should listen to your problems. I will tell you ahead of time that I am loathe to involve our kingdom in the affairs of another. If you have come seeking our aid in something we think your King should handle, then we will direct you do do just that." She settled herself in her chair a little more comfortably.

"That's just the problem" Chesmyse stated with a small wail. "Our King has tried to help us but is unable to resolve the problem. He knows that we are approaching you and we have his support." She reached back and her advisor handed her a scroll. "I have a letter from him asking for your assistance in this matter. He would like to keep his inability to help us as private as we can make it which is why we chose to approach you as informally as we did." The Queen was once again disconcerted with the developments; she couldn't see what they could do to help anyone from a kingdom so far away from them. But, she reflected, there was only one way to find out and that was to hear them out.

She sighed slightly and stated "Then I guess you should state what your problem is and what assistance you would like from us. I will look at your King's letter later. For now I will trust that it says what you claim it does."

"For over a year now my parent's land has been plagued by a number of magical beings that have disrupted normal life there. One of the worst things to occur has been an infestation by a horde of Pixies that torment people and steal anything they can. They have destroyed food crops and supplies and chased off livestock. They are not just simply doing this to feed themselves but appear to be trying to create such havoc so as to drive us off of our land. We have tried to deal with them ourselves but seem to be met with an opposing magic powerful enough to overcome ours. Every time we move the Pixies away, they are brought back and any magical traps for them are overcome in hours. We think that someone is directing them and we are looking for help to find and overcome that person. We have been led to believe that your kingdom has a Sorceress powerful enough to help us." She paused and indicated Lady Windlington. "As I mentioned, the King sent us some help but none of them were powerful enough to make a difference. He gave his approval for us to seek your aid only if we could keep the matter confidential enough that he wouldn't appear weak. He is currently tied up with a border dispute with our northern neighbour and is facing certain political factions about that quarrel. We have no proof that this neighbour is involved in our problems but it does seem too convenient that they began shortly after the clash started and are at the farthest edge of our kingdom from where the battles have been happening. It looks to us like an attempt to divert our strength away from the issue of the upper border."

The Queen frowned as she thought the matter over; she agreed that it seemed too coincidental that the problems would have started at the same time as the other clash but it could have happened that way. She would need to see further confirmation of the connection before she would be comfortable in linking them. She pondered the fact that she would be committing resources to a kingdom that they had little contact with and become involved in a disagreement that really wasn't her concern. She determined that she was unwilling to do too much even if the cause may seem just to her. The world was too unfair to everyone for her to try to right every wrong. But, she thought, these people came here avoiding a formal audience to put for their request so they might have concocted a plan that would allow her to help them without her appearing to be too connected with it. She decided that it would be okay to hear them out without accepting or declining any position on the matter until she was forced to do so. "I sympathize with your plight but am at a loss as to how we may help you. Do you have a strategy that you would like to propose?" She eyed Chesmyse with some interest but much speculation.

"Well, your majesty" Chesmyse ventured while she glanced around the room. "We would like for the Princess to visit our estate so that she can learn more about her northern neighbours. Of course if she and her advisors might happen to solve our problems for us, it would simply be a happy coincidence." Chesmyse ended her proposal by focusing her eyes on those of the Queen, having realized that she would be the one deciding the matter even though the lands were held in her husband's name. She attempted to look guileless but failed. Hargold snorted at the scheme but didn't make any further comment at the time. The Queen smiled a tight little grin at his outburst but gave the matter some thought. Such a scheme would allow her to disavow involvement and would also serve to permit Aurolla to exert some authority which might benefit her mightily. She considered what sort of danger she might be putting her daughter in but realized that Aurolla wasn't necessarily safe just being in the castle considering the assassination attempt that had already occurred. Plus Hargold had made limited success in ferreting out the religious group that might be a threat to her. Chesmyse had paused as she noticed the Queen pondering the proposal; she wanted to give the older woman time to warm up to the arrangement without trying to push too hard. Her family had spent a lot of time in attempting to prepare a proposal that the Queen could agree to and this had been their best idea. "It wouldn't have to be too big a party but of course your daughter would need protection, chaperoning and supervision." Chesmyse could see out of the corner of her eye that the Princess grimaced fiercely at the mention of supervision and was dismayed by her choice of words. She needed the Princess's goodwill for this to work and was unhappy that she'd upset the other girl. So she said hurriedly "That would allow you to provide her with as big a party as she would need to deal with our problem and allow you to include some specialized people that might be a help to her." She looked at the Queen wistfully and stated "We are entirely at your disposal in this matter."

The Queen grumbled somewhat about the imposition the request would be putting on her but started to believe that it might just put her in a position to agree with the plan. She looked firmly at Chesmyse and stated "You ask an awful lot of someone whom you've had no prior relationship with. What do we get besides the goodwill of your people if we do agree to your proposal?" She could see her husband fidget a bit as she asked this but waved her hand at him to keep him from interfering. She knew that he would be inclined to help the visitors mostly out of the goodness of his heart and she loved that about him but that was the reason that she did most of the negotiating for the kingdom rather than him. The King subsided at her signal and the Queen was confident that the visitors didn't pick up on his actions. She looked over at her daughter to see how she was reacting and was pleased to see that the Princess was displaying neither acceptance nor disapproval of the plan; she was just watching the proceedings in front of her.

Chesmyse nodded slightly and stated "Our King would express his gratitude to your assistance in any way he reasonably could do so. We currently have a great deal of trade routes to the areas surrounding us so there is much trade that could be funneled to your kingdom. He would certainly not be averse to allowing your merchants specialized access to our markets and would encourage our merchants to make the trip down to your kingdom in order to expand your choices in products that you may not be currently receiving."

The Queen pondered the offer for a moment and then recognized that she didn't know enough about Barcless to determine the largess of the agreement. "I don't know enough about your kingdom to assess the value of what you offer at the moment. Can you give me a quick outline on how much trade we may be talking about?"

Chesmyse pursed her lips slightly and said "Our experts have looked closely at what your kingdom has been producing and trading. Without attempting to slight your efforts, they are of the opinion that our kingdom benefits from trade to the extent of about forty or fifty times what your kingdom does. We have a large river that runs through our kingdom and that gives us an advantageous route for trade. They are also of the opinion that this is the main impetuous for the clash with our northern neighbour." The Queen raised her eyebrows at the estimate and looked over to Hargold to determine his opinion on the approximation; he shrugged to show her his lack of knowledge on the matter. She calculated that she would have to look into the matter before making the agreement but if it was true, she was being offered something of substance. That definitely sweetened the deal in her mind she thought with some glee.

"Well, we will give this matter some thought and then let you know of our decision. Meanwhile we should get you settled in some rooms so that you can rest up from your journey. I am sure that we all have some matters to discuss amongst ourselves before we meet again. I urge you to consider whether you will have problems working with Thelwyn and Gwendaleir because I am sure that they will be a major part of my daughter's retinue." She then called for a servant to lead them to their rooms and to get assistance in moving in their baggage. She waited for the visitors to vacate the room before addressing the people remaining. "Okay, we have much to discuss. I want to hear from everyone about any concerns that they might have and whether or not they feel that this venture would be worthwhile. I think it might be best if we start with you, husband, what are your thoughts?" She looked expectantly at the King.

He'd expected this and had been thinking about what to say; he knew that his wife was extremely interested in the carrot that had been dangled in front of them, namely the increase in trade possibilities. But he was not in favour of involving the kingdom in a far off conflict or in having their daughter risk herself for what he thought of as what could amount to a piddling sum of money. "I sympathize with their plight and would like to help them but I think we would be foolish to accept this proposal. It seems like a lot of risk for very little reward. Sure some of our merchants might benefit but what else would it do for us. I am unhappy that their King thought so little of their proposal to send only these children here to negotiate with us." He decided that he'd said enough and stopped there giving his wife a small smile. He thought that he'd set the example for the rest of the group to give their true feelings on the matter and for them to vote against it. He knew that the Queen would reluctantly agree with turning the proposal down if the majority of this group chose against it. The Queen nodded thoughtfully at him before she turned to their daughter.

"What are your feelings in the matter, Aurolla? After all, you are the one who is going to be at the most risk here. If you don't want to do this, let us know and we will immediately cease our discussion here. Your father obviously doesn't want you in any danger and I don't want to have to put you into too much danger either. But the assassination attempt on you earlier shows that no matter what we do, you are going to have to face threats to your well-being." She paused for a moment to let her daughter come to terms with that before continuing "Do you feel that this is a worthwhile cause for you to involve yourself in?"

Aurolla looked steadily at her mother, knowing that the Queen was interested in what was being offered to them; she recognized that the proposal for trade was a much bigger reward for the kingdom than her father seemed to think. She flicked a glance over at the king before stating "I think that these people truly need our help. When I look at our resources here, I believe that we have the ability to assist them. I recognize that their land is quite a ways from us and that we will not be able to have as close a relationship as those of our neighbouring kingdoms but I think a successful conclusion to this problem would profit us by showing our neighbours that not only do we care about other kingdoms, we can also protect ourselves quite well. The added bonus here is that if I am not able to do anything too substantial for these people, then I am just a young girl who was out of her league anyways." She saw her mother frown at those words and gave her a small, tight smile; she knew that her mother was politically wise enough to have seen that aspect on her own but wanted the Queen to recognize that she was wise enough to know that as well. She didn't look over at her father but continued "I also think that the offer of trade will do much more than just enrich a few merchants. If what they say is true about their own kingdom, I think that many of our people will benefit from the increased trade with them. And, as you say, I may not be in anymore danger travelling there than I am by staying home." The Queen grimaced and gave her daughter an intense look; that was not what she had said at all. As she eyed their daughter, she could tell that Aurolla was excited by the prospect of travel and adventure but was trying to suppress it as much as she could. She gave the Princess a small nod and then turned towards Hargold.

"What are your thoughts on the matter?"

Hargold coughed slightly and also flicked a glance towards the King before speaking. "This could be a very dangerous mission for the Princess to undertake. We don't know enough about what sort of magical powers have been employed or could be employed in the conflict. The Princess would definitely be in more danger on this trip than she would be if she stayed home." He paused for everyone to absorb that before saying "But it is a very good opportunity for the Princess to show what our kingdom can do. As she has said, even if she wasn't completely successful, it would still do our standing with other kingdoms a great boost. I also agree with the Princess that the trade being offered would benefit many of our people. I am aware that a great deal of the expensive spices that we import come through the Kingdom of Barcless as well as some other items that are fairly rare here. I think that the reward outweighs the risk. Especially if we make sure that the Princess is well equipped and protected on her venture." He sat back to show that he was done speaking for the moment.

The Queen turned to the Sorceress and enquired simply "Lady Windlington?"

Lady Windlington glanced around the room and said firmly "I won't try to deal with the economic aspects of this proposal because a number of you have better knowledge and understanding of that than I do. However, I will mention that a number of herbalist remedies come through Barcless and they are quite dear at the moment. An increase in amount and reduction of price would provide relief to a good deal of our people." She pursed her lips as she contemplated what she wanted to say. "I feel that if we ignore the magic that appears to be behind this assault, we will rue our actions in the future. If these visitors are correct and their northern neighbour is attempting to take them over with the help of what appears to be malevolent magic then they will certainly gain strength by taking over the rich trade routes that Barcless has and will be able to increase their attacks on more kingdoms. We might have the opportunity to nip a weed in the bud, so to speak."

"Do you think that you can contain the opponent's magic?" the Queen asked a little worriedly.

"I won't know until I get the chance to look at it and I would need to be there for that to happen. The three magic users that we met with have some power and apparently can combine their efforts, which is something I haven't come across before, but I think that I am stronger than them combined and Lagalaise is even stronger than me." She favoured her daughter with a loving smile and then said "Plus, magically, we have an ace in the hole in Thelwyn and the Pixies. It is evident that they haven't met anyone like Thelwyn before, judging by their reaction to her. And if they haven't seen anyone like that, chances are that their enemy hasn't either. I think that we need to see what we can do without fully committing ourselves to acting in their cause until we determine if we can help." The Queen nodded with respect for her words and then started to turn to Thelwyn but caught herself and faced Lady Ashmont.

"Lady Ashmont, your opinion on this matter" the Queen commanded in a somewhat cool manner.

Lady Ashmont was mildly startled; she'd expected the Queen to bypass her for Thelwyn but she said "I assume that since I am the Princess's public bodyguard and an officer of the Guards that I will be the one given command of this venture." She looked at the Queen for confirmation and the Queen gave a minimal nod of agreement. "Then I suggest that along with whomever you think should go to help the Princess, I take a group of twenty-five or thirty guards. They should be sufficient for just about anything but a pitched battle and I don't intend that we should get involved in anything like that."

Won't that seem excessive given that it is only supposed to be a visit by the Princess?" Hargold asked with a slight frown.

"Not if I take mostly younger troops and we let it be known that we are using this as some training for them. It will be expected that these might be more undisciplined troops that we want out of the kingdom for a while and that might lull our opponent somewhat into dismissing them."

"Do you have particular people in mind?" the Queen asked. "I would like for the commanders to have a say in who goes with you. Will that be acceptable?"

Lady Asmont nodded and said "Yes, I can work with them to fulfill all of our needs. They won't want to provide me with too green of troops because they will be guarding the Princess and I'm sure they don't want anything to happen to her." She turned and smiled at the Princess.

The Queen then turned to Thelwyn and stated "I hope that you don't feel slighted by being last, Thelwyn. I treasure your opinion as much as everyone else's." She gave Thelwyn an encouraging smile.

Thelwyn had been watching and listening carefully; she wanted to go on this mission but she had to think about what was best for the Princess. She could tell that everyone but the King was for proceeding. "I have a couple of concerns, your Majesty. I don't know how much of an ace in the hole I can be if any magic user can notice me as easily as these people did."

Lagalaise interrupted, stating "I believe that I can help you mute your magical signature so that you won't be detected, Thelwyn. I might also be able to do something with the Pixies. I covered up my magical strength once I saw they were magic users, like I did when I fooled the Pixies and I think that I can help you do something similar." She glanced at the Queen in apology for intruding before settling back in her chair.

Thelwyn nodded carefully and said "That might change matters somewhat. I think that there are a lot of good reasons for the Princess to go and see what we can do for these people. I trust that Lady Windlington, Lady Ashmont and myself can make sure that she is adequately protected along the way. But the decision lies with what you and the King believe is best for your daughter and the kingdom."

The Queen nodded and said "I would like everyone to think on it overnight. I will discuss matters further with the King and Aurolla. If we are still contemplating going ahead with the plan, I will arrange another meeting to discuss any further concerns that might have occurred to you. Good day everyone." She got up and held out her hand to her husband so that they could walk together to their chambers; Aurolla followed and the rest of the group went back to their tasks.

Meanwhile Chesmyse, Charlymi and Pellaynu, their magical advisor met with Kayseesee who was the trade advisor for the group. Even though she was younger than the two advisors, Chesmyse was in charge and she directed the meeting. "Do you think that we offered enough to the Queen for her to help us, Kayseesee?" she asked the older man.

He thought about the question for a moment before answering. He knew that they really couldn't offer too much more without causing some massive problems with their economy because of the other agreements that they had negotiated with surrounding kingdoms. He was aware of the potential danger that they faced and their need for assistance but he was also charged with keeping everything in perspective. "We're at the limit of what we can really propose. I got the feeling that the Queen was interested but that the King wasn't so it may depend on what the other advisors recommend and I wasn't able to watch them as closely to tell what they were thinking. You were speaking with the Princess for a bit in the courtyard, did you get any feeling for her?"

Chesmyse waved her hand and said "I'll get to that in a minute. First, I want to hear everyone's opinion on their reaction." She looked at Pellaynu and asked "What do you think?"

"I was watching the Queen and Lady Windlington. We're aware that the Queen appears to be the policy decider for this kingdom even though she defers to her husband in public and she seemed interested in the proposal. I got the feeling that Lady Windlington wasn't swayed by our trade offer too much but that she probably would want to help us because she might be one of the few that could. It could still be a fairly close run matter even with her help. I think we need to find out if they have any more resources that can help us. That wolf girl, Thelwyn, seems interesting even if she does consort with Pixies."

"I think we should keep as far away from the wolf girl as we can manage without offending them" Charlymi stated with a small sneer of disgust.

Pellaynu turned to him with a frown and asked "Why?"

"She radiates tremendous violence and has a Pixie. Do I really need to say more?" Charlymi almost shouted.

Chesmyse was going to reprimand him but Pellaynu waved her down and snapped "Yes, I do think that you need to say more. I studied her a bit in the meeting and agree that she radiates violence but she doesn't appear to be evil. Her

Pixie was well behaved during the meeting and even seemed to be paying attention to what was going on. I was quite surprised by that fact. The fact that she showed up so easily to us worries me but we can't have everything. Did you notice anything else about the group or were you just consumed with your dislike of the wolf girl?"

Charlymi flushed red in embarrassment and then said in a slightly unsure voice "I got the impression that when Lady Windlington first showed up, the young blonde girl with her was projecting a fair amount of power but then it seemed to decrease quite a bit. I wonder if Lady Windlington was lending out her power when she was interrupted by what happened." He shook his head slightly and continued "I didn't really see her power increase though. It was just as though someone or something left the courtyard and took its power with it. I wonder if they would share with us what was going on. It may be the magical advantage we are looking for if we can use whatever that was."

Chesmyse gave a slow thoughtful nod and then said "I think that the Princess might be inclined to help us. She seemed fairly confident and she wasn't panicked by our disagreement in the courtyard. She obeyed her bodyguard when the woman signalled her to move behind her but stayed in range to direct her people. What do we really know about that blonde swordswoman, Lady Ashmont? It was a bit curious that she remained in the meeting while the other bodyguards for the King and Queen were kept away, don't you think?"

Kayseesee said "Lady Ashmont has been in the Guard for a long while and has a very deadly reputation but after that assassination attempt on the Princess, she was made bodyguard for the Princess. You remember, the one where the young bodyguard died saving the Princess from the group of assassins?" The three others nodded as they recalled what they knew of the incident and Kayseesee continued with a frown. "If I recall matters correctly, there was some wonder that the young man had been so successful even though he lost his life. It was rumoured that he wasn't considered to be that good at fighting."

Pellaynu sat up straight as though she'd just been shocked and said "I wonder where that wolf girl was at the time. Could she have been involved? Is that why the Princess survived? We know she projects violence. Is she deadly?" The three others looked at her and contemplated what she alleged.

"Something to think about and investigate further, I think" Chesmyse stated. "Well, I think maybe I should see if I can meet with the Princess in the near future to see if I can convince her to help us while we wait for them to make up their minds. But I think that we will leave matters for right now."

THELWYN LEARNS SOME THINGS

As the royal family left to discuss matters, Lady Windlington suggested to Thelwyn that she join her and Lagalaise so that they could look into some things. Thelwyn was agreeable so she and Gwendaleir followed the pair of them to their quarters. The Sorceress suggested that they should all sit comfortably on some cushions on the floor. Gwendaleir wanted to perch on Thelwyn's knee but the Sorceress put a cushion beside Thelwyn and convinced her to sit there. She was unhappy about the fact but complied. Thelwyn didn't understand why the Sorceress wanted her separated from the Pixie but made no protest. Lagalaise brought over glasses of water for them and a doll's cup for Gwendaleir. "It is better that we stick to water rather than wine" Lady Windlington explained. "Wine may dull some of our senses and I would prefer that didn't happen." She looked Thelwyn firmly in the eyes and said softly "We need to try to determine some things here today. We may ask some questions of you that seem indelicate, even cruel or demeaning, but we don't mean them in that way. We just need to gather some information about you so we can factor that into what we are going to try to do. Please don't take offense." She paused and Thelwyn nodded her acceptance and understanding of the situation.

"So basically in this castle are four different types of beings" the Sorceress stated. "There are, for lack of a better description, ordinary humans such as Bettinka or even the Queen or Princess, even though they may have royal blood, that make up the vast majority of the beings in the castle. Then there are magic users such as Lagalaise and myself." She noticed that Thelwyn frowned at this and asked "What troubles you about that?"

"Wouldn't Gwendaleir be a magic user?" Thelwyn asked with curiosity.

"No" replied the Sorceress with a small tight smile. "Gwendaleir, as a Pixie, is a magical being. She can use some magic but exists because of magic." Thelwyn gave a reluctant nod of acceptance. "Then there is you. I have delayed in talking with you or trying to do too much with you because I have been trying to find out as much as I can about your tribe. I have a magical text that mentions your tribe but doesn't provide any more information than that. I have asked for some information from some other magic users that I am in touch with but none of them can provide very much in the way of information about your tribe either. We know that you are very different from ordinary humans and magic users and I don't truly believe that you are a magical being either but it is hard to categorize you." She paused to see if Thelwyn objected to what she had just said. Thelwyn wrinkled her nose slightly as she thought about the matter but then just shrugged slightly.

"Your major difference from the other three types is that you can change into a wolf. Ordinary humans or Pixies can't do that. Magic users may be able to provide the illusion that they are a wolf but they don't actually change nor can they bite like a wolf, which you can do. You also appear to be stronger, faster and more agile than other beings. Is there anything else that you've noticed is different?"

"I can take a great deal more pain and heal faster" Thelwyn stated. "Also, I believe that my hearing, eyesight and scent are better." She didn't make this sound boastful but just matter of fact.

Lady Windlington nodded and said "Then there is how magic works around you and affects you." Thelwyn frowned slightly once more and the Sorceress explained "You are able to see spell warded doors that only some magic users can see. We tried some items on you that ordinary humans and magic users can use and all they did was give you a headache. Then there is the matter of Lagalaise's disguise spell. Lagalaise has discovered that she can't use that spell on ordinary humans. It just doesn't work on them. She can disguise herself or me so that ordinary humans see us as how she disguised us but when we look at each other, we see the true form rather than the disguise." Thelwyn scowled at this because it was obvious that Lagalaise had been successful in disguising her before the assassination attempt on the Princess, so what was the Sorceress implying was different about her? Lady Windlington smiled slightly at Thelwyn's confusion and impatience and said "When Lagalaise disguised you, the spell worked extremely well, not only did you look like your disguise to ordinary humans, you looked like your disguise to us as well." She rocked back slightly as a thought occurred to her and asked "Gwendaleir, what did Thelwyn look like to you when she was disguised?"

"You mean when she looked like the little blonde girl?" the Pixie replied.

"Yes, then" the Sorceress replied with a smile. "Interesting that it affected Gwendaleir as well." She turned back to Thelwyn and sobered for a moment as she asked "Are any of the people who join your tribe normal humans or all they all special like yourself?"

Thelwyn frowned as she tried to determine what exactly Lady Windlington was driving at. She was shocked when Gwendaleir chortled and exclaimed "You think Thelwyn is a magical being like me!" Thelwyn could tell from the way that the Sorceress flushed that she did think that might be the case and was ashamed about having to ask about it. Then she wondered why it seemed that the Pixie knew that Thelwyn wasn't a magical being.

Thelwyn stated to Gwendaleir "You seem quite confident that I'm not a magical being like you. Why are you so sure?"

The Pixie flew up and faced Thelwyn stating "Wolf Princess, you are many things, most of them wonderful but you are as human as these magic users or Princess Aurolla. You don't have the same feel to you as other Pixies or even that beast we took care of have to me. I can tell when another creature's life is dependant on magic and you are human." She then settled back down on her cushion as the three women stared at her in astonishment.

"I guess that settles that question" Lady Windlington said in wonder.

Thelwyn gave a small smirk and said "Maybe it does but you would still like to know more about me so that you can figure out what might work on me and what might not, wouldn't you?" Lady Windlington nodded silently so Thelwyn continued "My father can turn into a wolf but my mother can not. She joined the tribe by marrying my father and there are a number of others who did the same. My mother was an apprentice shaman for her tribe before she married and knows some cures and such but can't work magic like you or Lagalaise. I mentioned that I was tall for members of my tribe. I am the tallest female that can change into a wolf and I am just about an inch shorter than my father who is the tallest male who can change."

Lagalaise interrupted and asked "Are you as tall as your mother?"

"Oh, no" Thelwyn proclaimed, with a small laugh. "Mom is over six feet tall. She towers over everyone else in the tribe. I guess my dad is attracted to tall women." She grinned at the two of them and they smiled back at her.

"Do you have any brothers or sisters?" Lagalaise asked, almost shyly.

Thelwyn nodded and stated "I have one sister who is about five years younger than me.

"Are all of the children able to turn into wolves?" Lady Windlington asked. "And if both parents are able to change, do the children have any more special traits?"

Thelwyn looked thoughtful and said "All of the children that I know about have the ability to change. There are only a few occasions that both parents are changers because we are basically all related in some ways and we know that too close a family relationship can cause problems but I don't think there is anything different about those children."

"Why has your tribe remained so small?" Lady Windlington asked. She was quite disconcerted when Thelwyn's face closed up and she looked down at the floor. "If you prefer not to discuss that topic, we can avoid it" she said kindly.

Thelwyn nodded and said "I would prefer not to discuss that at this time. It isn't because of any physical reason that should affect anything. Would you like to know anything else?"

Lagalaise looked like she was bursting to ask all sorts of questions but Lady Windlington said "I think that gives us a good base to judge you by right now. What should work on us should also work on you but we will keep watch to see if there are any differences like the magical items. I'm still not sure why they don't work for you." She shook her head slightly and said "No matter. Why don't we see how well you can visualize magic. We should all close our eyes, sit still and see if we can reach our inner power." She began to do exactly that so Thelwyn followed suit. She made her mind blank and meditated on her power. Lady Windlington said softly "Project your power and see if you can see us with your eyes still closed." She waited a minute and then asked "Do you see anything, Thelwyn?"

"I get a fleeting glimpse of what looks like four glows of light but I can't seem to hold it for very long before it fades away" Thelwyn replied, her voice a bit strained.

"Okay then, let's not bother with that anymore for today. Go ahead and open your eyes again and relax. It's good that you see that much and maybe with some practice, we can improve on it. You probably will never be a full magic user like us but maybe we can arrange for some things to help you out. Now Lagalaise is going to see if she can dampen your magical signature so that you can't be spotted by another magical user. She hasn't tried that previously since we weren't sure what it might do you're your differences to us. Gwendaleir, can you see the magic that all of us have?" Gwendaleir confirmed that she could so the Sorceress continued "Laglalaise, start doing your spell and tell Thelwyn what you are doing. Thelwyn, let us know if you start feeling anything different and we will stop what we are doing, okay?" Thelwyn nodded in confirmation.

Lagalaise said "I noticed that the Pixies were able to make themselves invisible to people who knew about them so I started researching how one magic user might be able to make another one overlook them. I found a spell and tried it out on myself." She gave a small smile as she looked over at her mother and stated "Mother almost had a conniption when she thought that I had somehow lost all of my power but it was just me hiding my signature away. That is what I am going to try to do for you. I haven't been able to try it out too much because I still see my own power and mother's when I try to hide them. Gwendaleir, how brightly do I glow in your eyes?"

"You are a very bright point of light" the Pixie confirmed.

Lagalaise spent a moment murmuring and moving her hands in a pattern. Then she asked "What do I look like to you now?"

The Pixie flew up from her cushion in agitation and exclaimed "You're not there anymore!"

Lagalaise nodded and asked "Mother?"

Lady Windlington said softly "I don't detect you either."

"Mother, I'm going to try to hide your signature now before I try to do it for Thelwyn." Lagalaise made her preparations and then asked "What do you see, Gwendaleir?"

"Both of you are gone" the Pixie replied in awe. "I can see you there with my eyes but not with my magic."

"Okay" said Lagalaise as she turned to address Thelwyn. "I am going to do the same spell on you. Tell me if you feel anything." She went through the same procedure and asked "Can either of you see Thelwyn's magical signature?" Both the Sorceress and the Pixie confirmed that they could no longer see Thelwyn as a source of magical power. Lagalaise asked "Did you feel anything, Thelwyn?"

Thelwyn grimaced a little and said "I saw a brief flash of orange light but nothing more than that. I don't feel any different." She sprang to her feet and pulled out her knives before sitting down again. "I feel as strong and fast as ever. Do you want me to see if I can change while you have me masked?"

"Yes, please." They averted their eyes while Thelwyn slipped out of her clothing but observed her magical signature as she changed into her wolf form. Thelwyn just held her change for a moment before morphing back to her human shape. She hurriedly put her clothing back on and then turned to look at their puzzled faces.

"Well?" she asked.

Lady Windlington said "You're still masked by the spell but when you actually changed forms, I could see a large flash of magic. What about you Gwendaleir?"

"I too saw a burst of magic when she changed her form but I can't detect her right now" the Pixie confirmed.

"Hmm" said Lagalaise who continued to see Thelwyn's magical signature throughout the procedure. "I may have to see if I can adjust it to cover you more when you change."

"If I have to change where someone can observe me then I'm probably not going to be too worried about them knowing that I have magic" Thelwyn ventured.

"Probably not" Lady Windlington agreed. "But there are some magic users that can see from a distance and they would be curious about those bursts of magic showing up in their sight. Let Lagalaise see what she can do to adjust the spell but I think that what she can do right now will still work well for us." She turned to her daughter and asked "How hard is it to hold that spell on Thelwyn?"

Lagalaise frowned a bit and stated "It is surprisingly easy to hold the spell on her, same as it was for the disguise spell. It's almost as though she's feeding the power for it. I find the spell harder to hold on you than on her but I can comfortably hold spells on all of us without feeling too much strain. Let me see if I can cover Gwendaleir's signature or not." She faced the Pixie and made her spell work. "Can you see her, mother?"

Lady Windlington said "No, I can't. Gwendaleir, do you feel anything?"

The Pixie stood up and then flew around for a moment before stating "Everything appears to be fine with me. Can you truly not see my magic?"

"No, dear, I can't" Lady Windlington confirmed.

"Does that mean I can sneak up on Queen Blossom in the dark and scare her?" the Pixie asked with a slightly evil chortle.

"Please don't try that" Lady Windlington said with a sigh.

Thelwyn and Gwendaleir returned to the Princess's Quarters to find that Aurolla had just gotten back from her own meeting with her parents. The maids were getting the room ready for their evening meal to be brought in since it had been decided not to have a formal welcoming dinner for the visitors until the next day to allow those visitors time to recover from their journey. Princess Aurolla knew that it was an unusual custom but she was glad that her mother insisted upon it; it made those dinners much better when the guests weren't falling asleep during them, she thought. Thelwyn went over to do her part but Aurolla called her over to talk so Bettinka and Annilee took care of her duties. Aurolla wanted to find out what happened with the Sorceress and to let Thelwyn know about her own meeting.

"So, what happened?" Aurolla asked as Thelwyn combed out her long blonde hair for her while Gwendaleir flitted about them. Thelwyn gave her a detailed rundown of what had been discussed at the meeting, including the fact that Gwendaleir had proclaimed her human. When she was done Aurolla asked "So Lady Windlington is confident that the spell will hide you from being detected by magic users?"

Thelwyn nodded and said "Yes, she thinks that it might be a good idea to see how these visitors react to me now when it appears like I have no powers anymore."

Princess Aurolla nodded attentively and said "It is probably in my duties to meet with Chesmyse in a less formal manner so we should send over an invitation to breakfast to her. I'd like to talk to her some more about her kingdom and her father's estates as well." She looked up and called "Annilee, would you please get a messenger in here." When the boy entered the room, she relay her message and sent him on his way, telling him to wait for a reply. The boy left speedily.

Dinner was arriving so Aurolla stated that they would wait to talk about her meeting with the King and Queen until they were all seated to eat; she hadn't wanted to talk openly where the maids could overhear about Thelwyn's meeting with the Sorceress because the maids and Annilee didn't know all of Thelwyn's secrets but since her own meeting would affect all of them, they could talk as they ate. The messenger returned with the reply that Chesmyse would be delighted to join them for breakfast in the Princess's quarters the next morning to start to get to know one another and she would be bringing her advisor, Pellaynu, with her.

Dezadillia and Annilee had fetched in the food as they were wont to do and were putting it on the table when Princess Aurolla and Thelwyn joined them. The five of them sat down and began passing the items around; Thelwyn took a lot of meat while the other four took less and filled up more on vegetables. One of the items that the visitors had brought with them was a barrel of sweet apples and Dezadillia had wheedled five beauties from the cook for their dessert. She'd placed them in a pretty wicker basket in the middle of the table so that they could admire them as they ate. Princess Aurolla let them all blunt their appetites somewhat before she started talking. She pointed to the apples and stated "Those look very nice, Dezadillia, almost too pretty to eat." The second maid smiled at her comment and nodded. "Hopefully, that is one of the things that we will be able to bring more of into the kingdom from Barcless so that more of our people can enjoy them. I talked with my parents and the Queen is getting Hargold to investigate their offer but if it proves to be as good as they say, we will probably be sent on a visit like they want. My father was against the trip but mother and I convinced him that it would be good for me to go." She sighed a bit and said a little wistfully "This may be my only chance to go visit another country before I am married and have to begin bearing heirs so I really wanted to take advantage of the opportunity. The Queen understood my desire totally and she supported me in my convincing of my father. So I need all of you to start preparing what we will need to take with us. Does anyone have any questions at the moment?"

The two older maids asked a bunch of questions about what sort of functions the Princess thought they might be attending so that they could plan what clothes to pack for all of them. Bettinka also asked if there might be time to get a new dress made for the Princess so that she would have something fresh to wear. The Princess and her decided that they should have enough time to get it done since the dressmaker already had recent measurements that she could use to produce a new item so Bettinka would go in the morning to take care of that. Annilee had very timidly asked if she would be going or would remain in the castle until they returned. The Princess assured her that she would be part of the travellers and she was quite excited because she'd never left the castle in her short life. Thelwyn didn't contribute too much to the discussion because she knew that she would be involved quite a bit with the security discussions and arrangements for the trip rather than the things the other maids and Annilee would be taking care of. The five of them all enjoyed the apples at the end of their meal and then took care of their evening duties before retiring for the night.

AN INTERESTING
BREAKFAST

The Princess was up slightly earlier than her normal time; she wanted to make sure that everything was set for the breakfast with Chesmyse and her advisor. Thelwyn normally woke at dawn and carefully slipped out of the bed so as not to disturb the sleeping Princess so she had already had some time to make sure she was ready for the meeting. She was calmly reading as she normally was when the Princess awoke but put the scroll aside so that she could attend the somewhat flustered Princess. Aurolla was a fairly level headed girl but she was excited by the fact that this was her first diplomatic meal to host; she wanted everything to go perfectly so when Bettinka, Dezadillia and Annilee arrived a few minutes later, Bettinka went to help the Princess choose her wardrobe while Dezadillia and Annilee joined Thelwyn in cleaning the already almost spotless room. They knew that they were doing that to please the Princess rather than actually achieving anything but were content with keeping Aurolla happy. Dezadillia had sent word to the kitchen to have the food hot and ready so when Chesmyse and Pellaynu arrived five minutes early, she, Thelwyn and Annilee went off to fetch it. Thelwyn had been slightly hesitant about leaving the Princess with the newcomers but Aurolla had insisted she would be fine. Thelwyn made sure to hurry them all back and was relieved when she entered the room to find the Princess in conversation with Chesmyse while Bettinka and Pellaynu looked on.

She brought her tray to the table and began to put the food on it out. Chesmyse spared her a glance as she did that before returning to her discussion with Aurolla. About ten seconds later, Chesmyse head whipped back around and she studied Thelwyn intently. Aurolla was surprised and blurted out "What's wrong?"

Chesmyse looked back at her briefly before returning her stare to Thelwyn; Pellaynu also scrutinized the wolf girl. "This is the girl that was in the courtyard yesterday, isn't it? I believe you called her Thelwyn" Chesmyse asked softly.

"Yes, this is Thelwyn" the Princess replied with a frown. "Is there something the matter?"

"She doesn't have the same feel to her that she did yesterday" Chesmyse replied as she continued to examine Thelwyn. "The wolf and the violence that we felt from her yesterday is gone." She looked very confused and asked in wonder "How can that be?" Pellaynu was also shaking her head in shock.

The Princess had forgotten that Thelwyn's magic was now being masked by Lagalaise even though Thelwyn had remembered. Thelwyn had been waiting for how long it would take the visitors to notice the fact but was somewhat surprised to find out it didn't take any time at all. That meant that they were used to surveying the area with their magical abilities, she thought a trifle smugly. She just smiled enigmatically at Chesmyse but didn't give an explanation. The Princess was a little disturbed not to explain the matter to her guest but took her cue from Thelwyn and didn't say a word. They remained there in an uncomfortable silence for a while as Thelwyn finished putting the food on her tray out. Dezadillia came up and began putting out the food on her and Annilee's trays without recognizing what was happening. Chesmyse realized that she wasn't going to get any explanation and slowly brought herself back under control and restarted her interrupted conversation once more but she kept glancing in Thelwyn's direction. It was obvious to Thelwyn that the girl was shaken by the situation and wasn't sure if they'd been mistaken about whether Thelwyn had had magic the previous day. The Princess was sharp enough to ask Chesmyse some questions about the political situation in Barcless that the girl might not have answered if she'd been fully attentive of the discussion. Aurolla found out that Chesmyse's father was quite powerful in the kingdom but had garnered some enemies amongst the other Lords because of his notoriety. She also discovered that Barcless had some major rivals among the surrounding kingdoms, not just the one that Chesmyse thought was the one in dispute with them.

However, Pellaynu quickly realized what was going on and monopolized the conversation with the Princess so that Chesmyse could recover her wits. Pellaynu made sure that the discussion was about less controversial topics like the weather, the geography and the people of Barcless than the political problems that they were facing. If the Princess directed a question at Chesmyse, Pellaynu answered it and steered away from providing any further information even if she had to make the answer be totally different from what the question was about. After a few more minutes of this, Chesmyse had recovered sufficiently to take back control of the conversation from Pellaynu even though she still spared a few intent looks at Thelwyn.

While this had been occurring, Dezadillia and Annilee had spread out the rest of the food and dishes for the breakfast. Annilee had been allowed to eat at the Princess's table with her and the maids since she had first arrived but she'd known that that wasn't the usual practice for servants; they were expected to eat after their masters not with them. Princess Aurolla saw no need for that to happen in her chambers or in any setting but the most formal ones so Annilee had grown accustomed to eating with the others even though she made sure that she was attentive in case anything needed to be fetched. But she assumed that since there were foreigners at this breakfast, that she wouldn't be joining them. She was surprised when she counted the place settings and came up with a total of seven; was someone else coming, she wondered. When the other women sat down, she remained standing and Dezadillia frowned at her and motioned for her to take the empty chair. She glanced over to the Princess to confirm this offer and the Princess paused long enough in her discussion to throw a nod to her. Therefore she sat down, happy to be included even though she knew that she wouldn't contribute too much to the conversation. She normally felt at a loss when it was just the five of them but was doubly sure that she wouldn't be able to contribute too much of use with people she truly knew nothing about. But she was ecstatic to listen and eat the wonderful food and she beamed her happiness for all to see. Chesmyse and Pellaynu noticed that she was sitting with them but chose not to mention the fact, accepting it as one of the Princess's habits. At their estate the workers very often shared tables with them because they all had to eat and it was too cumbersome to be too picky about where everyone ate, especially around harvest or planting when there were extra people about. Pellaynu tried to engage Annilee in conversation but found the young girl to be much too shy to hold up her end. She did notice that Bettinka was the one who chose to answer any question that Annilee wasn't able to respond about. Chesmyse and Pellaynu also noticed that Princess Aurolla steered any conversations that threatened to involve magic from that topic and therefore stayed away from that as well. They assumed that was because of the maids and Annilee since they also hadn't been included in the meeting the day previous.

Therefore they all had a nice meal and some interesting conversations as they compared the small differences in their two cultures. Bettinka and Chesmyse had a fairly lengthy conversation about the differences in fashion between the two kingdoms that the others all listened to with varying degrees of interest, Aurolla being the most interested. Dezadillia was interested in knowing how long and hard the trip had been and whether or not they had had any fascinating encounters along the way. Pellaynu took the lead in answering most of her questions to give Chesmyse some time to observe the Princess and her maids. Pellaynu became convinced that the Princess, by her speech and actions at the meal, was indicating to them that she was interested and prepared to return with them to help with their problem. She felt that the Princess was both intelligent and personable. She thought that the Princess might find a way to help them out and was glad. Chesmyse also began to feel more comfortable with the Princess even though she still felt that the Princess took advantage of her initial shock about Thelwyn's lack of magic to interrogate her about matters she hadn't wished to divulge. When the breakfast ended, both women left confident that the Princess would be returning to their estate with them.

The Princess was also fairly impressed with the pair of them and thought that she and Thelwyn would be able to work with them to find a solution to their problem. She knew that Lady Windlington and Lady Ashmont would also have to help but felt that it wouldn't be a problem for anyone. Thelwyn could tell that the Princess was favourably inclined to the visitors and began to think about what she might just have to do to ensure that the Princess would be as protected as she could be during the trip. She also began to think about the fact that they might just need the services of someone with whom she was not familiar with at the moment; she decided that she needed to have a discussion with Thugular to find that person. She pondered whether to talk with Annilee about that person beforehand but then decided that she wouldn't mention it until she did meet with the King of Thieves. She helped Dezadillia and Annilee gather and return the dishes to the kitchen while Princess Aurolla and Bettinka bid farewell the the visitors and then began to discuss a trip to the dressmaker later in the day.

A little more than an hour later, Thelwyn accompanied the Princess, her maids, Annilee and Lady Ashmont as the Princess made her way to the dressmaker. When they arrived the women discussed with that woman about the colours that they wanted for the new outfits that they wanted prepared for the trip. The Princess enquired about the length of time the woman would need to prepare her outfits and was convinced that there would be the time needed for the outfit she wanted. She also made sure that both Bettinka and Dezadillia would also receive at least one new outfit for the trip. Since neither Thelwyn or Annilee wore clothes that were too complex, the dressmaker assured the Princess that they could have four new outfits prepared by her assistants in the time allowed so the Princess ordered them. Both of them were pleased that they would be getting the new clothes for the trip. Since Thelwyn wasn't overly interested in clothes, she spent most of her time looking at the small selection of jewelry that the dressmaker had for sale in her shop. She was particularly interested in how some of them were designed and when she asked the assistant about them, the assistant stated that they were all made by one craftswoman. Thelwyn bought a few of the items that she found attractive and got the name of the woman so that she could commission some pieces for herself. Annilee was surprised when Thelwyn pressed a small silver dragonfly brooch into her hand before they left the shop but was very pleased to put it on her cloak as they left. Bettinka noticed the exchange and was very pleased about the fact. Thelwyn had bought each of the other women including Lady Ashmont a piece of jewelry but had them wrapped up for presentation to them later so as not to distract them. The Princess and Bettinka spent a few minutes choosing some accessories for all of the new outfits and then they went back to the castle.

When they arrived back, the Princess took Thelwyn with her to make a quick visit to the Queen to find out the progress in making the decision regarding the trip to Barcless. The Queen was busy with some of her advisors but made time to meet with Aurolla and Thelwyn to bring them up to date. She informed them that Hargold was still gathering information and that a decision wouldn't be made that day and maybe not the next. Aurolla nodded her acceptance of the fact and the pair of them went back so that they could continue with what they had been doing. Thelwyn informed the Princess that she and Annilee would be going off to visit the poorer section of town in search of some information, the Princess nodded her agreement.

Since the assassination attempt and the Queen's reward to Annilee and her family, Annilee's family had moved from the poor sector and into the castle. Her mother was a minor assistant in the kitchen but was thrilled with the position because it was such a step upwards for the family. Her father was a helper to the King's houndmaster and found his job to be rewarding as well. Two of her younger sisters were presently working with their mother in the kitchen but had been promised better positions once they grew old enough to hold them. The family was ecstatic about their improvement in life and were extremely proud of what Annilee had done. When she wasn't with the Princess and her maids, Annilee spent her time with her family. Therefore she no longer made too many trips down to the poor section of the town and Thelwyn had replaced her as contact with Thugular; Annilee had been asked by Thelwyn who her replacement should be and had nominated her friend, a young boy named Zagreth. Thelwyn and Annilee dressed in worn clothing for their trip to the poor area and then made their way to the Prancing Pony. They met with Zagreth just outside the tavern and Thelwyn sent him off to let Thugular know that she wanted to meet with him. When they had been at the dressmaker's shop, she'd gotten the opportunity to ask Lady Ashmont if she knew of a person whose specialty she was seeking and had been informed that the best person to talk to about it would be Thugular. Thelwyn didn't wear any of her jewelry and Annilee had also removed most of hers but the wolf girl was pleased to see that the young girl did wear the copper version of the necklace that the Queen had given her. Annilee was extremely proud about what it represented and didn't care if if might make her more susceptible to thieves, she knew all the thieves. The waitress in the Prancing Pony took them to the back room where they waited less than five minutes for Thugular to show up. It had been months since he'd first met here with Thelwyn but he was still very respectful of her after seeing what she was capable of; he had worked with her in trying to ferret out the religious conspiracy even though they hadn't achieved too much. He came over to the table, poured himself some beer and sat down asking "Thelwyn, what can I do for you?"

"I need your best thief" she replied.

He sat there and waited for her to continue but she didn't so he grimaced and asked "Best how? Do you want sleight of hand, smash and grab, skullduggery or what? It's like asking for a fighting man, do you want a swordsman, axeman or knifeman. They all have their own skills. What do you want this thief to do?"

Thelwyn sighed, she hadn't realized that it was going to be this complicated but she recognized the point that Thugular was making. "The Princess most likely is going to be travelling. I need someone to come along with us and to be available to steal items from other people that we meet. It might be on the road or in their homes. Can you provide me with someone like that?"

"Undoubtedly" Thugular stated while he twisted his face in concentration. "But the question is who might be best."

Annilee had been watching and suggested "Cassmetra?"

Thugular looked at her intently for a moment as he reviewed Cassmetra's skills in his head. Then he turned to look at Thelwyn and said "Annilee is right that Cassmetra would probably meet the skills you require. She's not the best at anything but is very good at pickpocketing and burglary. She would also be able to steal from a man after enticing him to bed if she needs to do so." He looked at Thelwyn and asked "Would you like to meet her?"

Thelwyn looked over at Annilee to see what she thought since she knew Thugular's people better than her. Annilee nodded her approval of the choice so she said "No, it Annilee and you think that she might be best then I don't think that I can find any disagreement in the choice by meeting her. She will probably have to go with us away for more than a couple of months and it might happen in the next week so have her ready as soon as she can be and send me a message at the castle. Okay?" Thugular nodded so she continued "Is there anything new on the Herasius conspirators?

"No, we're still tying up an awful lot of men and women watching the temple but we haven't seen too much since the attack on the Princess. I think that it maybe frightened them back into a hole" he replied.

"Then call them off. If the Princess is going abroad, they won't be doing too much that we can notice but continue to see if you can find any way of getting someone into their group. It will help with matters when we get back" she instructed and he nodded his understanding.

"Was there anything else?" he asked respectfully. She mentioned a few small matters she wanted taken care of stating that they should happen while the Princess was out of the castle and he nodded his agreement. Then Thelwyn and Annilee went back to the castle.

When they got back there, Thelwyn took Annilee back to the Princess's rooms and then made her way down to the practice yard. She felt in need of some some further fighting practice and she wanted to see if Lady Ashmont could meet with her.

She wasn't surprised when she saw Lady Ashmont practicing against three opponents and beating them all quite handily. Lady Ashmont had attended the Princess even when she was in her own rooms for about a month after the assassination attempt at the insistence of the Queen but it had proved to be too hard for her to keep her edge when she did that. She, the Queen, Hargold and Thelwyn had met to discuss the matter and had come up with the solution that the Princess's rooms be protected by two sets of sentries within view of one another so that they could support each other in case of attack. Hargold also arranged that one of his minor spies would be watching the Princess's rooms and that there would be a different one each day so the Princess wouldn't feel too constrained. Of course, the Princess had confided in Thelwyn shortly after a week that she was noticing the spies but they decided not to let Hargold know about that; Thelwyn told Aurolla that it was only for the Queen's sake that this was happening, the Queen wanted her as protected as possible. So now the swordswoman was able to get her practice in to keep her in top form as she was used to doing. Thelwyn chose to fight against different pairs of fighters and was impressed about how well those fighters were now becoming since they regularly practiced against her and Lady Ashmont. Of course, the Pixies quickly figured out that Thelwyn was practicing and since they liked to watch her, they came to join Gwendaleir to observe. Some of them got bored and went off to do some other things but five of them, including Queen Blossom stayed for the full session. During one of the breaks that they took at the same time, Thelwyn let the swordswoman know that she wanted to speak with her and Lady Ashmont agreed. After over an hour of fighting, Thelwyn spent more than a half hour practicing her archery. She was dismayed to discover she no longer could hit the same small area of the target with twenty arrows; she could only do nineteen with the other one being as much as a half inch away. She tutted in frustration to herself as Lady Ashmont looked on, having completed her own exercise for the day. The blonde swordswoman just smiled, recognizing Thelwyn's quest for perfection as similar to her own. Thelwyn put away her equipment and the two of them headed to Lady Ashmont's rooms to talk and have something to eat.

Lady Ashmont sent her serving girl off to get food for her and Thelwyn while she offered Thelwyn some water; Lady Ashmont believed that the water hydrated her muscles better after a workout and Thelwyn agreed with her. They both drank their first glass rather greedily before slowing down and taking only sips while they waited for their repast. Thelwyn started the discussion since she had been the one to ask for the meeting. "I talked to Thugular like you suggested and arranged for a thief to join us on our trip to Barcless." Lady Ashmont nodded to show that she understood even though she didn't necessarily think that it would be required; she felt that she would be able to get into most places that they might need to penetrate during the trip. She wondered why Thelwyn had a different opinion but decided not to make an issue about the fact at that time. "How have you made out in getting the people that you wanted to have in order to provide security for the Princess during the trip?"

"I've gotten most of the people I wanted and that is fine" the swordswoman replied. "The one or two that I had wanted but couldn't get released to me won't really make that much of a difference. I was pleased that the ones I felt were essential were available." She shrugged her shoulders a bit and her serving girl returned with the food for them and they set it out and began to eat. Lady Ashmont sent her serving girl off to the kitchens to eat so that they could have some privacy. When the girl left, Lady Ashmont retrieved the doll's cup and plate for Gwendaleir and the Pixie knelt on the table near Thelwyn for the meal.

Once they'd blunted their appetites, Thelwyn asked "Do you need for me to do anything to arrange for the trip?"

Lady Ashmont considered the offer for a moment as she reviewed in her head what needed to be done before replying "No, I think everything is being handled." She gave Thelwyn an intense look as she asked "How are you feeling about the arrangement the Queen forced on us? With me being the public bodyguard for the Princess."

Thelwyn met the older woman's eyes and said "I understand the Queen's reasons entirely and even agree with them. It is hard to know how many attacks your reputation might have dissuaded but I am sure that it is more than one." She paused and then asked "Has it seemed as though I resent the matter?"

"No" Lady Ashmont admitted. "You have agreed with anything that I asked of you and don't show any resentment if I disagree with you. You listen to what I say and I'm glad of that. I don't know how much training you've had in some things and try not to tell you things that you already know."

"You've mentioned some things to me that I have already been told but I would rather you repeat those things to me instead of assuming that I know them. You've had a good deal of experience in things that I haven't and probably my tribe hasn't, especially when it comes to things like leading troops. We haven't done that too much because we mainly work as solo guards. Also, you and Hargold have been very helpful in teaching me more about the spy trade and how to work with those type of people and I am truly grateful about that" Thelwyn said with a smile.

Lady Ashmont smiled and nodded and then asked "Would you like to know what my thoughts are for the tactics and strategies will be for our trip. It's not something that you necessarily need to know and probably you'll never have to do something like it but if you want to discuss it I will be happy to chat about the matter with you." The blonde swordswoman was pleased when Thelwyn nodded enthusiastically and they spent the rest of the meal discussing those matters. When the meal was finished, Lady Ashmont smiled and asked "I will be seeing you at the Princess's dinner tonight, won't I?"

"Only if you look down into the far end of the tables" Thelwyn said with a smile. "The Queen and Princess both wanted me to be part of the head table but the ladies in waiting were appalled by that and they couldn't explain why I should be there, now could they? I'd rather skip it but the Princess would be upset so I'll be there wearing the nice new outfit that Bettinka arranged for me. And speaking of the dinner, I better get going so that I can help out with the arrangements and then get ready for it. Bye for now."

Thelwyn walked into a busy beehive as Bettinka was directing people into making last minute adjustments to the arrangements and decorations in the formal dining room. "There you are. Where were you? I could have used your help an hour ago" the first maid snapped. "Could you please go out and make sure that they are cutting and arranging the proper flowers." She waved her hand at the tables that had flowers and stated "These are not the ones that I told them that I wanted. I don't have time to do it myself or I would."

Thelwyn knew that she didn't know much about flowers other than they smelled nice and looked good but generally weren't eaten. She knew that Bettinka knew that about her as well. She decided that Bettinka was just too caught up in what she was doing to recognize the fact that Thelwyn wouldn't really be able to do too much good in the garden but just needed someone to take some of the responsibility from her. She also recognized that the reason Bettinka was snapping at her was because her nerves were frayed from the attempt to make everything perfect for the Princess's first formal dinner and she forgave the first maid for that. She smiled at the other woman saying "Sorry. I'll go see what I can do." And she headed to the garden where she went up to discuss matters with the gardener. That man explained that there weren't enough of the flowers that Bettinka wanted in the arrangements so he was making do with some other ones for the lesser tables and would soon be cutting the flowers for the arrangements for the head and upper tables. Those flower arrangements would be as Bettinka wanted them. Thelwyn nodded at his reasonable explanation and told him to carry on, giving him a thankful smile. She stayed out in the garden for a few minutes before going back to see what else Bettinka wanted done. Bettinka had gone off to the kitchens to see about the food so Thelwyn just made herself busy with the other people helping out where she could.

When Bettinka returned the correct flower arrangements were on the head and upper tables so she turned and said "Thank you very much, Thelwyn. I knew that you could handle it." Thelwyn was about to tell her that she had done nothing, that the gardener had been taking care of everything but the first maid rushed off to deal with another crisis. Thelwyn just shrugged her shoulders and thought, I'll tell her later when she's not so busy. She helped out for a while longer before leaving to clean up and get dressed for the banquet.

At the dinner, Thelwyn was far down amongst the lower tables but had been given a seat where she could see the entire head table and keep an eye on happenings up there. She wasn't particularly worried about any problems up there because there were five bodyguards standing in back of the notables, including Lady Ashmont in a baby blue outfit that included a pair of tight breeches. Thelwyn smiled as she recalled the passionate discussion that had been held when the blonde swordswoman found out that Bettinka had determined that she should wear. Since Lady Ashmont couldn't come up with a reason other than embarrassment for not wearing the outfit, the Princess had sided with her first maid on the matter and the blonde woman was wearing the outfit including the matching small peaked cap. She didn't let her displeasure show on her face but Thelwyn knew that she hadn't liked the fact. Thelwyn wondered if she maybe felt a bit better about what she was wearing when she got to see how Bettinka had dressed the bodyguards of the King and Queen. She did have to admit that they looked decorative and that the bodyguards of Chesmyse and Charlymi were almost as ornamental. It made her feel a bit better about the dress that Bettinka had ordered for her to wear. It was a bit too skimpy in her opinion even though it covered more of her skin than quite a few of the outfits some of the other women were wearing. She also wasn't used to showing off her bare legs in public and Bettinka had insisted she do so but she got more used to the idea as the evening wore on.

She was also aware that Lady Windlington was seated by the Queen and would be able to provide any magical support that was needed; Lagalaise acted as her attendant for the meal. Since Lagalaise often attended her mother, no one looked at it as unusual even though Thelwyn knew that she was mainly there to provide magical support as well. Thelwyn did think it was fairly cute that Lagalaise wore a dress made as a copy of her mother's and smiled to herself. Gwendaleir had been banished on orders of the Sorceress and hadn't been happy about the fact. Lady Windlington had laid on a small party for the Pixies with cake and other goodies for them to keep them away from the celebration and Gwendaleir had been invited to that. She was loathe to leave Thelwyn's side and Thelwyn could tell that she was perturbed by the fact. Thelwyn told her that if she showed that she could obey the Sorceress's orders that she would receive a present for it. The dinner went fine with no incidents and Thelwyn was able to enjoy the wonderful food that was being served. She made a note to congratulate the Princess and Bettinka for their hard work. She and the Princess were very tired when they turned in for the night and they went to sleep without talking too much.

CONFIRMATION OF THE TRIP NORTH

Thelwyn woke at her usual early time, disengaged herself from the sleeping Princess without waking her and slipped out of bed. Thelwyn went over and performed her morning ablutions and then sat down with a glass of water while the rest of the castle woke up. She knew that the kitchen would be starting their morning routine and would have food ready for its workers. She wasn't feeling particularly hungry this morning since she'd enjoyed the banquet so thoroughly the previous night. She did note that Gwendaleir seemed a trifle piqued about something this morning and assumed that the Pixie was still upset at being excluded from the celebration. She spoke softly to the tiny creature so as not to wake the Princess "Gwendaleir, I have not forgotten my promise of a present and will try to get time today to arrange it. I will have to go to a craftsman to get it done. If you follow me into the shop it will spoil the surprise for you so when I tell you to wait outside a shop, please do it."

The Pixie began swooping about happily at that statement, not only a present but a surprise, she thought with joy. "I will do as you command, Wolf Princess" she chittered softly to Thelwyn. Thelwyn smiled about how happy the small creature was by the prospect of a present and began to think about her preparations for the trip north. Although the Queen hadn't officially accepted the proposal yet, Thelwyn knew that it was going to happen. There were just too many reasons for it to occur and so few that argued against it, she thought sensibly. She wondered if she should order Sammilla to go with them but then decided that the woman would be better off in the city. Sammilla hadn't done too much travelling in her work for Hargold so she wouldn't be too much help along the way. Thelwyn had her looking for a way to infiltrate the worshipers of Herasius and she seemed to be making headway in that respect, so she would remain behind.

As she was making that decision, the door opened and Bettinka entered with a yawning Annilee following, carrying a tray with some breakfast for them. She held a message in her hands that she'd taken from the messenger waiting outside and presented it to Thelwyn; the message was from Hargold and instructed her that the

Queen wanted her and the Princess to attend a ten o'clock meeting to make the decision on the trip to Barcless. After she'd read the message, Thelwyn joined Bettinka and Annilee at the table where Bettinka had divvied the food out for them. She picked up a piece of toast and smeared some strawberry preserves on it before biting into it. She smiled her thanks to Bettinka for bringing the food along. They'd developed this habit over time and Bettinka had long ago insisted she stop saying her thanks, that she was very happy to do the simple task. Thelwyn looked over at the still yawning Annilee and smiled at her "Did you have fun last night?"

"Oh, yes" the young girl nodded enthusiastically, her tiredness forgotten. "It was a wonderful evening and everyone looked very beautiful." She turned to look at Bettinka stating "Especially you, Bettinka. I liked what you did with your hair. Do you think you could put my hair up like that sometime in the future?" She looked earnestly at the older woman.

Bettinka smiled and looked at the young girl. "We shall see. I think your hair would need to be longer and we would need a reason to do it." She grimaced at them as she continued "You wouldn't believe how much time it took me and Dezadillia to create that hairdo." She smiled and said "It's not something I would do every day but it was fun to have a lot of people tell me it looked good." They continued chatting about the previous night as they waited for Dezadillia to appear and for the Princess to wake up. Bettinka spoke at length about the different fashions that everyone had been wearing and Annilee listened intently while Thelwyn thought about other matters.

A while later, Dezadillia arrived with the Princess's breakfast and asked cheerfully, as she brought it in, "Is that sleepyhead still in bed? It's time she got up and faced the cruel world."

"I'm awake" Aurolla grumped from under her covers. "I just haven't decided to join these chatter birds yet this morning. I prefer to ease into my day not throw myself off the cliff." She sat up and stretched. The others all smiled because this was her typical way to start the day, to insist that she needed time to get ready to join it, even though they had all seen her leap out of bed ready for action when the situation decreed it.

"Hargold sent word that we are to attend your mother at ten" Thelwyn let her know.

"Plenty of time yet" the Princess stated as she nodded her thanks to the tray that Dezadillia brought over to her. She started to eat her breakfast as the others continued their conversation about the previous night. The Princess was extremely happy that the previous evening had gone so well; she and Bettinka mainly, although all of the others had helped, had laboured very hard to make it a success. She relaxed contentedly and listened to the others chat about what had gone on. Soon she climbed out of her bed and joined the others at the small table they'd set up in her bedroom so that they could enjoy small meals and informal chats as they worked on the duties the others performed for her. She noticed that Dezadillia was mending some clothing for all of them while Thelwyn was sharpening different weapons, mostly her own. She joined in the conversation but didn't try to monopolize it as she began replacing the leather laces in all of their riding wear.

Soon it was time for her to get ready for the meeting with the Queen and she selected a fairly simple outfit for that, realizing that there probably be a larger meeting later with the visitors. She would save a better outfit for that meeting; she didn't want to be outshone by Chesmyse. That girl had worn a rather spectacular and daring outfit at the celebration the previous night and Aurolla had pondered whether or not she had the guts to order a similar outfit made for her. She hadn't made up her mind about that matter yet but relished what she thought the looks of the Ladies of the court would be if she did go through with the deed. She was grinning as she slipped on a nice comfortable dress. When she was ready, Thelwyn simply put away the long knife that she'd been working on and stood up to join her. Thelwyn didn't enjoy being a fashion plate like the Princess did and didn't change her clothes a few times a day like her.

As they left to go to the meeting room, Lady Ashmont joined them, looking none the worse for having to wear the glamorous outfit that she'd endured the previous night. The Princess grinned at her and stated "You looked very beautiful and enchanting last evening." Then she decided to tease the older woman and chortled slightly, saying "Maybe I should get you to wear that outfit at all of our public displays." She expected the blonde swordswoman to protest the matter.

So she was quite shocked and widened her eyes as she exchanged glances with Thelwyn as Lady Ashmont replied "Maybe I'll get some more outfits made like that and wear them more often. Some of the men really seemed to like to see me dressed like that." She gave the younger women a somewhat saucy grin and Thelwyn wondered briefly about what Lady Ashmont did for fun in her off time. There'd been rumours about what she enjoyed but Thelwyn hadn't paid too much attention to them, feeling that the woman was entitled to her privacy. The Princess knew a bit more about the swordswoman's affairs because of Bettinka and gave her a bold little smile. She made a note to tell Bettinka later that her insistence on the bodyguard wearing that outfit had apparently worked out well for her. When they entered the room, Hargold was already waiting for them and the others to arrive so they greeted him as they found seats.

The King arrived next and left his bodyguard out in the hall with the guards on the door. Finally, the Queen arrived with Lady Windlington and her daughter; she also left her bodyguard out in the hallway. The Queen looked over the group to make sure that everyone was here while Lagalaise got a glass of wine for her mother and the Queen. She gave Aurolla a broad grin and stated "Your dinner went very well last night. A lot of the Ladies and Lords told me how impressed they were by your efforts and how much they enjoyed themselves. There's going to be a lot of talk happening about that. I congratulate you for putting on such a spectacular celebration."

Aurolla blushed with pride and embarrassment, ducking her head slightly as she stated "Bettinka helped me a great deal and Dezadillia, Thelwyn and Annilee also did a fair amount of work." The Queen beamed with pride in her daughter for her maturity in acknowledging the help of others.

"Yes, I know they did, dear" she said regally. "They are definitely a credit to your leadership but you know that you're going to be the one to receive the compliments. Accept them with grace. I know that your maids wouldn't want you to bother explaining their part in the matter. They all want for you to be the focal point of their work and I am pleased that you have such caring people working with you." She paused and then sighed slightly as she said "But word of that success will also put some pressure on us to make a decision that many felt we should have made a least a year ago. Namely your betrothal. You know that you can't wed for love, dear." The Queen looked sympathetically at her daughter who looked up and met her eyes evenly. The Princess knew that she would be marrying for the good of the kingdom, not her own desires; she accepted that it was her duty and responsibility. She nodded her acceptance of the fact to her mother who was still watching her, proud of her daughter's maturity and poise in the matter. "We have at least six offers that we are currently considering and by this fall we are going to have to make a choice" she stated quietly and compassionately as she continued to watch her daughter's eyes.

Hargold interrupted them stating "There are three that we are seriously considering, Princess. They each would benefit the kingdom in their own ways and two of them could benefit you personally quite a bit." The Princess looked over towards him and he held her eyes as he said "The Queen is aware of the one I favour for you but she's not comfortable with it. She feels that your prospective husband is too young to accept the responsibility of marriage but since he is just two years younger than you, I think that he can make a fine husband for you."

"I told you she needs someone who can be her partner, not someone she has to mother" the Queen snapped at her counselor.

No one said anything for a moment, not willing to step into the fray and then Thelwyn decided that she had to ask "Would the assassination attempt have come from the possible marriages?"

Hargold broke off from the Queen and said "Certainly not from her possible matches but from enemies of them looking to circumvent her marriage as a means of weakening their opponent, certainly. I am almost completely convinced that it was not the duchy of Hellsford, even though it was men from that place. I think those men were hired independent of their country by someone else. But although I have a few suspects, I haven't determined who the responsible party is yet."

The Princess shook off her lethargy and asked "I assume then that you favour none of the prospects currently?" She'd directed the question at her mother, not even looking over at the King.

The Queen sighed heavily and looked intently at her daughter. She said slowly "As much as I love and respect you, Aurolla, if I felt that there was an ideal match for you that had been proposed, you would now be married and most likely pregnant." The two women continued to look at one another as they judged their own feelings and those of the other. Aurolla knew that her mother meant what she said even though she had some regrets about it. For her own part, Aurolla understood why it had to happen and was somewhat surprised that she was looking forward to having a husband. She cast a glance at her worried father and gave him a brief smile. Perhaps he would turn out to be as good a man as he was; she would definitely work to mould him in that manner. She gave her concerned mother a nod of understanding about her position in this matter and the Queen nodded back, once again feeling extremely proud of her.

Lady Windlington broke this up by saying "That is not the decision we are here to make today." She knew how pained the Queen was about the loss of her daughter to marriage and why she was being so picky about where she was going to be sent to. The Queen had cried over the prospect on her shoulder more than once over the past two years.

The Queen glanced over at the Sorceress and then cleared her throat and composed herself somewhat. "No, that is not the decision being made here today. I just want Aurolla to understand that this will be her last chance to make a trip like this. When she comes back, we will be making a decision about her betrothal and she won't be free to travel like she is currently." She looked at her husband briefly and stated "She's let us know that she is quite interested in making the trip if it benefits the kingdom so now we have to decide if it will profit us. Hargold, what have you found?"

Hargold started stating "I have talked to a number of sources within our own merchant community to see if they feel such an agreement as is offered would benefit them and almost all of them feel that it would. I talked with Merrigold to see what she knew about Barcless and have now formed the opinion that there statement that they were about fifty times our own trading size might just have underestimated them. I have the feeling that they are larger than that so we would benefit quite mightily from the agreement. The obvious downfall to agreeing to their proposal is that we would be accepting helping them against a very powerful enemy. One that they are having problems dealing with, even with all of their resources. We must weigh what we have to bring to their situation and decide if we can make a difference in their fight like they think we can."

Lady Windlington spoke up and said "I have talked with them to get a better feel for the possible strength of their magical opponent and what magical problems that have been occurring to get a feel for whether we can help them. It is hard to be certain until we get there and experience what is actually going on but I think that we have the resources in this room to make a difference for them. It is by no means certain and there is likely to be danger involved but I think we need to look at helping them." She gave a glance over to the King after she said this and saw him nod almost wearily at her. She was already aware of where the Queen's feelings were; she sat back to let the Queen take control of the meeting once more.

"Thank you for your input, Lady Windlington" the Queen said, smiling at her dear friend. "I take it that you recognize the need for you and Lagalaise to go with the Princess to assist her in this endeavour." The Sorceress nodded without looking at her own daughter; they'd discussed the matter and Lagalaise had been very interested in making the journey and seeing what they could accomplish. The Queen turned to Lady Ashmont and asked "Any input from you, Lady Ashmont?" The blonde swordswoman shook her head silently. The Queen looked over to Thelwyn but she had nothing to say on the matter, she was going wherever the Princess was, so she avoided making eye contact with the Queen. The Queen gave a small indelicate snort and then asked "Do you have anything further to say on the matter, Aurolla?"

The Princess looked over at her concerned father and said "Daddy, this will be good for me and although it may be dangerous, I will be well protected by the best people we have." She shook her head slightly and continued "We will be doing a good thing by helping these people and also will make a marked improvement in our own people's lives. That is what we are supposed to do, isn't it?" The king gave her a half-hearted smile and nodded his head at her. She turned back to her mother and said "You have the final say in the matter, mother."

The Queen nodded and sat back and up, straightening her carriage, as she proclaimed "We will have a meeting with the visitors from Barcless. We will offer them our help if we can give it but the decision will not be made until Lady Windlington has a chance to assess whether or not we can be successful. We will accept a trade treaty with them but will not hold them to providing us with too much unless we are able to assist them with their current problems." She looked at Lady Ashmont and asked "Are you prepared to accept that Lady Windlington is the one who will make the decision about helping these visitors?"

The blonde swordswoman looked surprised that the Queen would even ask her that question and replied "I am comfortable with accepting any decision at any time that Lady Windlington might choose to make. I trust her judgement totally." The

Queen nodded and glanced at Thelwyn who just nodded in agreement with Lady Ashmont.

Then she turned to the Princess and asked gently "Aurolla, are you agreeable that Lady Windlington will be making the decision to proceed or not instead of you?"

Princess Aurolla looked at her mother in shock and replied "Of course I am, mother. Lady Windlington definitely can assess the magical problems better than I can. Will she be the one who leads the party then?"

Lady Windlington jumped in and stated "This is your expedition, dear. I will be the one to handle the magical aspects of it but Lady Ashmont will provide and be responsible for the physical security while you handle the diplomatic duties. I will advise you in those matters in the same way that I do for your mother but you will make those decisions." She gave the young girl a smile.

Princess Aurolla flicked her eyes back over her mother to see if she agreed with what the Sorceress stated but couldn't tell if it was or not. Then she smiled back at the Sorceress and said "Thank you for your trust." The Queen dismissed them with her thanks and sent a message to the visitors informing them that there would be a meeting with them at two that afternoon.

At the afternoon meeting, they were in a slightly larger room because the bodyguards of the King, Queen and the visitors insisted on being at least in the room with their charges. They were positioned by the entrance where they could watch but not overhear the discussions. The Queen made sure that she was the last one to arrive once again, although this time Lady Windlington and her daughter were already in the room. The Queen took her time to comfortably seat herself on the chair that had been put out for her and accepted her glass of wine from Lagalaise with a slight smile. She knew that no one was going to object to her actions and didn't mind making them wait a bit longer. She looked over at the four people representing the visitors from Barcless and then proclaimed "You brought us a proposal asking for our help against a magical enemy who has been plaguing you with magical creatures and happenings. You offered us a favourable trade agreement in return for our help." Chesmyse nodded in agreement with the Queen's statements. "You suggested that we could send our daughter with a retinue as cover for this expedition. We have discussed this matter." The Queen paused and gave the visitors a steely glance. Chesmyse looked bewildered as she wondered if the Queen was going to reject their proposal. She'd gotten the impression in the time that they had been there that their plan would be looked on in a favourable manner and that their enticement had been sufficient to sway the matter. Now she wasn't so sure. She watched the Queen carefully.

The Queen saw that she'd planted a seed of doubt in Chesmyse and smiled inside, careful to keep her satisfaction off of her face. It was always good for people to be unsure of what she was going to announce she thought with glee. "After a great deal of discussion, I decided that my daughter would be the one to make this decision." Thelwyn hid her laugh as she saw the Princess start in shock knowing that this wasn't the case at all; the Princess carefully kept her eyes down on the floor in front of her so that she didn't give the game away. She began to realize that her mother was giving her a lot more credit for this decision than she'd actually had. Then the Queen said coolly "Princess Aurolla has agreed that she will travel to your kingdom and look the matter over for us. If she feels that we can give you the assistance that you require, she will offer it. If she feels that we can not, she will return home." Thelwyn saw the Princess's eyes widen as she realized what the Queen and Lady Windlington had meant by taking care of the diplomatic side of things; she would be the one credited with making the trade treaty for the kingdom. Of course, she recognized that the Sorceress would be very instrumental in guiding her towards that decision but it would be hers none the less. The Queen continued "If we do help you, whether we are successful or not, we expect you to provide us with the type of trade that you have intimated that you would do. We feel that you should show us some good faith by sending some trade down to us right away. Do you have any comments or questions?"

Chesmyse looked at the Queen carefully and asked "Would you give us a brief moment to discuss this amongst ourselves?" The Queen nodded regally and the four of them huddled for a few minutes as they talked over the matter. The Queen engaged in a conversation with Lady Windlington while the others just waited patiently until the visitors were ready. Finally Chesmyse broke the discussion up and looked back at the Queen saying "We had hoped for something more substantial than what you are offering but we need any help that we can get. We will accept your offer on those terms. Kayseesee has arranged for a trade caravan to make its way slightly northeast of here and will send off a messenger to bring them over here. They have a number of goods that you and your people should like. They will be here in less than two weeks. Can you arrange for some goods that you would like shipped back to them in that time?" The Queen was surprised by the rapid response they were getting; things must be worse for them than they were letting on, she thought. She looked over to Hargold and he nodded acceptance of the deadline; he would ensure that it was met.

"Okay, Chesmyse" the Queen replied. "Since we are going to be allies, we will lay our cards on the table for you to see." She looked over to Lagalaise and nodded to her. Lagalaise dropped the suppression of the magical signatures on her, Thelwyn and the Pixies, all of whom were in the room.

Chesmyse gasped in wonder at the well of power that was now coming from the little blonde girl standing by Lady Windlington. Charlymi, who had started to doubt the violence and power in Thelwyn, now saw it again in her and he stated tersely "I told you she didn't lose her power. She's had it all along but somehow hid it from us."

Pellaynu noticed the Pixies and said in an awed voice "They have nine Pixies in here and we didn't even notice them." Kayseesee, who had no magic, didn't notice the change but did see the wonder in his colleagues.

The three magic users scanned the group before them as they thought about the implications of the power that was in this room. Chesmyse began to feel much better about the arrangement they had just agreed to; she felt that this group could assist them a great deal with their problems. She asked "How were you able to hide that power from us? Could you teach us how to do it?" She shot an earnest glance at Lady Windlington.

The Sorceress replied calmly "We will try to teach it to you but Lagalaise can mask everyone here without too much trouble. You can see for yourselves that she has more power than I do. I have had more experience than she has so I will be guiding her as to how to cope with your problems." Chesmyse nodded enthusiastically about that. "We will also be bringing some Pixies with us so that we might be able to get them to talk with your tormentors and see if they can dissuade them." Chesmyse nodded a little less enthusiastically at this proposal.

"When can we start back?" she asked.

"We figure that we need a week to ten days to get everything ready "Princess Aurolla replied with a small smile. "If you wish to get back there faster, you can lead and we can follow."

"No" Chesmyse said as she thought about it. "It would be better for us to travel together. We can offer protection to each other and can learn best how to work together. That way we can sort out some tactics and options along the way. You wouldn't object to that, would you, Princess?"

"Oh, no" the Princess replied airily. "That works for us."

The Queen broke in and said "Lady Windlington will be taking three of the Pixies with her and Gwendaleir will be travelling with Thelwyn, as always. So you will have four Pixies altogether."

Chesmyse nodded as she watched the small creatures flitting about. "If you think that they will help" she said hesitantly.

"Oh, we will find these ones useful" Lady Windlington replied with a smile. "Now if you'll excuse me, I have some arranging to do of some items I wish to take with us on the trip. If you will excuse me?" The meeting broke up quickly after that and Thelwyn headed into town towards the craftsman that had made the jewelry she'd purchased at the dressmaker shop.

Thelwyn bade Gwendaleir to wait outside and the Pixie complied, she knew it was because Thelwyn was getting a surprise for her and she wanted to keep the surprise happening. Thelwyn went into the shop and the craftswoman came out to greet her; Thelwyn explained that she'd seen some items at the dressmaker shop and had purchased some of them. She explained to the woman that she wanted some pieces made for her and was here to enquire if the woman could make them. The craftswoman eyed Thelwyn with some suspicion because only people with quite a bit of money could afford to have jewelry made for them and this young woman didn't look overly prosperous even though she was wearing finely made clothing and talked about being at a dress shop that catered to Ladies and even Royals.

The woman stated "Commissioned jewelry is quite expensive. Could I see some proof that you would be able to pay for a piece before I spend any time trying to create it."

Thelwyn wasn't surprised that the woman wanted the proof, she'd expected that and had stopped off at the royal treasury to get some money to bring with her. She handed the woman a fine leather bag and said "Count that please." The woman took the bag, opened it and gasped slightly; there was gold in there and quite a bit of it. She thought about handing it back to the girl without counting it because seeing it made her sure that the girl had the means in which to pay her but she decided that she should do as the young woman asked and she counted it. There were two hundred gold pieces in the bag.

"Two hundred gold pieces" the craftswoman confirmed as she proffered the bag back to Thelwyn. "That is an awful lot of money to be carried by someone who looks unprotected like you do."

Thelwyn left the woman holding the bag out and said confidently "No one is going to try to take it from me. They would regret it totally. Now can we talk about what I want made?"

The woman continued to hold the bag out but said "Of course we can but this isn't my money until I earn it. Take it back. I now know that you have the means to pay for what you order. Two hundred gold pieces would buy you anything that I can do."

Thelwyn finally took the bag back and described to the woman what she wanted; she wanted a ring like shield made of gold with the image of a howling wolf on it. The woman sketched out a drawing of the wolf for her and they made some adjustments to it before both were satisfied with how it looked. The woman frowned when Thelwyn explained that she wanted the ring portion to be flattened somewhat but didn't protest the fact. She was unsure as to what the purpose of the item was because it was too big to fit the small girl's hands but wasn't going to make an issue of the fact.

"How much is that going to cost?" Thelwyn asked as they finished changing the sketch.

"The woman frowned as she calculated the material and time it would take her to make the item. "The gold alone would be fifty to sixty pieces and my efforts would add another twenty-five to thirty" the craftswoman stated.

"How long would it take you to create it?"

The craftswoman pursed her lips and thought. "To do a job like this in a material as expensive as gold, it would take me six weeks to two months" she stated, letting Thelwyn see the honesty in her eyes.

Thelwyn nodded in understanding, it was longer than she'd hoped but there was nothing to be done about that. "I am leaving for at least three months but would appreciate it if it was done on my return. Can you do anything for me in a cheaper material in the next week?"

The craftswoman drew a more rudimentary sketch and showed it to Thelwyn. "This done on copper or even silver could be completed within the week" she offered.

Thelwyn nodded and asked "Copper would make it easier for you?" The woman nodded in agreement so Thelwyn said "Make it copper then. How much?"

The woman once again gave Thelwyn her eyes and said "The design and effort are expensive no matter what the material. If you could wait my usual three weeks, this piece would be less than a gold but since you want it in a week, it would have to be a gold and fifty silver." She waited to see what the reaction would be.

Thelwyn bit her lip and thought about it; she got the feeling of honesty from what the craftswoman was saying. She knew that it would be expensive but she could afford it. She decided that she liked the honesty and forthrightness of the woman so she said "Done." She counted seventy-five gold pieces out of the sack and said "This if for payment of the copper piece and down payment on the gold one. Is it sufficient?" The woman nodded so Thelwyn put the purse away and left the shop.

Gwendaleir had been watching for her to exit and buzzed over with excitement; she'd made sure that she stayed on the other side of the road so that she didn't ruin her surprise. Thelwyn gave her a quick grin but didn't say anything to her because there were too many people around. She headed towards the Prancing Pony because Thugular had sent word that Cassmetra wished to meet with her. She entered the pub and was escorted back while Zagreth went to find Thugular and Cassmetra. They quickly arrived and Thelwyn studied the thief as she walked in and sat down.

"Well met" Thugular said as he poured them some beer. "Cassmetra would like to talk with you before she accepts the duties you wish her to take on." He sat back and let the thief talk.

She sat forward, nervously and asked "You are going on a trip outside of the kingdom. I have never been outside the castle before. What are you expecting me to do for you on this trip?"

Thelwyn looked at her carefully and replied "This is a trip with the Princess so it will be fairly comfortable and secure. I want someone who can get me papers from people if I need them or items that I may need. I will provide you with any assistance that I can or that others might be able to do. I can ask people to do things they might be hesitant to do just for you. I'll try to make it as safe as I can but there might be some risk. I will do my best to rescue you if you fail at any time."

Cassmetra nodded and stated "You hired Annilee." Thelwyn nodded, unsure if there was a question involved with her statement or not. "Annilee's family now have a very secure place at the castle because of that" Cassmetra continued.

"Not because I hired her" Thelwyn interrupted, protesting. "Annilee did a very courageous thing and was rewarded for that."

Cassmetra nodded, showing that she knew that, and said "But she got the opportunity to do that because you hired her. Will I get an opportunity to better myself if I do a good job for you?"

Thelwyn looked her full in the eyes and said "I will reward you handsomely if you do a good job for me. We can discuss what you may want after we return from this trip. Do you trust me in that?"

Cassmetra nodded and asked "When do we leave?"

"In a week" Thelwyn replied. She eyed the clothing that Cassmetra was wearing and stated "We need to get you some clothes so that you'll fit in better with the Princess's retinue. Come with me to the dress shop." The two of them bid farewell to Thugular and went off to get new clothes for the thief.

PREPARING FOR THE TRIP

The week that they spent preparing for the trip was a busy one for everyone. The Princess had to attend a lot of meals with her friends and their mothers so that everyone could say goodbye to her. Bettinka and Dezadillia were required to be at these sessions but Thelwyn, because of her apparent youth and her lower position, could skip them and she did that for most of them. Thelwyn only went to the gatherings the Princess went to with her three best friends because Thelwyn liked those women and they treated her well. After that, she begged off stating that she had a lot to arrange for the trip. The Princess knew that wasn't completely true but was willing to let that stand as the reason; she, Bettinka and Dezadillia enjoyed such gatherings and chatting about them afterwards but she knew that Thelwyn did not.

So one morning early in the week, Thelwyn was out and about in the castle when she thought that she should check in with Lady Ashmont as to what she might be considering for the trip. She made her way over to where the blonde swordswoman had her rooms and caught her half-dressed, kissing a man as he was leaving her apartment. Thelwyn was shocked and tried to make her way away from them but Lady Ashmont noticed her and broke away long enough to call "Thelwyn, did you want something?" The man glanced over at her and Thelwyn thought that he looked like the bodyguard for Chesmyse. He gave Lady Ashmont a quick goodbye kiss and made his way past Thelwyn; she could now see that it was definitely who she thought it was. Lady Ashmont watched him leave, then sighed and said "You better come in." Thelwyn hesitantly went in and they sat at the table. Lady Ashmont looked at her and noted the surprised and almost furtive look on her face. She growled angrily "Do you have something to say?"

Thelwyn flushed somewhat and asked meekly "Can I ask you a question?" She'd been pondering something since she'd gone to the dress shop with Cassmetra and didn't feel comfortable asking the Princess or her maids about it. Finding Lady Ashmont in this type of situation seemed like it might allow her to ask about it. The thief had requested all of the outfits that Thelwyn was having made for her to be extremely tight and revealing, telling Thelwyn that men liked that. She'd wondered if she should be dressing somewhat more like that or not. She knew that the Princess and her maids didn't dress like that but she wondered if she should. Lady Ashmont nodded her head as she considered what Thelwyn might ask. "What...how...um" Thelwyn stuttered.

Lady Ashmont had been prepared to defend her actions but now let the anger seep out of her as she realized that Thelwyn wasn't questioning those actions but seemed to be seeking advice about herself. She could tell that Thelwyn was confused and embarrassed about what she wanted to ask so she suggested gently "Relax and take your time, Thelwyn."

Thelwyn gulped a bit and then mastered herself. "How do you handle your interest in men and their interest in you?" she asked finally.

Lady Ashmont looked at her with a touch of trepidation; she didn't know how much the girl knew about affairs between men and women and she wasn't sure that she was comfortable having this talk with her. She reviewed in her head who among the people that Thelwyn knew would be best to handle this conversation and the only person that came to mind was Lady Windlington. She knew the Sorceress was currently extremely busy getting ready for the trip so she decided to start the talk with Thelwyn and then suggest that the girl talk with the Sorceress when she felt it got too personal. "What do you know about men and women?" she ventured cautiously.

"I know about the mechanics of it" Thelwyn said bluntly. "I just don't understand the you know..."

"The emotional part of it?" Lady Ashmont supplied with a slight smile as Thelwyn nodded. She understood now what the girl wanted and recognized that she could help her with it somewhat. "Have you ever been in love with anyone?"

Thelwyn looked at her plaintively and stated "I'm not sure. I've been attracted to some men but they haven't been attracted to me."

"Are you sure?" the blonde asked her. She was aware that some young men had expressed interest in Thelwyn but that she'd ignored them; she hadn't brought the matter up previously because she felt it was none of her business. Thelwyn frowned at her in response and Lady Ashmont continued "I've seen at least four men express interest in you but you didn't return it or give them any encouragement. Do you know how to tell when someone is interested in you?" She asked this last question as gently as she could so as not to upset the girl.

"When has anyone shown interest in me?" Thelwyn asked, confused.

Lady Ashmont nodded thoughtfully, knowing now that Thelwyn couldn't tell when interest was shown in her. "Are you looking for a lord?"

"Would a lord even be interested in me?"

"Probably not" Lady Ashmont admitted. "They'd be more interested in the company you keep than you." She paused and asked "Are you okay with that?"

"I doubt that a lord or I would have very much in common." She looked at the blonde swordswoman and said "I'm not looking for a pretty face or anything and don't think that a man looking for that in return would be interested in me either."

Lady Ashmont nodded, relieved that Thelwyn understood her own looks so well. "You're young and you look even younger" she said. "That can put some men off. You should be looking for someone to have some fun with and gain some confidence with right now rather than attempting to jump into a serious relationship. Is that what you're looking for right now?"

Thelwyn thought for a moment or so and Lady Ashmont let her take her time about answering. Then Thelwyn nodded and said "I think that you are right in what you say and that would probably be best for me right now." She dropped her eyes and asked "How do I do that, Lady Ashmont?"

"If we're going to have a heart to heart talk like this, you better call me Rachealle. Sit comfortably. Do you want some wine or anything?" Thelwyn shook her head so Lady Ashmont just poured some wine for herself. She took a sip as she thought about the best way to approach this problem. "If a young man asks you about what you think, compliments you for any reason or finds an excuse to touch you, you should look at that as him showing interest in you. If that happens, you should look him in the eyes and touch him back. I don't mean that he gropes you or that you grope him. I mean gentle touches to the arm or the face. If you lightly touch his face and he smiles at you, lick your lips. That will signal to him that you want to pursue his interest." Lady Ashmont spent a while more instructing Thelwyn about what she should do but she cautioned the young girl to take matters slowly and not try to rush things. Thelwyn nodded in understanding and determined to think matters over for a while and maybe practice a bit by herself before attempting anything.

"What have you been up to?" Thelwyn asked.

Lady Ashmont smiled as she recognized that the young girl wanted to move onto safer topics and replied "I have chosen my people. There will be twenty-eight of them and I have started teaching them the tactics that I will want them to employ. We will continue training while we travel. And you?"

"Oh, I've been avoiding the Princess's friends gatherings" Thelwyn admitted with a slight grin. "But I've also been preparing for the trip. Gwendaleir and I have been working with the three Pixies so that they will work together better on the trip. Lady Windlington asked me to do that because she was going to be so busy with her own preparations. Well thank you for the talk, it's given me something to think about."

As they left Lady Ashmont's rooms and were alone, Gwendaleir decided to tweak Thelwyn a bit about her hesitation with the opposite sex. "So is the wolf girl going to find a man to try out her new knowledge on?" she said slyly.

Thelwyn turned on Gwendaleir quickly and hissed "If you want to stay with me, you will keep a civil tongue in your head. I will not discuss my personal matters with you. I will banish you the next time I have any talk like that in the future." She looked intently at the small creature.

Gwendaleir cringed at Thelwyn's fury and said contritely "I'm sorry, Wolf Princess. I didn't realize that it was such a sensitive topic. I will behave myself." The Pixie was truly sorry and she decided that sometime in the future she would see if she could help the young girl to find what she was looking for. She looked hopefully at Thelwyn and said softly "Please don't banish me from you." Thelwyn snorted but didn't say anything more and just continued to walk back to the Princess's rooms.

Gwendaleir stayed very quiet during the week as Thelwyn practiced her archery to get back to top form, gathered items that she thought might be useful for all of them on the trip and went to get the clothes that had been made for all of them. Thelwyn knew that the Pixie was contrite and forgave her for her missteps. Just before they had to leave, the craftswoman that Thelwyn had commissioned to produce the shield for Gwendaleir sent word that it was ready so Thelwyn went down and picked it up. She was impressed by the quality of it, even though they had simplified the design quite a bit, and so she asked "What if I wanted broach pins with the design that you are doing for me in the gold ring? I would want at least one done in gold and three or more done in silver." She thought that those items would look very nice on the Princess, her maids, Annilee, Lagalaise and maybe Lady Ashmont.

The craftswoman looked at her attentively and replied "If you wanted more jewelry following that same basic design, that would reduce my costs for my effort of producing them. The price that I quoted you was for a one time item because that was what we were discussing. I can't change the cost of the materials but if I can make more than one item, I will reduce the costs of my errors." She began wrapping the copper ring up so that Thelwyn could take the package with her.

Thelwyn nodded her understanding and said "How much of a deposit would you want to start making a gold broach pin and four silver ones after you have finished the gold ring?"

The craftswoman thought furiously for a moment and scribbled down some numbers on the edge of her sketch. She looked Thelwyn in the eyes and said "One hundred and twenty gold pieces more as a deposit for those items. I will produce a bill for you for all of the items once they have been crafted. I will not have them all done if you come back in three months though."

Thelwyn nodded and said "That will be acceptable. I will send some men from the castle to deliver the coin to you, not bring it myself. Is that all right?"

The craftswoman had widened her eyes at mention that the men would be from the castle. She was aware that Thelwyn had money enough for what she was asking but wasn't aware that she was associated with the castle and the royalty within. She didn't want so obvious a delivery of money to her workshop though, so she replied quietly "It would be better if they delivered it to me at the money lender's shop around the corner. He is set up to protect it better than I am and I already have coin on deposit with him from your first payment."

"Then I will arrange that" Thelwyn stated as she nodded about the sensibility of the request. She left the shop and headed back to the castle with her package as Gwendaleir buzzed excitedly around. Once again, the Pixie had remained outside so as not to spoil the surprise. Now that Thelwyn actually had the item though, the Pixie was extremely anxious to receive it but Thelwyn had told her that she would not acquire it until they were ready to leave for their trip. She'd also chosen items for Annilee and Lagalaise when she'd been in the craftswoman's shop and was going to give all of her traveling companions a gift at the start of the trip. She still had the items that she'd purchased at the dressmaker's for the Princess and her maids because she'd forgotten to give them out. She didn't feel comfortable giving any items to Lady Windlington or Lady Ashmont because of their station. She hummed happily as she journeyed back to the castle where she arranged for the payment to be delivered to the craftswoman.

THE START OF THE JOURNEY

They had decided that they wouldn't start the trip from the castle at the early break of light because they would probably be doing that for most of the journey. They also had an inn in mind for the stop for the first night and had sent a rider ahead to ensure that they would be ready for the group. The inn was just over a half day's ride from the castle so they wouldn't have to push themselves to reach it. Lady Ashmont expected them to be a bit slower at the beginning of the trip until they sorted themselves out so she wasn't planning to make large inroads into the excursion at the start. She figured that it would take them three weeks to complete the trip. The road that they would be travelling on was built more than two hundred years ago by sorcerers at a time when the kingdoms were more at war with their neighbours. It was a magically enhanced road that a group of sorcerers were responsible for maintaining its wards and signalling to the kingdoms that it spanned when it needed repairs. Those kingdoms would raise the needed labour to repair any parts that required it. It was still a fairly lightly travelled road because most traffic used the roads more in the eastern parts of most kingdoms where there were more towns and inns. Darkcloud was too far west for this more popular road to run through so it was thought of as being too far off the trail for most people to visit. Cream Mountain, the capital of Barcless was about the only spot where the main road ran through it and the military road was only fifty miles away. There was an off shoot that ran from the military road to that capital. The carriage that they were going to use to travel in and the wagon for their luggage had both been built to travel rougher roads and were built to be higher and stronger than normal ones. Chesmyse assured them that they should be able to handle the poorer areas of the road.

So Thelwyn got up at her usual time. Gwendaleir pounced as soon as she slid out of bed and begged "Can I have my present now, Wolf Princess?"

Thelwyn smiled at the anxious creature and shook her head saying softly "Later. Come we don't want to disturb the Princess." The Princess was going to be woken earlier than her usual arousal time but that was still some time away. She shooed the Pixie in front of her as she made her way over to the table. Gwendaleir buzzed around, tremendously excited, causing Thelwyn to feel her own enthusiasm level rise; she thought that it was fun to give presents when the recipients were so eager to have them. She tried to read a scroll as she waited but Gwendaleir kept buzzing by her ear and swooping in front of her eyes in order to keep her attention on the fact that she wanted her surprise. Thelwyn decided that there was no reason to be mad about the fact, she'd created this situation. She also figured that since she would have to give the Pixie her present without the others around since most of them didn't even know about Gwendaleir, that it made sense to do it now. Besides, she felt that she'd tortured the Pixie enough. "Fine" she said, attempting to be grumpy. "I'll give you your present now." The Pixie spun in the air in joy and landed on the table in front of Thelwyn with her arms outstretched.

Thelwyn smiled and retrieved the Pixie's present from the Princess's trunk. She brought the wrapped package over and placed it in Gwendaleir's arms. "Oh, it's heavy" the Pixie shrilled. She put it down and tore through the packaging. When she uncovered it, she let out a piercing shriek of happiness; Thelwyn looked quickly over to see if the shrill sound had woken the Princess. She saw the Princess's eyes were open and she was watching them with pleasure. She was going to apologize but the Princess just shook her head and continued to watch. "It's a shield with your symbol on it" Gwendaleir crooned enthusiastically. "It's beautiful and I will carry it with me at all times." She lifted it and frowned about how much it weighed. "Oh no, it's too heavy for me to fly around with."

Thelwyn said gently "I think you should only carry it at ceremonial occasions when you can ride on my shoulder." The Pixie smiled and nodded happily before going back and admiring her gift.

Princess Aurolla sat up, yawned and remarked "It's definitely beautiful, Gwendaleir. It shows you how much Thelwyn appreciates you and what you do for her." Gwendaleir nodded happily once again as she agreed.

The Princess and Thelwyn watched as the Pixie carefully traced the design on the shield with pride as she crooned with pleasure for a while. Then they heard the door opening as Bettinka, Dezadillia and Annilee arrived. Thelwyn quickly moved the shield back to the Princess's trunk and Gwendaleir watched her put it away sadly. The Pixie knew what Thelwyn was doing and that she'd get to admire the gift more at a later time but she felt regret that she couldn't carry it with her forever. Thelwyn gathered the gifts that she had for the others and brought them to the table with her. She handed them out to the others to exclamations of delight. They opened their packages one at a time, starting with Princess Aurolla and ending with Annilee. They all thanked Thelwyn profusely. Thelwyn had to be careful not to let her eyes drift too much to where Gwendaleir was flipping in the air with happiness as the others all appreciated their gifts. The Pixie noted that she was the only one blessed with a wolf symbol and was impressed by the fact.

The women quickly ate the meal that was brought in and put away their final items that they wished to take with them; the majority of what they were taking had already been packed away and was on the baggage wagon already. They finished their morning routine and then went down to prepare for their departure. The Princess and her maids all retrieved their horses from the grooms that had saddled them; one groom would be going along to help them but the Princess and her maids knew that they would be expected to give most of the care that their own animals would need and were content with having to do that. They were aware that the rest of the party would also have to perform a lot of their own duties as well. Thelwyn and Annilee didn't have animals to take care of because they would be riding in the carriage of Lady Windlington; both of them had been informed that they would have to help with the kitchen duties on the trip and were okay with it.

Soon they were all on their way and a number of people had turned out to wave farewell to the Princess and her group. There were the Princess and her two maids, Lady Ashmont and her twenty-eight fighters, Chesmyse and her group of seventeen all on their horses, the carriage carrying Lady Windlington, Lagalaise, Thelwyn, Annilee and Cassmetra with its driver and three helpers and the baggage cart with three more people. There were a number of remounts being brought along for when they might be needed. It took a little while for them all to shake out into the formation that they would be travelling in but there were surprisingly few problems.

Lady Asnmont let them travel for over an hour and a half before she stood up in her stirrups and shouted loudly "Practice. Arrows from the front left." She had warned everyone before the trip that there would be training going on and had instructed everyone as to their duties. There was a brief hesitation in the riders at the front as they sorted out which pair should be rushing to where the arrows were coming from and the rest shook out into their defensive formations to support them. It took the Princess a moment to determine where she should be but Bettinka grabbed the bridle of her horse and started leading her back towards Lady Windlington's carriage. Chesmyse and the rest of her entourage hesitantly moved back to that area also while the occupants of the coach slipped out of it and sheltered under it. The drivers of the vehicles and the helpers also got down around the horses pulling their vehicles to protect and calm them. Lady Ashmont called out further instructions to see how her people responded. She'd worked them out a bit in the training yard but now she wanted to see how well they had learned their duties. She wasn't impressed with the speed of how they reacted but didn't really expect any better than what they were doing. She knew that they would get better with more training. She did acknowledge that most of the people eventually got to where they should be by the instructions that she'd called out. But there were a couple of people who got in the way of others as they forgot where they were supposed to go. She called for everyone to halt as she surveyed where everyone was and how prepared they were for their duties. She noted the people that she would have to talk to, including the Princess for being slow to get into protection, but was a good enough leader not to call them out in front of the others. She would only do that if people constantly didn't perform well; she found that it was better to talk to and teach people than simply yell at them. "Okay, people, that was pretty sloppy and we need to get better. I will be talking with all of you about your performance and how you can improve it. We should get back underway now. Don't think that there might not be another practice or two today just because we had this one. I will determine when they happen" she called out loudly as she rode up where the Princess was.

Princess Aurolla remounted her horse when Lady Ashmont called the halt to the exercise; she was feeling a bit embarrassed that she'd been caught offguard when it started and hadn't performed very well. Lady Ashmont rode up to alongside her and spoke quietly "That wasn't a very good performance by you, Princess."

Aurolla nodded sheepishly and acknowledged "I know, Lady Ashmont. You definitely surprised me and I wasn't thinking. It took me a moment to remember what you wanted me to do. Bettinka reacted better than I did fortunately so I didn't look as bad as I might have. I will do better in the future." Lady Ashmont nodded and then rode on to speak to the next person; there was no point in stressing the matter with the Princess when she already knew that she'd done badly and was counted on as being a leader.

They sorted themselves out and got underway once more. Lady Ashmont made sure that she talked with all of the people who'd done the worst and received assurances from them that they would perform better. She decided that she would leave talking to the ones that had only made minor mistakes later when they stopped for the night. She'd purposely chosen a portion of the road where some woods encroached on the route because that was likely to be the terrain that some attackers would choose to use. She let them all travel until she called a halt so that they could stop for lunch. She knew that if she was simply travelling with a fighting group and not with the Princess that they wouldn't have stopped but would've eaten while in the saddle. But the Princess was used to eating at certain times and even though it would be more primitive than she was used to, they would have to stop so that she and her people could eat in some comfort. The blonde swordswoman didn't begrudge that to the Princess, she'd known that that was how they would have to operate. So they stopped, quickly prepared and ate a meal; while everyone was eating, she went around to talk with them and ensure that there were no issues.

As they were packing up the leftovers, Lady Ashmont called out "Arrows center front." There was a slight hesitation and then the correct pair rode out to investigate while the others formed into their support formation. The Princess had been somewhat surprised once again but recovered and scurried over to where she would be protected. Lady Ashmont called out some further attacks and was pleased by how everyone was responding. They were still slow but now they were all doing the correct responses to the attacks she was calling out. "Okay people. That was better but still slow. We need to practice so that our response is instantaneous and almost instinctual. We have no way of knowing if or when we might be confronted by enemies so stay on your toes. Now finish putting things away and get ready to move out. You have five minutes and we will be departing."

They travelled the distance to the inn where they were going to spend the night without any interference and Lady Ashmont didn't call another practice while they traveled. Thelwyn had spent the day in the carriage, practicing her limited control over magic under the tutelage of Lagalaise. Both Annilee and Cassmetra were somewhat surprised by what was happening in front of them but they didn't really understand what the two of them were doing. Both of them decided that it would be best just to ignore the matter; each of them had trust in Thelwyn. They also realized that Lady Windlington was giving instructions to things that they couldn't see. They were dumbfounded when items and food disappeared right in front of them. But that was none of their business in their minds and they just occupied themselves with their own interests. Bettinka had decided that Annilee should learn to read and write and had been teaching her over the last few months so she practiced her printing. Cassmetra was interested in what she was doing and the young girl was pleased to share what she was undertaking, showing the older woman how to print out the alphabet.

When they reached the inn, the innkeeper and his family came out to greet the Princess warmly; they were ecstatic to have the royal party stop at their inn even though it would mean a fairly large rearrangement to accommodate them. They had emptied out the barn so that the warriors could sleep in it; the horses would be placed in the corrals overnight because it was a warm enough night for them to endure it. A couple of travellers had to be shifted so that rooms together could be arranged for the Princess and her party as well as Chesmyse and her immediate group. Only one man complained and the innkeeper simply informed him that he was quite welcome to journey onward if he had such a problem with the arrangements. He chose to share a room with another merchant as he had been offered rather than do that. Since they'd had some warning of the party approaching, the innkeeper had requested that a couple of the local foresters go out and hunt and there were three deer cooking over outdoor fires as the Princess arrived. The Princess descended from her horse and greeted the people waiting to welcome her. Lady Ashmont remained in her horse as did eight of the guard while the others dismounted and began arranging belongings for the night. Lady Ashmont felt that this guard would be able to react to any threats in a quicker manner if they remained mounted and it also allowed them to see any activities from a higher vantage point. She hadn't wanted to allow the Princess to interact with people on the road but the Princess had overruled her on that matter. The Princess felt that it was important to show herself and interact with her people as much as she could rather than trying to remain completely aloof from them because they could be dangerous to her. She trusted that Lady Ashmont, her guards and Thelwyn would ensure her safety. Lady Ashmont was appeased by the fact that the Princess had actually waited for Thelwyn to come up to her from the carriage before she actually dismounted. Lady Ashmont knew that Thelwyn could intervene in any sudden attack and was completely capable of fending off many attackers by herself. Her surprise appearance would allow the support to defeat the enemies before they could be effective. So, Thelwyn was busy scanning the people who were out greeting Aurolla for any signs of problems as the Princess shook hands and greeted her subjects. The innkeeper suggested after about ten minutes that he should show the Princess and her party to their rooms so that they could prepare themselves for dinner. The Princess smilingly agreed with the affable man and soon they were guided to their accommodation.

Shortly the Princess and her immediate party were in the dining room, which also doubled as the taproom for later in the evening, along with Chesmyse and her immediate party. The rest of the group would be dining outdoors but nobody complained about the fact. Lady Ashmont was in the dining room with them and they all ate a quite satisfying meal served by the two servants that regularly worked at the inn. Annilee was happy that she got to sit and eat with the rest of them rather than having to fetch food or drink for them. Thelwyn and Lady Ashmont kept a close eye on everything even though there were four guards at the entrances to the room to discourage any problems. There were no incidents during the meal and the Princess and her maids retired early so as to return the inn back to its usual activities. They didn't want to disrupt the inn any more than they had to and there was really nothing of interest to them that would be happening. So after the Princess retired for the night, the innkeeper was able to feed the rest of his customers before changing over to the taproom for the evening. Lady Ashmont made her rounds, checking to see that everyone was aware of what their duties would be and was prepared to carry them out. Some of the people who would be standing guard later in the evening were having a pint of beer before going off to rest for their duty. Lady Ashmont cautioned them not to drink too much but otherwise left them alone.

The inn had a bathhouse attached to it and the innkeeper had ensured that there was an adequate supply of hot water so the Princess and most of her party decided that they were going to make use of it. There was no sense in wasting the innkeeper's labours even though it was only the first day and they would have many on the road, most of them without the bathing facilities offered currently. The Princess went down to the bathhouse with her maids, Annilee and Cassmetra; they were joined by Lady Windlington, Lagalaise, Chesmyse, Pellaynu and Lady Ashmont. The Princess had wondered if Chesmyse would bring her brother when she invited her to join in using the bathhouse and was slightly relieved that she hadn't. She'd bathed with men present before but she'd had complete trust in them; she didn't hold the same opinion of Charlymi right now, he hadn't earned it. But she'd left the matter of whether he would be joining them to his sister who hadn't bothered to include him. The women washed up thoroughly though quickly so that whoever else of their party might want to use the facilities would get the chance to do so. The Princess had enjoyed the chance to have an informal chat with Chesmyse about her home; it was amazing, she thought, how much you could find out about each other while washing one another's backs.

The Princess's party returned to their rooms and Bettinka started combing out the Princess's long blonde hair while Annilee combed out hers. Thelwyn ran a quick comb through her dark hair and was content with it because she wore her hair in less fancy fashion to the Princess and her first and second maid. She joined the trio on the Princess's bed and started working on Annilee's hair; she'd noted that Annilee always tried to copy the hairstyle that Bettinka wore and was simply following what the young girl was doing to the first maid's hair. Dezadillia was working on her own hair but was giving some gentle pointers to Cassmetra who would be staying with them in the rooms. There had been some discussion as to whether or not the thief should be in the Princess's rooms with Bettinka being the one most against the idea. The Princess had been ambivalent to the matter but let her first maid state her case. Bettinka objected to having a person known to be a thief stay with them and be tempted by their riches. Bettinka was shocked to see Annilee's face cloud over when she made this argument. Dezadillia sided with Bettinka but was less strenuous in her objections. Aurolla looked to Thelwyn to get her opinion and she'd stated that the woman might be a thief but she was their thief and wouldn't be stealing from them; that she had other objectives and wouldn't jeopardize achieving them. Bettinka had meanwhile beckoned Annilee to her so that she could comfort her but had been ignored by the young girl. That was a first because Bettinka doted on Annilee and the young girl relished their relationship. So Bettinka had changed her mind on the fact and told the Princess that Thelwyn knew the woman the best and probably was right on her opinion of her. Dezadillia didn't bother to say anymore, having determined that the decision was already made. After Bettinka had stated her changed position, Annilee went over and sat in the older woman's offered lap and they had embraced with some joy. Bettinka recognized that Annilee still considered herself to be in a similar position as the thief and had thought that if Bettinka didn't trust Cassmetra then she probably didn't trust Annilee. The first maid knew that she trusted Annilee completely and that the girl had shown her courage and strength of character with her actions during the assassination attempt; she was determined to make sure that the girl never doubted her love and respect for her. So Cassmetra had been invited to sleep with the Princess and her entourage; she was extremely surprised because she'd expected to be asked to sleep with the guards. She accepted with all of the grace that she could manage. They all chatted for a little while but since they were going to be getting off to a very early start and they were all somewhat emotionally tired from their excitement over starting the journey, they made an early night of it.

Thelwyn came instantly awake, her ears straining to hear any noise; something had woken her up and she was reviewing in her mind to see if she could determine what it had been. Obviously it wasn't something too loud since no one else was stirring but it had been enough to disturb her. She lay there quietly to see if there was any repetition of whatever it was but didn't hear anything. After about two minutes, she decided that she was disturbed enough to get up and investigate matters so she slipped out of the Princess's bed and crept to the door. Gwendaleir saw her movement and joined her silently, aware that everyone else was still sleeping. Thelwyn could see well in the dark and she knew that Gwendaleir did also so she just nodded at the Pixie, acknowledging her. Thelwyn paused at the door for a brief time, listening to see if there was someone on the other side of it. She didn't sense that there was a presence on the other side of the door. She whispered quietly to the Pixie "If I open up the door a bit, can you go out and see if there is anything amiss out there?" The Pixie was aware her high-pitched voice might arouse the others so she just nodded knowing that Thelwyn would see it. So when Thelwyn opened the door slightly, the Pixie slipped quickly out and began searching on the outside of the door; Thelwyn quickly closed and latched the door while remaining alert. Gwendaleir buzzed around noting that the two guards were awake and keeping guard on the staircase up to the rooms as they had been instructed to do. She didn't sense that they were disturbed by anything so she calculated that there was no immediate danger.

She went back to the door and stated quietly, knowing that Thelwyn's acute hearing would pick her up, "Nothing amiss, Wolf Princess." Thelwyn opened the door enough to admit the Pixie once again. She remained leaning against the door as she thought about what she should do. As she was figuring out her possible moves, her sharp hearing heard a disturbance from below. It didn't sound overly threatening, more of a murmur of sound. She glanced at the Pixie who shrugged off knowledge of what it might be; she'd seen nothing that would've caused the sound. Thelwyn strained her hearing once more and heard cautious steps up the stairs; she thought that she could hear the two guards remaining at the bottom of the stairs so this didn't seem to be someone unauthorized coming up the stairs.

There was a very gentle tap on the door and Lady Ashmont whispered "Thelwyn, are you awake?" Thelwyn opened the door and slipped out, startling the blonde swordswoman a bit by her speed in answering the question.

"Something happened" Thelwyn stated flatly as they moved away from the door slightly so as not to be heard.

"Yes" Lady Ashmont acknowledged. "It would appear that at least three people attempted to creep up on the guards. If there were only three of them, they weren't attempting an attack so they must have been trying to gather information. The guards killed one of them but the other two got away although one of them was wounded in the process. No one saw more than two individuals getting away but it might have been missed in the confusion."

Thelwyn nodded and then realized that the other woman couldn't see her in the darkness like she could see her so she asked "This happened a few minutes ago? That must have been what woke me up."

Lady Ashmont let her eyes widen in astonishment as she replied "Yes it was a few minutes ago. I had to be aroused and spent some time looking over the scene before coming here to let you know what was going on. I didn't expect you to be alert and awake, though."

Thelwyn smiled slightly as she recognized that the swordswoman wouldn't have let her face betray her surprise if she thought that Thelwyn could observe her reactions but felt covered by the darkness. "I'm not sure if I heard anything but my senses woke me for some reason" she admitted. "We were checking it out when you came to tell me."

"We?"

"Gwendaleir and I" Thelwyn replied. She saw the swordswoman nod in understanding and recognized that Lady Ashmont hadn't realized that the Pixie was with them. "Should I come down and examine the body?"

"You're more than welcome to do that if you want but he wasn't carrying anything in his pockets. Not even any coin. I have decided that I will look closer at the body in the light. It is hard to see too much by lantern light. Do you want to go look at the body?"

"No, you're undoubtedly right that morning is time enough to look things over. Was there anything else?"

"No" Lady Ashmont replied with a smothered yawn. "I'm heading back to bed myself."

"See you in the morning then" Thelwyn replied as she and Gwendaleir re-entered the Princess's rooms and she slid back into bed and was quickly asleep again. She didn't notice that Cassmetra was quietly watching her.

THE JOURNEY CONTINUES

Thelwyn got up at her usual time in the morning and slipped out of bed. She knew that the rest of them would have to be woken in a short amount of time but figured that they might as well get as much sleep as they could. She stretched slightly, waking up her muscles and frowned as she had the feeling of being watched. She let her eyes roam the room casually and saw that Cassmetra was watching her from the covers in the bed that she was sharing with Dezadillia. She turned her head and looked intently at the thief to let her know that she knew that she was awake. Cassmetra noticed the intent look and flushed as she recognized that she'd been caught. The woman slipped carefully out of bed and quickly dressed. Thelwyn put on her clothing and the two of them exited the room, making as little noise as they could. Thelwyn noted that the thief was almost as silent about moving as she was and was impressed by the fact.

When they got outside the room, Cassmetra asked quietly "Something happened during the night, didn't it?"

"Yes" Thelwyn replied, keep her voice down but feeling surprised. "Did you hear anything?"

"No" the thief admitted softly. "I woke up when you opened up the door a crack. I didn't know what was going on but felt that I should just observe in case I needed to do something. I dozed slightly until you crept back into the room."

"Hmmm" Thelwyn muttered intrigued by the fact that she hadn't detected the woman's observation of her the night before. It made sense, she thought, that the thief would be able to hold still given her profession but it was still interesting. "There's a body out in the stable that I was going to look over. Would you care to join me? You might be able to pick something up that I might overlook."

"If you want me to, I would be happy to do so" Cassmetra replied even though she was definitely beginning to doubt that she would detect anything that this very intriguing young woman would overlook. The two of them made their way down to the barn and had to wait because the guard wouldn't let them do anything until Lady Ashmont had been fetched. Thelwyn knew that they were just doing their duty and she was fine with waiting for that. Lady Ashmont walked up to them, stretching and yawning slightly as she informed the guard that although she appreciated the dedication of the guard, he was to let Thelwyn and whomever she might be with examine anything that she desired. Cassmetra raised her eyebrows slightly at this pronouncement as she began to re-evaluate Thelwyn's importance. She knew that Thelwyn was more to the Princess than it seemed but hadn't realized that her importance with the guard and Lady Ashmont was that high too.

"He was only doing what you commanded him to do" Thelwyn told the swordswoman calmly.

"I know. I was only readjusting my orders for the oversight that I made" Lady Ashmont stated in an equally calm voice. "He knows my bark would be much more intense if I felt that he was doing wrong." She smiled at the guard and at Thelwyn before looking curiously at Cassmetra. She didn't say anything or make any sort of gesture towards the thief but just examined her briefly. The three women made their way to the stall that the body lay in and began examining it. They ignored the fact that the man had a gaping wound in his abdomen; they knew how he had died and were just interested in who he was and who sent him.

"The clothes look like they come from Hellsford" Lady Ashmont offered. "But so do a lot of mercenaries so that may not mean too much."

Cassmetra had knelt and pulled at the clothes as she examined their quality and their fit on the body. "The clothes look more like they come from Crossmountain not Hellsford but the man is likely from Hellsford" the thief contradicted softly as she looked up at Thelwyn. Thelwyn glanced over in Lady Ashmont's direction to see her reaction to this announcement.

The swordswoman frowned as she thought about the information for a moment and then she squatted beside Cassmetra to look at the clothing closer. The thief indicated some stitching done under the arm and a repair to the pants without saying anything out loud. Lady Ashmont snorted slightly and said "She's undoubtedly right about that." She gave the other woman a smile to show that she appreciated being corrected on the matter. Thelwyn was pleased to see Cassmetra start to show a bit more confidence in herself.

Cassmetra studied the man's palms and asked Lady Ashmont "What profession were you thinking that he was?"

The swordswoman looked quite thoughtful and replied "I was thinking military, most likely scout. His hands aren't rough enough to be handling a sword constantly like most guards do. What is your thinking?"

Cassmetra pursed her lips and said "He most likely isn't military so not a mercenary. I think that he is a thief who also does rough work such as mugging or highway robbery. Those sort of people can be hired from Hellsford as well." Lady Ashmont nodded thoughtfully as she absorbed this new information.

She looked up at Thelwyn and said "So most likely a thief from Hellsford clothed to look like a man from Crossmountain. Still doesn't get us any farther on discovering who might be hiring and sending these people if it is the same person as the one who sent in the assassins." She looked at Cassmetra and asked "Unless you have anything further that you see than we do not?" Cassmetra shook her head silently. "Should we get Lady Windlington to look over the body in case there is any magic involved in it?"

Thelwyn replied "Wouldn't hurt but I don't think that she'll find anything more." So a messenger was sent to fetch the Sorceress and she arrived with Lagalaise. They looked over the body and after a short while admitted that they didn't have anything to add to the knowledge. The leader of Chesmyse's party also came over with an associate to examine the body; he'd been made aware of the incident when it happened but had agreed that it would be better to look matters over in the light. They could add nothing to the information that they already had.

So they went off to inform the Princess and Chesmyse as to their findings. They met in the Princess's room since it was the largest and most secure. The two maids and Annilee were sent to make sure that the Princess's and their things were packed away properly. Lady Ashmont took control of the small meeting since she was in charge. "Princess, Chesmyse, there was an incident in the night. We think that three people were trying to gain as much information about us as they could for unknown people. We are not sure which of you this might have been targeted against but it is likely one of you. We managed to kill one of them but the other two got away with one of them being wounded. We looked the dead man over and have some idea about him but nothing that would definitely pinpoint who hired him." She paused and looked at the Princess "We think the man is from Hellsford like those assassins but Hargold wasn't convinced that they had been sent by the Duke. I don't think that this implicates the Duke either. It is just too easy to hire people from Hellsford because a great deal of them want to leave that duchy." She rubbed her chin and said "I don't think that this changes anything in what we do other than reinforcing that we need to keep a close watch over things."

"Why do you think that they were only after information?" Princess Aurolla asked, curious.

"Because there were only three of them. Too small a group to attack the number of guards that we have. If they were assassins, they wouldn't have been near the barn but would have been trying to get in here to get to either of you. I think that they will be reporting whatever they managed to learn to someone who will plan a more extensive attack at a later date" Lady Ashmont replied. There was more conversation about the information but nothing of real import was decided or discussed and soon they were once again on their way.

They travelled along the road for the whole day and Lady Ashmont called three practices during that time. Everyone was mindful of the incident in the night and made sure that they reacted to the best of their abilities. Lady Ashmont felt they were still a little slow but she was pleased with their progress and their intensity. When dark was close, they found a small clearing just off the road and they made camp in it. It was cramped but they made do. They had a good supper because the innkeeper had sent quite a bit of food with them. He hadn't wanted payment but the Princess insisted on making sure that he was reimbursed for his efforts. She knew that he and his family was quite proud to have hosted her and she was please that he should feel that way.

Morning came and they quickly got underway once more. The Princess groaned and said that she wanted her feather bed; everyone laughed at her joke. But all of them were quite happy to start along the road. They had another uneventful day with a few practices thrown in and then found a rather large clearing with a small river running through it. Lady Ashmont looked it over and decided that it would be the best place to spend the night so they set up camp and began to prepare their evening meal. Thelwyn was busy stirring the stew that all of them would share while Annilee, Cassmetra and some of the guards portioned out the other items for the meal. Thelwyn didn't mind helping in preparing the food and was humming slightly to herself.

Suddenly Gwendaleir buzzed her ear, squealing slightly "We're being observed. In the trees. A Pixie."

Thelwyn nodded and said calmly "Go tell Lady Windlington and do what she tells you to do. Okay?" The Pixie nodded enthusiastically and sped off towards the Sorceress. Lady Windlington gave a tiny pack containing a set of clothing and a cup to Gwendaleir to deliver to the unknown Pixie. She also gave her one of the steel needles that had been converted into a Pixie sword for the new Pixie. Gwendaleir and the other three Pixies had spent most of the trip wrapping fine thread around the eye of the needle to provide a handgrip for it. Gwendaleir made her way carefully over to where the other Pixie was, approaching it carefully so as not to scare her away.

She stopped a respectful distance away and put the pack and sword down on the ground before backing off a bit. "Ho, unknown Pixie in the woods, I come in friendship and peace. We wish to offer you this gift if you will agree to talk with us." She was quite proud of those words because she had spent time with Lady Windlington to craft them.

"What are you?" the Pixie in the woods demanded. "You look like a Pixie but you don't have magic like I do. Why should I believe and trust you?"

Gwendaleir had forgotten that Lagalaise was currently masking the power of all of them. "I am a Pixie same as you are" she said carefully. "You don't see my magic because it is being masked by a powerful sorceress so our enemies can't determine where we are."

The Pixie flew out into sight a bit more and eyed the pack and sword in a greedy fashion. She did keep an eye on Gwendaleir, ready to flee if the other Pixie came too close and she asked "What do you want for those goods?"

"They are gifts to you if you will agree to listen to our Sorceress. She wants the chance to talk to you and see if you will agree to join us. Even if you choose not to accompany us you may have these items. If you do decide to come with our group, she will offer you much more and we will help each other out with any problems" Gwendaleir said soothingly. She'd argued with the Sorceress that any Pixie that they met would just take the goods and flee but the Sorceress had insisted that they do things this way. She didn't want the Pixies to feel like they were trapped but that they had a choice in the matter. Gwendaleir had agreed to perform in the manner that Lady Windlington wanted her to do but she was somewhat anxious about her ability to do that. The Pixie now came closer, testing to see what Gwendaleir would do but Gwendaleir maintained her distance.

"I have friends. Would they be offered anything if they came to talk with this Sorceress of yours?" the Pixie asked cautiously.

"Yes, they would be offered the same as you are" Gwendaleir replied. "My name is Gwendaleir, what is yours?"

The Pixie considered the matter for a moment and then decided that there was no harm in giving her name. "I am Fir" she replied proudly.

"Nice to meet you, Fir. How far away are your friends? I know that the Sorceress would want to meet them in the daylight and it is almost dark now. Would it be better to meet in the morning? How many are there so we can bring the right number of gifts?"

Fir considered the matter with some care. "It would take me a while to get to all of them. There are six of them" she acknowledged. "So it would be better to meet in the morning." She looked wistfully at the pack and sword and asked "I take it I don't get those until the morning then?"

Gwendaleir had been carefully schooled by the Sorceress to answer that. She said "You may take them with you. If you chose to show them to your friends it may help convince them to meet with us. Until morning then." Gwendaleir turned her back on the other Pixie and didn't look back as she headed back to camp. Fir couldn't believe that she could just take the goods and maybe not return but soon her greed overcame her and she sped out and grabbed them before heading back into the woods. She expected some sort of trap and was surprised that she got away with them. She flew around for a while to see if anyone would come out after her but no one bothered with her. She flew off to let her six friends know about the opportunity.

Meanwhile Gwendaleir had returned to camp to let the Sorceress know that the Pixie would be possibly bringing six friends with her in the morning. Lady Windlington had been waiting for Gwendaleir to summon her to meet with the Pixie and was surprised that she hadn't called for her. Now she understood why and was pleased that Gwendaleir had done as she'd suggested. She looked forward to meeting the Pixies in the morning and didn't share Gwendaleir's belief that they wouldn't show up. She knew that the Pixies would want the swords and packs that she was offering them and then it would be up to her to convince them to accompany them.

The camp was stirring at dawn, getting ready to depart. Gwendaleir was keeping an eye on the woods in case the Pixies did come. She was still quite surprised to detect the seven Pixies that flew up to the edge of those woods but went to inform Lady Windlington. Lagalaise removed the magical mask off of her mother and Gwendaleir so that the Pixies could see their power. The Sorceress slowly and carefully walked out to meet the newcomers; she carried the six gifts that they had promised them. Gwendaleir flew beside her even though she was tempted to rush out there. Lady Windlington walked up to about ten feet away and arranged the six gifts on the ground before backing up five feet and sitting down to await the Pixies. Fir flew out cautiously while keeping an eye on the human and Gwendaleir who had seated herself on Lady Windlington's shoulder. "My friends have come as you asked them to do. I see that you brought the gifts that you promised. Can they come out and look at them?"

"They are welcome to come out and examine them" Lady Windlington said in a cheerful manner. "After they have had a chance to try them out a bit, I would like to talk to all of you and let you know about the further benefits that we can offer you if you agree to help us." She hadn't got all of her words out before the other six Pixies sped out of the woods to claim their prizes. Two Pixies fought a brief tug of war over one pack until they recognized that there was one that no one was claiming. The six newcomers cooed with pleasure over their new items; they had been very jealous of Fir when she'd shown them her new belongings the night before. Fir kept an eye on the human and Gwendaleir while her friends quickly tried out their new possessions but neither of them moved from where they were.

Lady Windlington let the Pixies admire the gifts for a few minutes before she called out "You promised that you would talk with me in return for those items. Please come over here so we can do that." She waved quickly to an area in front of her. The Pixies slowly made their way over to the spot indicated but remained alert to flee if there should be a trick involved. When they were near the Sorceress stated "My name is Lady Windlington and I represent Princess Aurolla. We are making a trip to help some new friends of ours and one of their problems is to do with some Pixies. We would like it if you help us deal with that issue."

"So you're looking for a Pixie army to fight another group of Pixies?" Fir asked suspiciously.

"No, we definitely hope that it will not come down to that. If there is to be fighting like that, my daughter and I are powerful enough to handle that issue even though we don't want to handle it that way. We would prefer a more friendly approach like we are doing with you."

Fir regarded the pair of them and then realized something. "Hey, you got your powers back" she blurted to Gwendaleir.

"Like I told you yesterday, I never lost my powers, they were just masked by this woman's daughter" Gwendaleir stated evenly. "You should be able to determine how strong she is with magic. She will help you with any of your problems if you help us with ours. She can even offer you some permanent space in a castle that has lots of fun things in it if you want."

Fir looked at them and then at her friends. She said "We are going to go over there to discuss this matter. Once we have decided, we will return to tell you our decision. We will be taking the gifts with us. Okay?" She indicated a spot very close to the trees.

Lady Windlington nodded and said "Okay but Gwendaleir is going to go back to the camp to get my daughter so that she can show you what she can do." The Pixies went off to talk of the matter, watching to see what the human was going to do and Gwendaleir flew off to fetch Lagalaise. The Sorceress watched as the Pixies talked animatedly for more than five minutes as Lagalaise made her way over to join her mother.

Then the Pixies came back and Fir, who had been elected their spokeswoman, stated "We took a vote and by a score of five to two against, we have decided that we don't want to help you." The Pixies were poised to flee if the humans made any sudden moves but Lady Windlington just nodded.

She asked "Does the fact that my daughter has more power than I do make any difference?" Lagalaise dropped the mask on herself and showed them her power. The Pixies flew around a bit as they absorbed this information.

"We will take another vote" Fir stated and they flew off to do that. Lady Windlington sent Gwendaleir back to camp again as she and Lagalaise sat there watching the discussion. The Pixies kept a close eye on them and the camp as they argued the matter. They were somewhat relieved to see Gwendaleir return with another small girl as she brought Thelwyn over as per the Sorceress's request. Fir could see that Gwendaleir was linked to this new person.

After a few more minutes the Pixies returned and Fir stated "We feel that what you are talking about only affects you and not us. We have voted four to three against joining you." The Pixies hovered in a crowd with Fir slightly in front of them.

The Sorceress mulled over trying to argue that the Pixies would be affected by whatever the humans did but quickly determined that they wouldn't be swayed by her words. She wasn't sure if Thelwyn's presence would make any difference but it wouldn't hurt so she said "Unmask Thelwyn please, Lagalaise." When Lagalaise dropped the mask on Thelwyn, the Pixies were curious. They exploded in flight with two of them actually cartwheeling across the sky and Fir backed up a couple of feet. Lady Windlington and her group were astounded by the reaction of the Pixies and pondered why they had reacted that way.

The Pixies eventually came back behind Fir and she came closer once more. Lady Windlington waited for them to explain their actions, giving them time to calm down again. The Pixies were all looking intently at Thelwyn and then three or four crowed "A Wolf Princess. She's a Wolf Princess." Lady Windlington looked at them perplexed by their response.

"You are a Wolf Princess, are you not?" Fir asked Thelwyn keenly.

"Gwendaleir calls me a Wolf Princess" Thelwyn admitted carefully. "But what do you mean by that?"

"Wolf Princes and Princesses are warriors that can turn themselves into wolves when they want to" Fir stated.

"Well if that is your definition then I do fit that bill" Thelwyn stated evenly. "Have you had contact with someone like me before?"

"No we have only heard about people like you but you are obviously a Wolf Princess" Fir stated as they heard one of the Pixies exclaim "We're supposed to help Wolf Princesses and they will aid and protect us." Fir tried to shush that Pixie so that she could talk with Thelwyn. The humans looked amongst each other, perplexed, none of them had heard that previously and the castle Pixies and Gwendaleir hadn't told them about that. Thelwyn glanced over to Gwendaleir who was looking as confused about the matter as the humans were. Fir stated "We have to go discuss this new development." The Pixies flew back to their spot.

They came back just over thirty seconds later and Fir pronounced "We agree to follow the Wolf Princess. The vote was six to one for." Lady Windlington was quite happy with that decision and was about to get back on her feet.

Then she heard Thelwyn flatly say "No." She looked over at the girl and gestured for her to accept the offer but Thelwyn refused to look in her direction.

"You refuse our help, Wolf Princess. But why? You've been telling us you want us to agree to help you and you say no" Fir wailed, confused.

"I'm not refusing your help" Thelwyn stated evenly. "But I will not accept that you will follow me. Princess Aurolla is our leader and you should agree to follow her. She is my friend and I aid, protect and advise her and so should you. I will teach and protect you to the best of my abilities and expect you to pay attention to my instructions. You should also agree to follow the instructions of Gwendaleir as she works well with me." Gwendaleir straightened in pride as she announced this last condition; she was pleased that Thelwyn was showing them she trusted her so much.

The Pixies went off to vote on this change and came back within a minute or so with Fir announcing "Okay, we voted unanimously that we will meet this person who has your respect, Wolf Princess. If she is someone you admire and follow, we feel that she would be someone we should also. Please bring her over here." The Pixies had been made aware that Lady Windlington didn't want everyone in the camp to see them and were quite fine with that; they didn't want to be seen by everyone either.

Gwendaleir was about to fly to get the Princess when Lady Windlington said gently "Perhaps it would be best for Lagalaise to go get her, Gwendaleir. She's rarely alone and Lagalaise can take her from her group easier than you could. Stay here with Thelwyn and me. Lagalaise, please bring back another outfit for each of the Pixies from the more colourful ones we made. " Gwendaleir looked a little crestfallen but nodded that she understood and Lagalaise left to fetch the Princess.

Soon the pair of them made their way back over so that the Princess could greet her new subjects. Princess Aurolla sat gracefully down and looked at the seven Pixies who were now all dressed in the clothing given to them; the clothing was in greens and other earth colours so they would blend into the forest better. She smiled at them and greeted them with a nod. They looked back at her intently, trying to spot why Thelwyn put so much stock in her. They were somewhat confused because she had no magical powers that they could detect and thought that Lagalaise must still be masking her. Lady Windlington introduced the Pixies to Aurolla and she accepted their pledge to work for her. When they were done, Lagalaise gave each of them a new outfit and they spent a few minutes enjoying the bright colours of them. Then Fir mentioned that they all had some possessions that they would like to take with them so Lady Windlington sent Thelwyn back to get bags for her and Lagalaise. Each of them would go with some Pixies and gather the belongings to bring back to the camp. Soon Thelwyn headed south with three of the new Pixies and Gwendaleir while Lagalaise headed north with the other four. Lady Windlington and Princess Aurolla went back to the camp.

Lady Ashmont approached them as they returned and asked "When can we get underway again?" She'd had the camp partially dismantled in preparation for their leaving; she knew what Lady Windlington had been up to, having been informed of what might happen the previous evening. But she assumed that they would now be on their way and was already thinking about that.

"I'm afraid that we will be spending the day here" Lady Windlington said, giving her a small smile as she frowned. "Our new Pixies have some items that they wish to bring with them and Thelwyn and Lagalaise will be gone most of the day helping them retrieve their goods so we might as well put off leaving here until tomorrow morning. I hope it won't cause you too much trouble. I'll go over and inform Chesmyse and her people that we will be staying here while you tell your people." Aurolla found it slightly amusing as Lady Ashmont grimaced about telling her guards to put the camp back together while the Sorceress hurried off to let Chesmyse know the change in plans. But Lady Ashmont knew what was important and she quickly called her people together and let them know what was happening; just that they were remaining there for the day, not why since they had no need to know that particular piece of information.

So when Lagalaise returned later in the day, she found that Lady Ashmont had sent out some people to hunt and they had bagged a couple of deer that were now roasting over fires for the evening meal. She reported in to her mother and the new Pixies were now in the carriage, sorting out their possessions and storing them. About half an hour later, Thelwyn came in with the rest of the Pixies and Gwendaleir took charge, beginning to inform the newcomers about what was expected by them. Lady Windlington was pleased that both of them had encountered no difficulties in their journeys with the Pixies.

TRAVELING THROUGH KURSTMIAS

They left early the next morning and the Pixies were excited to be travelling in the carriage since it was a new experience for them; Gwendaleir spent most of the day explaining things to them and showing them the best places to watch the scenery go by. She was immensely happy about her role and Thelwyn was pleased for her. Lady Ashmont had drilled her troops in reacting from an attack while they were set up in camp the previous day for a number of times since there wasn't much else for them to do. They were actually grateful to be underway once more even though they started very early. They were traveling through northern Darkcloud and since there weren't many large towns along the road up there, they didn't stop in any town but rather camped out at night. It took them three days to approach the border with Kurstmias.

Lady Ashmont had sent two riders out front just to scout the road and give warning of any problems and they rode back to her when they were near the border to report that there were some people waiting at that spot. They told the swordswoman that there were nine or ten people waiting dismounted at the side of the road and that they had a number of cook fires burning, more than they would need for their number. It was nearly mid-day but those fires made her have some concern that there might be more troops nearby. There hadn't been any incidents with their northern neighbour for a number of years and Hargold had assured her that he considered relations with them to be very good. Roads through the kingdoms were generally considered to be safe and passable by all without the requirement of permission from the kingdom in most cases. Kurstmias had never required anyone to have authorization as far as Lady Ashmont knew but she wondered if that had changed recently. She decided that she should go ahead and check out if there was an issue in front of the main group. Since there were about ten people visible to her scouts she decided the polite thing would be to bring less people with her so she chose six other people along with her two scouts to go with her; she would leave a pair behind to watch and report back to Lady Windlington if her party ran into any problems. The small group rode forward to discover the intentions of the waiting party.

They rode slowly up along the road and as soon as the group came into sight, Lady Ashmont ordered the pair to wait and observe as she continued on. She kept her eyes roving to see if there were any noticeable threats; she could see one person rise from where he was by the fire and slowly stride to a position near the road. It was done carefully and obviously and was not the motions of a person looking to surprise a large party travelling on the road. She frowned and looked over the rest of the group. She got the impression that they were somewhat tense but trying to stay calm. It became clear as she rode up that the waiting person was a man but the rest of the group were all women. She wondered about that because as far as she knew Kurstmias had some but not a lot of women in its army. To have that many females in the party had to have some meaning, she thought as she puzzled about it. The man continued to stand easily by the side of the road as her group rode up.

As she got within hailing distance and was getting prepared to stop, the man held up his hand in a friendly fashion and said firmly "Greetings, my king and queen along with the rest of the royal family wish to express their respects to you and Princess Aurolla. We would like to offer her this token guard to ensure that no harm comes to her along our portion of the road that she travels on." Lady Ashmont looked at his smiling face and pondered questioning his assumption that she was part of Princess Aurolla's guard. She got the impression that this wasn't a guess on his part and that he undoubtedly knew about her. She didn't reply but made an obvious study of the women in his party. They all looked back at her with friendly smiles and she didn't get the impression that any of them were forced; that each of these women were happy to see her.

"I am Lady Ashmont" she stated finally as the man nodded at her introduction, acknowledging it rather than learning it. "The Princess is on her way along the road and I came forward to garner your intentions. I note that you have some cooking fires along with quite a bit of food in evidence. Are you intending to greet the Princess with a feast?" She kept her eyes on his friendly face.

"That is exactly our intention" he replied calmly. "As I said, we are here simply to make matters easier for the Princess. We don't expect her to have any issues as she travels our part of the road and acknowledge that she has immunity while travelling it but our people want her to know that we approve of her and her family and offer nothing more than respect."

Lady Ashmont nodded in acknowledgement and said shrewdly "You have a fair number of women with you, I didn't realize that your army was as integrated as that."

The man smiled at the implied question and said "These women are all volunteers for this task. There was quite a competition for the honour of being in this party. The highest placed female in our army is a captain which we felt was sufficient rank to greet the Princess." Lady Ashmont noticed that he was a captain as he said this and frowned as he continued "She would be here but unfortunately my wife is indisposed as she is heavily pregnant with our second child. I came in her place with the approval of these women." Lady Ashmont could see the women nodding in agreement and detected a fondness and respect in their actions. This was a man who these women felt comfortable being led by.

"Thank you for your greeting and your offer. I will accept on behalf of the Princess" she stated easily as she nodded her head towards one of the people she'd brought with her. The man rode back towards the main party to let them know what she'd discovered and bring them forward. The blonde swordswoman dismounted and the rest of her party followed suit. One of the very young women in the greeting party came forward to take their horses off out of the way. She was grinning hugely at the group of them as she did that. The captain offered her a seat on the blankets that had been spread on the ground and she sat down gracefully. He joined her and they chatted easily as they waited for the main party to arrive.

The main group arrived and all of the women stood and saluted the Princess as she dismounted. Aurolla was surprised by the honour but made sure to go up and greet each of them individually to their delight. She could see that these women were truly happy to see her and she could feel the warmth of their welcome. Captain Breiting got to his feet as the Princess began to make her way over to where he sat with Lady Ashmont. He grinned and gave her a salute of his own as she approached. She formally introduced herself and began to chat with him about happenings in his kingdom. The rest of the party took care of the horses and then arranged themselves on the spread blankets. The captain noted that Lady Ashmont still arranged sentries and he nodded to her in approval of her caution. The women with the captain arranged so that they were scattered amongst the larger party and were freely answering any questions put to them. It was a very friendly gathering and the food was good. Lady Ashmont was content to let her people enjoy themselves with the friendly folk from Kurstmiar for a while but after an hour she began suggesting that they get back underway. Captain Breiting immediately began to start his people into packing up what was left of the food and the Princess and her party started rearranging themselves for travel once more. Captain Breiting and his senior lieutenant asked to ride along with Lady Ashmont, Princess Aurolla and Chesmyse so that they could chat about issues that their king wanted to raise with them along the way.

The senior lieutenant introduced herself as Lieutenant Pulmite and stated that she was a member of the King's intelligence corps; she stated that she was neither an operative or diplomat in that service and that she would never be posted outside of her kingdom so there was no harm in them knowing what she was. She indicated that the King and her boss, whom she didn't name, had informed her that she was to share any knowledge that they had with the Princess and Chesmyse and that she would answer any of their questions as honestly as she could but wouldn't reveal any names or spies that might exist in their kingdoms. The others nodded their understanding and agreement with the restrictions that she was placing on their discussion; all thought that was extremely fair and understandable. Lieutenant Pulmite started by asking "What do you know about Kurstmiar, Princess?" Princess Aurolla spent about fifteen minutes relaying her understanding of the current political and economic circumstances within the kingdom. Lieutenant Pulmite listened intently and was impressed by what the young Princess did know and when the Princess was finished, she spent a couple of minutes updating or expanding what the Princess knew. Then the lieutenant indicated that she would like to spend some time later, talking with Lady Windlington since it was known that she was a close advisor of the Queen; she mentioned that she wouldn't mind talking with anyone else not in their current group at that time either. Princess Aurolla was about to mention Thelwyn but she caught the minute headshake of Lady Ashmont indicating that she shouldn't; she didn't think that Lady Ashmont wanted to keep Thelwyn in the dark about the information that the lieutenant was relating but just wanted to keep Thelwyn a secret to them.

So she said smoothly "I will arrange that for you. Would you want to ride with her in her carriage or would this evening when we stop for the night be better for you?"

"Whichever makes it easier for Lady Windlington" Lieutenant Pulmite replied. "But do you have any more questions for me at the moment?"

Lady Ashmont glanced over at the Princess to see if she wanted to continue directing the conversation or not. When it appeared that the Princess wasn't going to take charge, she asked "What about your relations with your three northern neighbours? I understand that there have been some skirmishes that have occurred. Also you have had some incursions by what seems to be bandits, have you not? Can you fill us in on these?" The lieutenant nodded and thought for a moment before telling them quite a bit about what was happening. She relayed that most of these incidents did not include regular troops from the kingdoms indicated but could have been someone else taking advantage of certain groups disposition to cause trouble. She relayed that their intelligence group wasn't entirely sure about who the perpetrator to this was for sure but they had some suspicions about that. She did mention three of their main suspects and suggested that at least two of those could be the ones who might be stirring up the trouble in Barcless as well. Chesmyse was surprised by the two that she named because she didn't think that her king had considered them. They spent a further half hour discussing these matters as they rode along. The Princess took careful note about the information so that she could share with Thelwyn later; she was pleased to note that Lady Ashmont also seemed to be absorbing the information intently.

The lieutenant took a moment to slake her parched throat and Captain Breiting stepped into the conversation. It was apparent that the captain wasn't part of the intelligence network but that he'd been trained somewhat in the diplomatic endeavors of his kingdom. He asked carefully "Is there any news as to your possible betrothal, Princess?"

Princess Aurolla frowned as she considered the question and then replied "My mother and her advisors are the ones mainly involved in that matter. They haven't yet talked to me too much about possible matches yet. My mother feels that the ideal match hasn't been offered yet and she wants the best for me. Is your King concerned about the matter?"

The captain smiled broadly and said seriously "Yes he definitely is. It will be a very important factor in diplomatic relations between the kingdoms." He noticed the Princess's puzzled and concerned look and continued "You're not aware that there has been a great deal of competition amongst a number of kingdoms for your hand for the last five or six years?"

"I didn't realize that was happening or that it had been going on for so long" the Princess admitted with a frown creasing her face. "Could you enlighten me as to why your King and his advisors think that it is so important." She did notice that Lady Ashmont appeared ready to step in to steer the conversation to a different subject but then she subsided and didn't say anything.

Captain Breiting noticed the movement of the swordswoman and paused as he thought about what information he should relate to the young woman. He sighed slightly and said "Take this as you will, Princess. My king is concerned about where you end up because you will affect the strength of whatever kingdom gains you as part of their royalty especially if you were to become married to the heir. If you pardon my crudeness, you would immediately improve their bloodlines, their prestige and their diplomatic influence. So who you and your family decide to choose is important to us." He sighed and said "There is also the matter that we have a Princess who is a year younger than you who's own betrothal is being held up because she would likely join one of the kingdoms that wasn't successful in achieving you."

The Princess turned in her saddle and enquired coolly "Why is your King holding up the betrothal of his daughter simply because of me?"

The captain smiled easily and stated "He's not the one holding it up, Princess. It is the other side that is hesitant to make the agreement because they think they still have a shot at you. You are the main prize here and our Princess is a secondary prize." He noticed her disapproval and continued "Our Queen and her daughter are aware of this fact and they aren't upset about this fact. My Princess would like to know what her future might hold so she is a bit anxious but we aren't looking to try to involve ourselves in the matter. I only bring it up to let you know that we are interested in the fact." He gave her a friendly grin.

"Why isn't your kingdom included in the ones that are so eager to get me if you state that your King and his advisors are so impressed by me then?" Princess Aurolla asked with curiosity.

"My King would love to have you join his family, your majesty, but his three older sons are all a bit older than you and are happily married. He wouldn't ask them to put aside their wives for you. All he could offer you is a Prince that wouldn't rule and he doesn't think that you or your mother would agree to that. However, if you were willing, he would introduce you to a number of important people in our kingdom in hopes of you choosing one of them as your husband. He would certainly make sure that you were gifted with a large land grant if you did agree to that." He grinned once more as she looked slightly disdainfully at him.

"Who would your king like for me to marry?" Princess Aurolla asked bluntly.

The captain smiled and said "My King would be happy to discuss the matter with you if you wish. I can not speak for him in this matter. I understand that you are in a bit of a hurry but if you stop and spend a week or so with us on your way back, we could enlighten you further as to our preference."

Princess Aurolla regarded him for a moment before replying "I will think on the matter. I might give you an answer before you leave our company but it might be made after we conclude matters in Barcless." The captain nodded in acceptance.

Lady Ashmont decided to interrupt and asked Lieutenant Pulmite "What do you know about the assassination attempt on Princess Aurolla?"

The lieutenant looked sympathetically at the Princess and replied "Not too much unfortunately. Probably not any more than Hargold already knows." She saw the slight look of surprise on Aurolla's face at the mention of her mother's spymaster and continued "Yes, we know that Hargold is your mother's spymaster same as he is sure of the name of our King's spymaster. That is information that can be hard to keep secret, especially since we tend to trade knowledge amongst ourselves. It is our understanding that Hargold thinks that the assassins were men from Hellsford but were mercenaries and not sent by the Duke. We agree that the Duke was probably not involved but there might have been some distant relatives involved. We are not sure that they were doing it entirely on their own or were doing it as a behest of another nation." She paused for a moment and Princess Aurolla interrupted with a question.

"Why wouldn't the Duke be involved but his relatives might be?" she asked, looking intently at the woman.

The lieutenant looked back at Aurolla and stated "Because the Duke is one of the main people who wants you to join his family. He is a stubborn, pig-headed man who doesn't have much nice to say about most women but he has a grudging respect for your mother. We have a firm belief that he holds you in the same regard. We know that he has offered quite a bit for your hand in marriage to his son who is a few years older than you and will be his successor. We think that some of his relatives would like it better if you didn't strengthen his bloodline or improve his approval with the people like you are apt to do. So they might be involved but we don't think they would have thought of it on their own. And we don't think they would have had the courage to do that by themselves." She grimaced a little as she said this to Aurolla.

"What is the Duke's son like?" the Princess asked with a frown.

The lieutenant grimaced and glanced at the Captain before replying "I best not say what our opinion of him is. You should make up your own mind on the matter without any interference from us." She was ignoring the Captain's hard glare at her for saying anything at all.

Princess Aurolla was savvy enough to know that the lieutenant gave her opinion of the Duke's son by saying nothing at all following the old saying that if you had nothing nice to say, say nothing. She was also smart enough to wonder about something else and she rounded on the captain and demanded "Are you really married to the only female captain in your army?"

Captain Breiting laughed for a moment before replying "Yes I really am, your majesty but you are wise to question the fact. I am also one of the King's chief advisors in a diplomatic vein. It was a happy coincidence that I was tasked to meet you. My wife really did want to come talk with you and she really is very pregnant." Princess Aurolla nodded her acceptance of those facts even though she still harboured some doubts; they discussed other matters until they were ready to stop for the night since Lady Windlington had sent back word that she would meet with Lieutenant Pulmite after the evening meal.

When it was growing close to dark, they found a clearing that they could use to camp for the night, so they stopped and began setting up camp. Princess Aurolla quickly informed Bettinka that she wanted her first maid to sit in on the talk that Lady Windlington was having with the Kurstmias lieutenant; she was just to listen, not volunteer any information. Then she informed Thelwyn that she would bring her up to date on the information discussed while the lieutenant was occupied with Lady Windlington. So after supper, the Princess and Lady Ashmont discussed what they had found out with Thelwyn. The wolf girl could tell that the Princess was excited and somewhat apprehensive to find out that she was in great demand for marriage. She was interested in the fact that the Queen hadn't been totally forthcoming about the marriage negotiations with her daughter and wondered about the reason behind that. She decided that was a matter for another day and concentrated more on the fact that relatives of the Duke of Hellsford might be the instigators of the assassination attempt. Lady Ashmont cautioned that they should not take that information as fact but to keep it in mind. She felt that there might be someone else behind the attack but didn't know who that might be as of yet.

When they were just about finished, Lady Windlington and Bettinka joined them. The Sorceress relayed what she'd discussed with Lieutenant Pulmite and it wasn't anything that the Princess hadn't already talked with her about. Bettinka mentioned that the Lieutenant had seemed to be regarding her quite closely and she didn't know why there was all the attention to her. The lieutenant had then mentioned the assassination attempt and that Bettinka had been rewarded quite handsomely for her role in foiling it. Thelwyn thought about the information for a moment and then suggested that maybe the lieutenant believed that Bettinka was a hidden bodyguard for the Princess. Bettinka was thrilled to be thought of in that way but became less so when Thelwyn cautioned her that if people assumed that she might become a target for the Princess's enemies. Bettinka didn't want that to happen. After a bit of discussion, they decided that they couldn't do too much about it since they didn't want the lieutenant to know about Thelwyn. They finished their conversation and then headed to bed.

The next morning they got underway once more and the Princess continued talking with the lieutenant and captain; they filled her in on quite a bit of background information about the nations surrounding Darkcloud but there was nothing too startling in what they relayed to her. She found the captain to be charming and easy to talk with and understood why his King had decided that he be a member of his advisors and why he had sent him to talk with her. They continued on at a good pace for the whole day, only stopping briefly for lunch; Lady Ashmont hadn't wanted to call a practice for the group with the members of Kurstmias's military amongst them. Their presence would only cause confusion and she didn't really want anyone outside their party to be aware that they were preparing for attack. It was not that she distrusted the people from Kurstmias but the fewer that knew of her tactics, the better, she thought. In the evening, they made camp and once again, the Princess let Thelwyn know about what had been discussed. Thelwyn recognized that the people from Kurstmias were being extremely forthcoming about what they knew about the political situations in the surrounding nations and was pleased. She discussed with the Princess what their motives might be for doing that and they decided that it was likely that the King of Kurstmias was only looking to improve his relations with the Princess and her mother. If that was all that they were looking to do, Thelwyn would be happy with the situation.

In the morning, the Captain and his people took their leave of the group. He had warned the Princess the night before that they would be doing this because the party was within a few hours of crossing into the kingdom of Marchnium. The captain said that Kurstmias's relations with Marchnium were fairly good but that his King didn't want to instigate any possible problem with their northern neighbour so they shouldn't approach the border. He mentioned that Marchnium usually maintained a small guard on the road at the border but that they didn't typically interfere with travellers. He thought that the Princess and her party wouldn't have a problem with them. He also took the opportunity to request that the Princess stop to visit his King and the royal family on her way back after she'd finished her visit to Barcless. He hinted that they were aware that it was more than a simple visit but wouldn't elaborate further. He also requested that the Princess send word of their meeting to her mother and that Kurstmias would like to talk about increasing their cooperation and trade with Darkcloud. The Princess recognized that this was the price that they were requesting for giving her all of the information that they had. She didn't have a problem with that because it seemed like it would benefit both kingdoms to have closer relations with one another. So the ten people from Kurstmias headed back southerly while the Princess and her party headed northeast.

AT THE BORDER OF MARCHNIUM

A few hours later, the scouts came back and reported that there were some men at the border like Captain Breiting had told them but that it was a small group of five or six. Lady Ashmont was aware that the King of Marchnium was one of the people who wanted his son married to Princess Aurolla so she didn't think that he would do anything to interfere with her on her trip. Still she thought that it was better to check into it rather than assume that all would go well so she headed forward with the scouts. They approached the group and Lady Ashmont was hit with the immediate impression that the older man in uniform commanding the small group was quite nervous so she surveyed the immediate area, alert for any possible attack. All she saw was a grey-haired man who was seated by the small watch fire and she wondered about him. It was apparent that the group which was assembled by the road would usually be gathered by their fire but the presence of the man prevented that from happening. She decided that he must have some influence from the attitude of the border guards and she wondered why such a man wouldn't have a number of guards of his own. She stood up in her stirrups and started scanning the area, not bothering to disguise her actions. The man at the fire noticed and walked slowly over to the border guards; he spoke to the commander who nodded and ordered his men back to the area by the watch fire. The man stood at ease at the side of the road, waiting for Lady Ashmont to ride up to him.

Lady Ashmont sank back into her saddle and pondered the situation for a moment; she thought that the man was trying to demonstrate that he was not a threat and that he simply wished to talk. After a moment, she signalled the scouts to remain where they were and approached the man on her own. The man waited till she was close enough to talk before speaking; she noticed that he wasn't smiling like the people from Kurstmias but that he wasn't scowling either. "Do I have the honour of addressing Lady Ashmont?" he asked neutrally. She was convinced that he knew that she was the person that he thought she was but was just being polite in his greeting.

Still there was no reason to deny it so she replied "Yes I am Lady Ashmont. I am in charge of Princess Aurolla's party and we wish to travel along this road on our way to Barcless. Will we encounter any problem in doing just that?"

"Of course not. The King of Marchnium honours the agreement to let people travel along the road without any harassment from his armed forces. He simply puts out a token force to inform people of possible laws that they might not know about and to help direct them to areas of Marchnium that they may wish to visit. They are there to allow us to monitor any large groups that might threaten our country." He hesitated slightly before stating "Not that we believe that the Princess's party is a threat to us. However I do request that she grant me a boon."

"What do you want from her?" Lady Ashmont asked flatly.

"I simply wish to greet the Princess and her party and pass on my greetings from my King. I would like to interrupt her trip for a short while to speak with her. I am an advisor of the King and am authorized to do this for him" he said without any hint of threat in the matter.

Lady Ashmont decided to push him a bit to see what he would do and replied "What if she doesn't wish to stop and talk with you?" She watched him intently to see his reaction.

The man didn't let his face or tone change in the slightest as he replied "My King would be most disappointed if she were to choose to do that but I have orders not to interfere with her trip in the slightest way." He paused to let her think about the matter for a bit and then asked "Will that be her answer?"

Lady Ashmont continued to examine him, noting his expensive gloves and clothes as well as the attitude of the border guards. This man wasn't just a minor advisor of the King, she thought, he was probably a very close advisor of that man. She pondered the consequences of avoiding this meeting and decided that there would be little to gain and maybe much to lose if they simply rode by him. "I don't know what her answer will be" she stated. "I will ride back and find out."

As she turned her horse to head back to the group, she heard him say softly "Thank you." She rode back to the scouts and told them to stay where they were and keep an eye on what the man by the road did while she rode back to the Princess's group. Then she made her way back to where the group had stopped to wait for her to return.

She rode up to the Princess, who was in a group that had dismounted their horses, and said carefully "There is a man at the border who says that he is an advisor of the King. He wishes to meet with you and have a brief talk. He says that he is authorized by his King to speak for him. I asked what would happen if you declined and he said that they would simply be disappointed but would take no action." She paused to let this sink in and then continued "He is not just a minor functionary. He is used to being obeyed without question. The border guard is nervous about him being there but he doesn't appear to have any troops with him. I think that we should talk with him and see what they want but that we should keep our guard up. What is your feeling on the matter?"

Since they were stopped and had moved away from their horses, Thelwyn had come up to the Princess to advise her; she had brought a drink from the carriage and then spent some time polishing the Princess's clean leather boots to justify her presence. The Princess glanced quickly in her direction and caught her quick nod that she agreed with the actions Lady Ashmont was advising. The Princess took her time, looking around at the group around her, before replying "I think that you are right about what we should do, Lady Ashmont. Your judgement is good and you have the best knowledge of all of us on this matter. I would like to meet this man but I am not going to get too close to him in case there is any intent on his part." She looked at Thelwyn and said to her "I think you should bring up my cloak in case I should need it." Thelwyn understood that the Princess was simply giving her an excuse to be up near her when they met with the man.

They got started and quickly joined the scouts who reported that nothing had happened; the man had simply waited there by the road waiting for them to return, he hadn't spoken to the border guards at all. So the party rode up to near the man and the Princess dismounted a ways away so that she could approach him on foot. Thelwyn carried the Princess's cloak up from the carriage and ended up just in front of her and to her left when she stopped to address the man. Lady Ashmont and six of her guards had also dismounted and arranged themselves near the pair of them. The man stood there waiting while they did this without moving or speaking.

"I am Princess Aurolla. I understand that you wish to speak with me on behalf of your King. May I have your name?" the Princess asked him as she looked him over. She agreed with Lady Ashmont that this man was not a minor advisor and that he was used to being in charge.

"My name is Janiswhym, your majesty" he replied, giving her a bow. "It is my pleasure to welcome you to Marchnium of behalf of its royal family and people. We wish you a speedy successful trip to Barcless." While he was speaking, his eyes roved around the group around her as he assessed them. The Princess, Thelwyn and Lady Ashmont all noted his scrutiny but none of them believed that he was looking for weaknesses in the Princess's protection but that he was simply looking for whatever information he could glean from them. Chesmyse had walked up with them and Janiswhym nodded at her to acknowledge that he knew who she was.

The Princess stepped in and said "Thank you for your welcome, Lord Janiswhym."

"You give me too much credit" Lord Janiswhym said dryly. "I am simply an advisor to his majesty and bring you his greetings." The Princess widened her eyes to tell him that she didn't believe that for a moment and he was quite pleased that she managed to convey that opinion without stating it out loud. "We don't think that you will run into any dangerous circumstances while you are in our kingdom but would like to warn you that we have heard that there is a group of robbers that have moved towards an area near the road north of us. There have been reports that they are harassing groups and individuals travelling along the road. I doubt that they would attack a group as big and well-armed as yours but felt that you should know about it." His eyes wandered the group again and came back to rest on Thelwyn where they rested for a moment.

"Thank you for that information" the Princess said politely. "Was there anything else?"

"My king was hoping that you might carry a message from him to the King of Barcless" he said calmly as he looked over the group once again. Once more his eyes came to rest on Thelwyn and she could feel his intense scrutiny of her and wondered why he was so interested in her.

"Why would your King wish me to carry his mess..." the Princess began, confused. "Oh, he would like to suggest to the King of Barcless that I do his bidding" she stated, slightly miffed about the matter.

"I am sure that he didn't want to suggest any such thing" Lord Janiswhym said smoothly. "He simply felt that you might do him this favour since you were already headed that way." He felt a great deal of satisfaction that the young woman in front of him had seen through the ploy without any of her advisors having to step in and inform her. "It is of no import and if you don't wish to do it, he will understand." He stood there easily awaiting her reaction.

The Princess glared at him and asked, a trifle coolly, "Do you have any more games you wish to play, Lord Janiswhym?"

"I'm afraid I don't know what you are implying, your majesty" he replied with a slight hint of glee. He was definitely impressed by the opinion that the Princess was engendering in him; she was very much like what had been reported about her, smart and forthright. Then he sobered back up and said "One more thing that my King would like to do is to invite you to come visit him and his son on your return trip. He would like for you to spend a week or two in our kingdom so that you can meet our people and see our nation. We believe that you would benefit mightily from doing that." He paused and looked around the group once more, giving Thelwyn a wink as he paused on her. "But I am keeping you from being on your way; so once again, I bid you a safe trip." He stepped back and bowed once more.

"I will think about your offer of visiting your kingdom on my return trip" she stated as she went back to get her horse. Thelwyn looked intently at the Lord as she went back to the carriage so that they could proceed again. She was pondering his actions and felt that he'd made a decision about her and she wondered what it was. Then they were on their way once more.

After they had travelled for more than a half hour, Lady Ashmont and Princess Aurolla rode back and joined Lady Windlington and Thelwyn in the carriage. Lady Ashmont gave her horse to Lagalaise to ride for the time that she was in the carriage and Princess Aurolla put Annilee on her gelding. The young girl was apprehensive about being on the horse so Bettinka came back and led the horse at a slow pace. Annilee was thrilled to be on the large animal by herself because she'd only rode on a horse in front of Bettinka previously. Lagalaise knew how to ride horses and was only in the carriage to assist her mother in case anything occurred; she rode Lady Ashmont's fine stallion with glee. Lady Ashmont glanced over towards Cassmetra, wondering if she should request the thief ride with the drivers up top while they talked but Thelwyn shook her head negatively about that so the thief stayed. Thelwyn had been impressed by what Cassmetra said about the dead man who'd been killed at the inn and by the observations the woman had made about things that happened subsequently. So they began to talk about their encounter with Lord Janiswhym.

"He's very obviously one of the King's top advisor" Princess Aurolla stated confidently. "What was his purpose in meeting with us? A lesser official could have delivered the information just as well."

"He chose to do this so that he could get a look at you, Princess" Lady Windlington said firmly. "He wanted to see if the reports about you were accurate or not. That is why he tried to play you. To see if you would notice it and what you would do about it." Thelwyn noted Cassmetra nodding in agreement.

The Princess frowned thoughtfully and asked "If that was his purpose, did I pass his scrutiny? I assume that he was doing that for his King and not someone else."

"Oh, I think that we can be sure that you passed in his opinion" Lady Windlington said with confidence. "He wouldn't have made the offer to host you on your return if he didn't feel that you were up to the standards he was looking for. And I am pretty sure that he is the King's top advisor so his recommendation would carry a lot of weight." The Princess looked pleased about the fact.

"You think he was checking out whether or not the Princess would be a good match for the Prince, don't you?" Lady Ashmont said to the Sorceress. Lady Windlington nodded without saying anything and Lady Ashmont nodded in return as she considered the matter. The Princess looked at them with some astonishment.

Thelwyn broke in and stated softly "He seemed to be somewhat concerned with me. He kept looking us all over and then ending with me. He did that a couple of times and he winked at me the final time." Lady Ashmont, Lady Windlington and Princess Aurolla all looked at her with some puzzlement on their faces.

Cassmetra said quietly "He was looking to see who was standing where so that he could determine their role in the Princess's life. He was worried about you because he expected to see a large man who could handle a sword extremely well to be standing in the place that you were. He couldn't understand why you were there, Thelwyn, and then he realized that you couldn't be what you appeared to be. That is when he winked at you." The others looked at her, stunned as they thought about what she had said.

Lady Ashmont slowly said "What Cassmetra says makes a lot of sense. He is quite a perceptive man who could figure something like that out. We will have to watch that but we won't be running into too many like him." She glanced meaningfully at Thelwyn who nodded her understanding. "Okay" she said briskly. "I need to get back to commanding my troops." She leaned out of the carriage and called Lagalaise to bring her horse back. The Princess soon followed her and they continued on until they stopped for the night, all of them ruminating about Lord Janiswhym.

When they were all done eating supper and were just getting ready to turn in for the night, Gwendaleir flew up to Thelwyn and asked quietly "A Pixie is watching us. Should I go over and meet with her or do we have enough Pixies at the moment?"

Thelwyn replied "Let's go over and discuss this with Lady Windlington but I think that she wants to gather all of the Pixies that she can while we are travelling." They went over to talk to the Sorceress and soon Gwendaleir was heading to the woods with a gift of a pack and sword to offer the new Pixie. When the Pixie came out to meet her, Gwendaleir noted that the Pixie appeared young and somewhat bedraggled. It was obvious that she was on her own and seemed to be just hanging on. It didn't take any persuasion at all by Gwendaleir to get the Pixie to join them; simply the promise of regular meals was about all that it took. Since she really didn't have much in the way of possessions in her home and Gwendaleir promised that they would supply the few things that she already had, the new Pixie flew into the camp with Gwendaleir. Lady Windlington and Thelwyn were surprised that they hadn't been called over to talk with the Pixie but welcomed the newcomer as friendly as they could. The Sorceress noted the new Pixie's condition and took her off to check her over and see if any of her medicines could help to improve her condition. She would also make sure that the Pixie got the items she would need to exist on a daily basis since she wasn't bringing anything with her.

The next morning they were on their way once more and they travelled the morning without any incident but Lady Ashmont called for a practice defending against an attack. She was pleased that they responded fairly quickly now. After their mid-day meal, they were travelling again. Cassmetra noticed a group of four riders overtake them; she was suspicious about how they were dressed and how much surreptitious attention they appeared to be paying to the Princess's party. She concentrated on reviewing in her mind why those riders seemed to spark interest in her and she determined that they might be scouts for the group of robbers that Lord Janiswhym had warned them of. He'd said that they were operating north of the border and they weren't at the border yet; they would probably cross it the next morning. She decided that she was disturbed enough that she felt that she had to let Thelwyn know about her feelings.

"Thelwyn" she began hesitantly. "I'm concerned about those riders that just passed us. They seemed to be observing us too closely and I wonder about the information that Lord Janiswhym told us about the robber group operating north of the border. They might have moved down south to surprise us." She looked anxiously to see how Thelwyn was taking her apprehensions. Thelwyn was considering her fears; she'd been quite good at interpreting matters previously so serious thought should be given in her opinion. Then she made her decision and leaned out of the carriage window to call over one of the riders to let Lady Ashmont know that she wished to speak to her.

Lady Ashmont came back to speak with them and Thelwyn told her "Cassmetra feel that the riders who just passed us may be scouts for the group of robbers that we were warned about. She thinks that they might have moved down the road to try to take us unawares. I think she could be right and that we should take some precautions in case she is. What do you think?"

Lady Ashmont thought about the matter for a moment and replied "It is possible she is right and it certainly wouldn't hurt us to prepare for an attack. I'll go warn my people now." She rode up to let the guards know that they should keep watch for a possible attack and to get their light wooden shields that would work against arrows ready at hand. Cassmetra looked gratefully at Thelwyn, happy that her concerns had been taken with such seriousness. She hoped that she was wrong and that nothing would happen but was content that she'd warned the group.

The attack came over an hour later as arrows came flying out of the woods in front of them. Because of the training that Lady Ashmont had been forcing them to perform, the guards reacted almost immediately as four pairs of them rushed at the spots that the four archers were shooting from. The archers were quite shocked at how fast the riders reached them. They had been prepared to flee but didn't have the opportunity to do so before the riders attacked them. Their battles were over quick as the guards killed the lightly armed bowmen. One archer on the far left had an arrow cocked as the two horsemen came at him but as he was trying to draw a bead on the lead female rider, she slipped to the side of the horse making it impossible for him to hit her. Her horse ran quickly towards him but off to the side and when she came by him she popped back into her saddle and struck at the side of his neck with her sword. He was dead before her partner rode his horse over him. The second guard slipped off his horse to ensure that the archer was dead and saw that there was no doubt about it. He picked up the body and put it across the saddle of his partner who'd returned.

Another archer tried to turn and run before the horsemen reached him. The man riding the horse aimed his sword for the middle of the fleeing archer's back and with the horse's impetus skewered the leather clad man. The other two pairs of guards managed to kill their foes with only one guard receiving an arrow to the shoulder before killing the archers. But the arrow attack was just a feint to draw off the guards from the Princess's party.

The main attack had thought that the group would continue on enough so that they could attack them from behind but the Princess's party had responded so quickly that the group of men that came out of the woods was still in front of the carriage and immediately conflicted with the main body of the Princess's group. They were surprised that the group of people in front of them were larger and more alert than the rearguard that they had been expecting. Nevertheless they were committed to their attack and rushed at the group that had dismounted to protect the Princess, her maids and the carriage. The attackers weren't used to fighting an organized, trained group like Lady Ashmont had assembled and the fact that they didn't outnumber their prey also hampered them. Lady Ashmont spotted the movement out of the corner of her eye and she made her way over to help the guards that were near the forest. Her troops had quickly turned to face the attackers. The guards had been trained to work in pairs and to protect each other and they quickly fell into those formations. The lead attacker rushed one man and swung his sword at him; the man speedily parried the blow and tried a counter attack but was foiled. The two men clashed swords for a while until the woman guard to the right of the attacker managed to disengage herself from her opponent for a moment by hitting him with her shield and stuck her sword into the attacker's armpit. The man groaned and looked over at her as the man he'd been fighting struck at his exposed neck, killing him. The female guard had returned to her opponent and managed to stab him in the leg before cutting him across the throat. One guard was being fairly hard pressed by a large man and had been slashed along the arm. The attacker raised his sword to finish the guard when Lady Ashmont arrived and stuck her sword into his throat. The attacker gurgled and fell. Thelwyn slipped out of the door of the coach and surveyed the attack. She was prepared to join in the fray but was concerned that there might be another group ready to attack the carriage and she was the only one who was in place to prevent that. She watched as the guards speedily foiled the initial rush and slaughter almost half of the adversaries confronting them.

The remainder of the opponents turned and fled back into the forest. A couple of the guards made to follow them but Lady Ashmont immediately called them back to their places. She didn't want them to try to pursue the men through the forest where they might be vulnerable. Their job wasn't to eliminate the robbers but to ensure that the Princess was protected and able to do what she wanted. Both she and Thelwyn scanned the area to see if there might be an even larger attack launched on them. They didn't see any sign that that might occur and the riders came back with the archer's bodies in case Lady Ashmont wanted to examine them. Lady Ashmont assigned some people to keep sentry while they investigated the situation. She was quite pleased with how the encounter had gone; her people had reacted very speedily and well and the Princess and her maids had rushed to the protection for them with alacrity. She spent a few minutes talking to her people to let them know of her approval of them.

Thelwyn and Cassmetra were already checking over the bodies to determine what they might be wearing or carrying to identify them. Lady Windlington had already checked to see if there was any magic associated with them and having determined that there wasn't, had given them the go ahead. Lady Ashmont came over and stood by the Sorceress, Princess Aurolla, Chesmyse and her bodyguard as they watched the proceedings. There had been two men who hadn't been killed outright but they weren't going to survive their wounds so Thelwyn had dispatched them, determining that they wouldn't regain consciousness to answer any questions before they likely died. She didn't feel any queasiness about her actions having done similar in the past. The men hadn't been carrying too much but they brought the items that they had gleaned over to the group.

Lady Ashmont and Lady Windlington both handled and examined the items that Cassmetra was holding out in front of them for a few minutes before they began discussing their thoughts. "Not very much here" Lady Ashmont remarked as she put a fancy knife back in the basket that Cassmetra was holding. "Less than I would expect from a group of robbers, in fact" she stated as she surveyed the bodies once more.

"I don't think that these men were robbers" Cassmetra ventured carefully. "Most robber bands would have included some women and there are none. Also, these men are a little too well fed and in too good of condition to have been existing on their own in the woods for any length of time. These men seem to be members of someone's army. They had too much coordination in their attack to be anything else, even though it really didn't do them too much good. Your people certainly surprised them by their response, Lady Ashmont."

The swordswoman nodded her acknowledgement of the compliment and said "I think that you are right, Cassmetra. Those archers have too good of bows not to have been in the militia of someone. If we hadn't been prepared for them and hadn't attacked them back as quickly as we did, they could have wreaked some havoc on our people. As it is, we only have about four people wounded who will all recover fairly quickly. Do you or anyone else have an opinion on who these men might belong to?"

Everyone but Cassmetra shook their heads, denying knowledge but the thief grimaced slightly and said "Lieutenant Pulmite suggested that relatives of the Duke of Hellsford might have been involved in the assassination attempt and could be involved in further actions against the Princess. I think that maybe these men could be traced back to them. They have the look of men from Hellsford but not necessarily the look of mercenaries like the other body we examined." She looked intently at Lady Ashmont and stated "I think this but am not totally confident that it is the case." The swordswoman nodded understanding that Cassmetra was only giving her best opinion on the matter but felt she could also be wrong.

"It's the best opinion that we all have. Thank you Cassmetra" she replied. They discussed matters for a few more minutes but couldn't come up with any better information or opinions. Lady Ashmont had some of the guards drag the bodies off to the side of the road; they wouldn't waste any time in burying them but would let the border guard know about where they were. They were quickly on their way once more and let the men at the border know about what had happened and where as they crossed into the next kingdom, Zobreska.

TRAVEL THROUGH ZOBRESKA

They travelled for a few hours more but there was still a few hours of light left when the forward scouts came back to report that there was a caravan from Barcless ahead. They rode forward and had a brief meeting with the caravan master who indicated to Chesmyse that he had news from her father and their king. Lady Ashmont decided that they might as well camp together for the night for mutual protection because the robber band that they had encountered might not have been the one that they had been warned about. Since the robbers that had attacked them were actually guardsmen most likely from relatives of the Duke of Hellsford, they might not be the robbers that people had been reporting in this area and both parties individually might have made inviting targets. Combined they would be too large to take on in the swordswoman's opinion. The caravan master agreed and the two groups began setting up camp together. There was a babbling brook nearby and people went off to fetch water. The caravan master indicated to Chesmyse that he would pass on his messages to her later and went off to direct his people. Princess Aurolla let Thelwyn know about this exchange as they were arranging her tent and Thelwyn went off in search of Cassmetra.

"Do you think you could sneak up close enough to hear what is being said in Chesmyse's tent without being caught?" she asked the thief. Cassmetra thought about it for a moment and then nodded that she could. "I want to know if Chesmyse is told anything of import that she doesn't share with us but don't take any chances with being caught. If you can't do it, that will be fine" Thelwyn cautioned. Cassmetra went off to work her way over to her target area.

There was a bard that was travelling with the caravan for protection; he was a fairly handsome man with a strong, melodic voice. As Lady Ashmont was directing her people he came over to her and crooned slightly "Ah, my Lady, if I could crave a boon to whisper in your delicate shell-like ear."

Lady Ashmont grimaced a bit but said neutrally "If you wish, sir. What may I do for you?"

The bard glanced around as slyly as he could and said quite loudly "I would like to perform for the Princess and wonder if you would grant your permission." Before she could answer, he stated quietly "The north wind warms our fields."

Lady Ashmont looked at him, startled slightly for a moment and then said "I think the Princess would like that." She completed the recognition phrase is a low voice saying "The southern sun casts many shadows."

The bard smiled and said "I will take my leave to go prepare for entertaining the fine Princess then."

"You may wish to take a walk after your performance" Lady Ashmont stated, indicating to him that someone would contact him during that walk. He nodded and left.

Lady Ashmont made sure that everything was going well and that her people could finish without her before making her way to the Princess's tent. She went into the tent as the maids were putting the finishing touches on it for the Princess. She walked up to where Thelwyn and Princess Aurolla were standing and asked "Thelwyn, do you think that you or Cassmetra could do something for me later tonight?"

Thelwyn frowned somewhat and replied "I'm afraid that Cassmetra might be busy doing something else. I certainly could do it though."

Lady Ashmont nodded, figuring that no one would pay attention to either woman if she went off and met with the bard whereas her own meeting with him might cause some notice. "The bard is an agent for Hargold. He is available to carry a message back to him and I want to pass that message on to him. He might also have some knowledge of what we might run into on our trip that he wishes to pass on to us. He will go for a walk after he sings for the Princess and I want you to meet him out there and retrieve whatever he knows. I will go off now and write out the scroll for him to carry on to Hargold." Thelwyn nodded in acknowledgement of the simple task and Lady Ashmont took her leave.

Shortly after they had begun setting up their camp, Lady Windlington and Lagalaise had come over to Thelwyn and spoke with her. Lagalaise had detected some magical charms that a small trader, who purported to be from Crossmountain and had joined the caravan from Barcless for security, was carrying in his wagon. She was concerned as to what they might be and wanted to have a look at them. They had asked Thelwyn if Cassmetra could attempt to steal them so that they could examine them. It was possible that they were simply some sort of benign charms but they could be more dangerous than that and they wanted to make sure. Thelwyn told them that she would discuss the matter with Cassmetra and they had left.

Cassmetra returned to the tent shortly before they were ready to eat their evening meal. She informed Thelwyn that she had managed to overhear the conversation in Chesmyse's tent and Thelwyn told her what the Sorceress wanted her to do. Cassmetra agreed to attempt the theft. They went off to enjoy their supper. As was their usual practice, Chesmyse, Charlymi and Pellaynu joined the Princess and her immediate party for dinner; they brought the caravan master and the bard with them. When they were done, Chesmyse relayed the news that the caravan master had told her in her tent earlier to the group. The main news was that there was still a major problem with Pixies at the estate and that there had been some other magical incursions in the kingdom. Chesmyse's father was waiting for their arrival quite anxiously. The king had warned that there were further attacks on the northern border and now some magical protection and attacks were also occurring there so they might have to travel to that area. The caravan master had reported having little problems along the road down from the kingdom but felt that it might just be because no one was concerned about people travelling south from Barcless. It might be different for them because they were headed towards Barcless. There were a few other items but nothing of note. Cassmetra listened to what Chesmyse said and when she was done, she nodded her head to Thelwyn to acknowledge that it was essentially all that had been said; there only had been some minor messages of a more personal nature that Chesmyse hadn't bothered to pass on. Thelwyn had no qualms about checking on Chesmyse's honesty but was happy that she'd been forthright with them.

The bard started singing some songs and entertained them for over half an hour before he excused himself and went for a walk in the woods. Thelwyn had slipped out to meet with him while Cassmetra had left to burgle the wagon soon after the bard started. Cassmetra had stolen the small chest with what she thought would be the magical items and taken it out to where Lagalaise waited for her in order to inspect them. When Lagalaise confirmed that the chest contained the items that she was interested in, Cassmetra opened the simple lock so that Lagalaise could look more closely at them. Lagalaise quickly determined that they were minor charms that would help to relieve the pain of the wearer and nothing more. She had Cassmetra return them to where she'd found them. Thelwyn meanwhile waited along the path that she was sure that the bard would take with the scroll from Lady Ashmont. When the bard came close she slipped out from the shadows in the trees and surprised him.

"Whoa, where did you pop out from?" he asked startled. He took a closer look at the small figure and finally recognized that she was one of the Princess's people even though he hadn't paid her too much attention.

"Lady Ashmont asked me to meet you and give you this" she said as she held out the scroll. "She felt that no one would notice me leaving whereas she would be spotted. Do you have anything you wish me to tell her?"

"As the caravan master said, we didn't encounter any problems on the road but there was some ruckus in the last town that we left and you may have some issue with that. I don't know what it was about but there were some men that appeared to be grouping together to discuss matters. That was about five days ago that we went through that town. We spent two nights there." Thelwyn nodded and then slipped back into the woods and made her way back to the camp. The bard strolled for a few minutes more and then returned as well.

Thelwyn reported her success to Lady Ashmont and passed on the information to her. She also was informed of the information that Cassmetra and Lagalaise had discovered. Then the party all bedded down for their early start in the morning. There were no disturbances in the night.

They started off on the road in the morning. The scouts spoke of noticing some people watching from far off but they weren't disturbed by anyone on their trip. They travelled along until they stopped for their mid-day meal. Lady Ashmont commented "I think that maybe the men watching us might be from the robber group that we were warned about. I am less convinced that the attack on us was by the group that had been reported operating here and was a targeted attack on us in particular. But they are keeping their distance, probably because of our size so we won't worry too much about them." They all nodded in acceptance and continued eating.

Gwendaleir and the rest of the Pixies had been practicing over in the woods where they had room to move around more than in the carriage. Thelwyn walked over to watch them as the rest of the party began packing up to continue on. Shortly after she arrived, Gwendaleir detected a Pixie deeper in the woods and came over to ask Thelwyn if she wanted to go see if she could contact the newcomer. Thelwyn went back and asked Lady Windlington if she wanted to try to contact the new Pixie. Lady Windlington looked over the party as it was completing its preparations and said "We want to get all of the Pixies that we can so go out with the Pixies and see if you can make contact. If the Pixie flees, just let it go and return here and we will be on our way. I'll go tell Lady Ashmont to delay our departure until you return. Lagalaise will give you the gift we have been offering." So as she went to talk with the swordswoman and Princess Aurolla, Thelwyn got the gift from Lagalaise who decided that she would come with them and they headed out.

When she got back to the group of Pixies, Thelwyn told them to spread out so that they could make contact with strange Pixie. She told them not to approach the Pixie too aggressively but to try to make friendly contact. She told them that if the Pixie chose to fly off, just to let her do that. So they headed off. The Pixies flew forward openly and calmly with their weapons sheathed. Lagalaise was still masking their magical signatures. The Pixie became quickly aware of the approaching group by their obvious movements and stopped to observe them. The group paused so as not to startle the other Pixie into flight and Gwendaleir made her way forward slowly. The Pixie watched her a moment and then headed to meet her. She stopped a distance away and called "What are you doing in my woods? And why can't I see your magic?"

"We have come to see if we can talk with you. My name is Gwendaleir. If you don't want to talk, we will leave and not bother you. A sorceress is covering our magic so that our enemies can't detect us" Gwendaleir replied calmly.

The new Pixie looked over the group of twelve Pixies and said "What do you wish to talk about?"

Gwendaleir had been looking over the other Pixie and noted that she appeared to be doing quite well for herself, she had a good set of clothing and it looked like some metal knives but not a steel sword. She didn't appear to be starving but looked in good shape. She held forth the gift and said "We would like to offer you these items as gifts and would like to sit down and tell you what we are doing. Our humans would like you to join us if you agree with us but you can keep this gift even if you decide you want to stay as you are."

"Are you traders then" the Pixie asked, curious.

"No" Gwendaleir said with a small frown. "Do you deal with human traders?"

"No, there's a group of twenty or so Pixies that live in a community a little ways away that I trade with" the Pixie admitted. "I don't know where they get their goods but I got these knives from them. Is that a sword, I see?" She was looking quite intently at the offered gift.

"Yes, it's a sword and you can have it if you wish."

"Those are your humans, then?" she asked as she waved towards Lagalaise and Thelwyn. "I suppose it wouldn't hurt to talk with them. Have them come up here and have the other Pixies remain where they are." She was still eyeing the sword with interest. Gwendaleir put the pack and sword down where she was, turned her back and flew back to get Thelwyn. She half expected the other Pixie to grab the gift and fly off but the Pixie remained politely where she was as she waited for Gwendaleir and the humans to return. Thelwyn and Lagalaise made their way slowly forward, trying not to pose a theat.

They came up to a respectable distance from the Pixie and stopped, standing close together so the Pixie could observe them easily without having to look around. "Hi, my name is Lagalaise" Lagalaise offered with a friendly smile. "I am going to remove my mask of our magic now so that you can see our power." She removed her spell and watched the Pixie carefully.

The Pixie was impressed by the power she saw in the young sorceress but quickly noticed Thelwyn. "A Wolf Princess" she said in awe as she looked Thelwyn over quite intently. "Well, I never expected that. Are you asking me to join you, Wolf Princess?"

"My name is Thelwyn and yes, I would like for you to join us" Thelwyn replied in a friendly fashion. "I represent my Princess in this matter. What would you like us to call you?"

"I go by the name of Purple Cedar" the Pixie replied. She looked wistfully around her and said, sadly "I've got such a nice area here and I really don't want to give it up. But if you are asking for my help, I feel I must honour your request." She paused and looked more intently at Thelwyn, asking "Do you want more Pixies to join you?"

Thelwyn said instantly "Yes, we would like as many as we can get. Do you know of some that might assist us?"

"The group that I trade with might be willing to join you, especially if you do the asking" Purple Cedar replied. "It would take me over a day to fly over to meet with them, though."

The Pixie was still looking quite sadly around her so Thelwyn said softly to her "If you don't like your circumstances when we are finished with your help, I can bring you back here if you want." Purple Cedar brightened considerably at this offer while Lagalaise glanced over at Thelwyn and frowned in disapproval. Thelwyn ignored the other girl because she felt that the Pixie deserved that choice. "Let us go back and talk with some more of our people so we can decide how we are going to proceed" Thelwyn offered. "I think that maybe I can cut down on your time to contact the other group and maybe help in convincing them as well. Would you accompany us to talk with our other people?" They went back to talk with Lady Windlington and the others.

Lady Windlington considered the matter for a moment; she wanted the Pixies but she didn't want to have the party wait for too long to go get them and convince them to join. She said "I'd like to recruit those Pixies but it will take us to long to go to them. Perhaps we should just continue on without them." She sighed to show her displeasure at having to make that decision.

Thelwyn said carefully "Perhaps I can go get them and catch up with you further up the road. It seems like I might be the only one to convince them on my own anyways, being the Wolf Princess they adore."

Lady Windlington frowned at Thelwyn and started to ask "How can you..." Thelwyn made trotting motions with her hands and the Sorceress understood; Thelwyn could go in her wolf form and travel faster than the humans or the Pixies. "How will you be able to find us?" she asked.

"Gwendaleir can guide me to you and Lagalaise if she removes the mask on your power" Thelwyn replied.

Lady Windlington thought about it for a moment; she knew that leaving their power exposed might attract the enemy to their position but she thought that he probably already had the idea that they were on the road. She weighed the pros and cons of what Thelwyn was proposing and decided that the risk was worth trying. "Okay, go ahead. Since Lagalaise has the most power she'll leave herself unmasked for Gwendaleir. You might as well get on your way right away. We'll spend the night here and leave in the morning. You know that the road runs mostly north and somewhat east from here for the next few days right? So you can intercept us along it up north of here." Thelwyn nodded knowing that Lady Windlington was letting the mother in her show up.

Thelwyn gathered what she would need and put it into the small sturdy pack that she would carry in her mouth. Since she would be carrying gifts for the Pixies she decided to forgo her dress that she normally took but she did pack her small eating knife. Lagalaise went out into the woods with her so she could bring Thelwyns clothes back with her and she removed the mask from Thelwyn and herself just before Thelwyn changed to her wolf form.

"Oh my" Purple Cedar exclaimed as Thelwyn shifted. She was thrilled that she would actually get to ride on the back of a real Wolf Princess. Gwendaleir attempted to show nonchalance about the trip but she was quite excited about it as well. The two Pixies settled themselves comfortably on Thelwyn's shoulders with Purple Cedar responsible for guiding them on the right paths to the Pixie settlement. Since all of them could see quite well in the dark, they would travel through the night and hoped to be there for the morning.

Thelwyn trotted through the dark forest but didn't encounter any problems on their trip; she had detected only normal woods inhabitants and had to pay attention as she perceived a bear but it was a distance away. Purple Cedar had managed to guide them quite well and they arrived at the home of the Pixies. Since she was unmasked, the Pixies were aware that Thelwyn was approaching and were extremely curious about the fact. They flew out to check on her as she approached and Purple Cedar called a greeting to them.

"I've brought a Wolf Princess to meet with you" she gushed. "She's brought you some gifts as well." Since the Pixies didn't challenge her to stop, Thelwyn continued trotting into the main clearing of their camp. She glanced around, noting that this group of Pixies shared trees for their homes which was quite different than the smaller groups she'd seen before. They appeared quite prosperous where they were and Thelwyn wondered how they had been managing that and where they got their small metal tools from which appeared to be their major trade good. When she reached a good spot in their camp, she stopped, put down her pack and waited. Purple Cedar wasn't aware of what Thelwyn wanted so she continued to sit on her back; however, Gwendaleir flew up and then told Purple Cedar to do the same. When both Pixies were in the air once more, Thelwyn changed back to her human form. She looked around at the impressed group of Pixies and smiled at them in a friendly fashion. She heard comments like "A real Wolf Princess," "Wow" and "Impressive" from the Pixies.

One Pixie flew forward and asked "What can we do for you, Wolf Princess?"

Thelwyn started taking the gifts out of her pack and arranging them in front of her as she replied "Purple Cedar was kind enough to guide me to your settlement. I simply wish to talk with you to see if I can persuade you to help us. I understand that you are traders." She looked around noting the number of metal items that these Pixies had but she didn't see any swords. "You have quite a number of knives, axes and plates. Do you make them yourselves?"

The head Pixie just waved her hand and didn't reply to that question; she was looking slightly greedily at the swords that Thelwyn was offering to them. She didn't want to admit that they exchanged singing for the metal goods with a nearby dwarf and that the dwarf refused to make them swords. "Those are very nice swords you are offering. May we have a closer look at them?"

"Of course. I brought what I hope is enough for each one of you. Feel free to take them and one of the packs as well. You should find them of some use" Thelwyn replied as she watched the slight scramble the Pixies made for the gifts. As they were admiring what she gave them, she described the situation and what she wanted for them. It took her over twenty minutes to do that.

When she was done the head Pixie asked "Could we have some time to discuss this amongst ourselves. You must be tired and in need of some food. Feel free to help yourselves to whatever is around." She pointed to a nearby area by the babbling brook.

Thelwyn looked over to the area and said "Thank you. Do you mind if I see if I can catch a fish?" She was granted permission and headed over there. She gathered some wood and began a fire so that she could cook the fish if she caught one. Then she changed into her wolf form and waded into the cold brook. She had seen some fish jumping so she knew that they were in the stream. She stood still for nearly two minutes watching the stream. A plump trout swam by and she plunged her head down and snatched it up with her mouth. It flopped in a desperate attempt to free itself but she managed to carry it over and drop it by the fire. She changed back into human and gutted the trout. She was just spitting it nicely over the fire on a willow branch when she became aware that there were more Pixies watching her than just Gwendaleir and Purple Cedar. She looked them over and found out that there were four other Pixies there. They looked quite young and had already begun wearing their gifted outfits.

Their leader flew forward saying "That was quite impressive Wolf Princess. We are not able to catch fish ourselves. Would you be able to catch another one so that we can taste what they taste like?" She grinned at Thelwyn.

Thelwyn thought about it and then replied "Sure. Gwendaleir, would you keep an eye on this one?" Gwendaleir nodded that she would and Thelwyn returned to the stream. It didn't take her long before she returned with another trout and soon it was cooking along with the first. "Why are you over here and not at the meeting?" she asked the Pixies curious.

"Oh" replied their leader as she watched the fish cooking. "They're over there discussing whether or not to go with you and we've already decided. We are going with you whether they agree to or not." She looked over at Thelwyn and stated "We are convinced that it is the right thing to do but we know that they wouldn't listen to our arguments anyways because we are the younger members of the tribe. Besides it was fun to come over here and watch you catch fish." Thelwyn grinned at them and tended to the fish. When it was cooked she took it off the fire to cool slightly. She could feel herself drooling slightly at its wonderful smell and the Pixies were all watching it quite raptly. After a moment she portioned it out, keeping the majority of it for herself but giving all of the Pixies a piece. The second one was still cooking and they could all share it when it was done too. They all ate their fish and then Thelwyn pulled the second one off of the fire. When it had cooled she offered the Pixies a second piece and all but one took her up on her offer. She'd talked a bit with the new Pixies in just a general get to know you type conversation without pressing them too much for any information.

When they were done eating, she could see that the other Pixies were still arguing about whether or not to join her so she decided to take a nap. She asked the Pixies to wake her if the others came to a conclusion and then shifted to her wolf form and settled down to sleep. Gwendaleir flew over and cuddled against her neck. Purple Cedar looked at this for a brief moment and then she also snuggled against Thelwyn. Thelwyn was a bit surprised when three of the new Pixies also joined her but made no protest in the matter.

She woke up about forty-five minutes later feeling refreshed and moved about gently to wake up the Pixies. They had already been awake but only moved away from her when she starting moving about. When they were all off her, she changed back into human and asked "Have they made up their minds yet?"

"No" reported the Pixie that had remained on watch. Thelwyn nodded and went down to the brook to get a drink and to wash her face. When she returned to the small fire, the leader of the Pixies had flown over to tell her that they had decided on what they would do. So she followed her back over to the settlement so that she could hear about it.

The leader waited until Thelwyn was settled and then she started to speak. "We have decided that most of us will go with you, Wolf Princess. We are aware that legends say that we should help you and we will. We have twenty-three Pixies here. I know that these four will go with you no matter what." She indicated the Pixies that had joined Thelwyn in eating fish. "Another fourteen of us will go with you for your trip but we want to return here after you are done and are on your way back to your home kingdom. That will leave the five oldest and least mobile here to protect our homes. Is all of this acceptable to you?" The Pixies all watched her intently to see what her reaction would be.

"That would be perfectly acceptable" Thelwyn replied reasonably. "I thank you for your help and will guide you back here afterwards if you need me to do so. When can we leave? I want to rejoin my people on the road as soon as I can."

"We know that the road is north and just slightly east of here. There is a creek that crosses it that we know about. It will probably be our best place to intercept them. We will guide you to it" the leader stated. "Since we will be returning we won't be carrying too much with us so we can be ready to go in about a half hour if you want. But we can only travel at our speed." Then she snorted slightly, and said "Unless you plan to carry us like you did the two you arrived with."

Thelwyn quickly considered the matter; there would be twenty Pixies and their stuff. She'd brought as much as their stuff in her small pack as gifts so that would be no problem. The twenty of them could hold onto her fur and travel on her back and she would be able to get them all there quicker, she thought. "Okay, I will carry all of you but you'll have to hold on tightly" she said. The Pixies all looked at her in shock but they became very enthused about the idea. They scurried off to pack what they were taking with them. Soon they were on their way and Thelwyn could hear the excited chatter of the happy Pixies; they'd never travelled on wolf back before.

About four hours before dawn they encountered the stream that the Pixie leader stated would carry them along to the road and Thelwyn followed it for a couple of hours until they reached the road. When she determined that it was actually the road she stopped and the Pixies all flew up off of her. She changed back to human and asked Gwendaleir "Can you determine where Lagalaise is?"

Gwendaleir flew around a bit and concentrated on where Lagalaise might be. She felt her pulse of magic just on the edge of her range and she pointed towards it. "She is that way."

Thelwyn nodded, happy because Gwendaleir was pointing to the southwest, and said "Okay, then they should be coming here and we can join them. There isn't too much use in our backtracking to them so we can rest for a while. Can you tell how far they are or when they might reach us?"

Gwendaleir shook her small head and said "They are at about the limit of my range but I don't know how far that might be. I also don't know how long it might take for them to reach us." She shrugged her shoulders at Thelwyn in apology. Thelwyn nodded and suggested that they might as well rest up until they arrived so she led them along the stream back off of the road and set up camp. The Pixies were all anxious to try fish so she went off and caught three trout after starting a fire for them.

After they had eaten, Thelwyn asked Gwendaleir to keep a watch on whether Lagalaise was on the move because it was starting to become light. She directed Gwendaleir to wake her if the Princess's group was coming close and settled down for a nap for a few hours to regain her vitality. She was pretty close to being on her reserves but the meal and a few hours of sleep would put her right again. She shifted to her wolf form so she would be warmer while sleeping. When she woke up just over three hours later, she discovered that most of the Pixies had settled in against her to nap on their own. She moved about gently and they woke up and left her warm body. She got up, stretched and yawned mightily. Then she changed back into a human and asked Gwendaleir "Are they still a ways south of us? Can you guess how far they might be?"

"They are still a ways south of us. I would guess it will be three or four hours before they reach here but that is just a guess" she replied with a small frown of concentration.

"Are you tired, Gwendaleir?" Thelwyn asked carefully, she didn't want the Pixie to overtax herself and she had been keeping watch for quite a while.

"No" replied the Pixie. "Purple Cedar and Blue Fox have been helping me keep watch. I have only been checking on Lagalaise every once in a while. I didn't think there was a need for me to try to keep her in focus constantly. Just check to make sure she was heading this way. Did I do right?" the Pixie asked slightly anxiously.

"Of course you did right" Thelwyn replied, impressed that the small creature had determined that herself. She was really learning how to be more and more of a help, she thought happily. "Do you think that you could fly down the road and get into the carriage to tell them where I am and that they will have to stop for us?"

Gwendaleir did a quick assessment of how she felt and then replied "I'm sure that I can do that. See you later." And she flew off down the road, slightly stunning Thelwyn who thought that she might want to eat before leaving. Still, if she feels alright she might as well go ahead, Thelwyn thought as she went down to the stream to clean up a bit. She contemplated her condition and decided that another meal might hit the spot so once more she changed and hunted fish. The Pixies were quite delighted to help her eat them when she had them cooked.

Gwendaleir flew determinedly down the road to intercept the Princess and her party. She was resolute that she was going to accomplish this task to the best of her abilities. She was somewhat concerned about trying to get in the carriage if they were travelling fast but decided that she would worry about that once she found them. She travelled for over an hour and a half before she saw the front riders; she noted that they weren't approaching her very fast and she wondered about that. She was able to easily swoop into the window of the carriage, avoiding the covering shade to keep the dust out a bit and flew over to Lady Windlington.

Lady Windlington noticed her and started slightly while asking "Gwendaleir, where did you come from? Is Thelwyn all right?"

"She's fine, Sorceress" Gwendaleir panted out, feeling a bit worn out. "She's up ahead of you and will be waiting for you to reach her. She's by the stream that crosses the road. It took me an hour and a half to reach you from her. Why are you travelling so slowly?"

"We thought she would be coming up from behind so we were giving her a chance to catch us" Lady Windlington replied and then opened the shade, leaned out and called to the nearest rider to let Lady Ashmont know that she wanted to speak to her. The rider passed the message forward and soon Lady Ashmont had dropped back to the carriage. "We need to speed up and then stop at the creek that crosses the road for our mid-day meal. I'll explain why later." Lady Ashmont nodded and went to pass on her orders. Lagalaise was busy giving Gwendaleir some food and water so she could recover.

When Lady Ashmont gave her orders to speed up, Princess Aurolla was concerned about why they weren't waiting for Thelwyn to catch up to them. But as she thought about it, she realized that Lady Windlington must have had word that Thelwyn had somehow gotten ahead of them. She looked forward to having her back even though nothing untoward had happened when she was gone. She ignored the puzzled looks of her two maids about the orders and urged her horse forward to hold her position in the party, gesturing for them to do the same.

Soon they were reaching the stream and unpacking to have a meal. Lagalaise didn't help them but rather went down the stream with a bundle of clothes for Thelwyn. She met up with Thelwyn and passed on the clothing. She was amazed at the number of Pixies that were accompanying Thelwyn and greeted them as they chattered in their excitement. One of the Pixies excitedly told her "We journeyed here by wolf back. It was great. I wonder if we can get a regular wolf to do that for us." Thelwyn was putting on her dress when the Pixie said this but snorted slightly, thinking good luck with that, wolves had tremendous pride and wouldn't be agreeable to such treatment. Soon Thelwyn was ready and they went out to join up with the group once more.

The Princess wanted to go up and hug Thelwyn as she came out of the woods but realized that it would draw attention to her so she restrained herself. She did beam a bright welcoming smile to her though and Thelwyn grinned back at her before starting to tend to the fire like she had been with the party all along. Nobody said anything about her having been gone but there were a fair number who were aware of the fact. Lady Windlington went with Lagalaise and the Pixies to talk with them in the carriage since it was the most private place they could talk. She spent some time with them discussing what they wanted them to do and how they should train for the duties; Lagalaise brought them all some food to eat. Annilee waited for a few minutes after Thelwyn showed up, looked around to see that no one was paying much attention to her or Thelwyn and went over to give her a hug to welcome her back. Thelwyn smiled at the young girl's expression of affection and hugged her back firmly, letting her know that she appreciated it. She realized that she truly liked the group of women that she spent most of her time with and it warmed her heart a good deal. Soon they were on their way once more and she enjoyed travelling in the carriage once more rather than having to run.

AN ATTACK ON THE ROAD

When they stopped for the night, there was once more a small creek nearby. After they had everything set up and their meal was cooking, Cassmetra came up to Thelwyn and asked her if she would like to go bathe with her. Thelwyn initially wondered if the thief was hinting that she needed a bath and was slightly offended because she had washed up while waiting for the party to meet with her earlier that day. Then she recognized that Cassmetra wanted to go off with her by herself because she wanted to talk with her. So she agreed with a friendly smile and got her towel. They went off to a sheltered area of the creek, not too far from the camp and began to wash up. Thelwyn waited silently for Cassmetra to initiate whatever conversation that she wanted to happen; she hummed happily to herself. They had been accompanied by Gwendaleir, Purple Cedar, Blue Fox and the other three young Pixies from the settlement and the Pixies were delightfully playing in the stream. Finally, Cassmetra settled back a bit and asked cautiously "Maybe this is none of my business and you may tell me to ignore it if you want to but it is obvious that you, Lady Windlington and Lagalaise see and interact with some things that I don't see. I don't think Annilee can see them either but she ignores the fact that you do. What can you see that I can't?" She looked wistfully at Thelwyn, imploring her to answer.

Thelwyn ran her towel over her face as she contemplated what Cassmetra was asking and whether she should answer it or not. She trusted the thief and felt that she had been contributing quite a bit with her forthright talk about what she deduced from incidents that had occurred. Thelwyn came to the conclusion that the thief was very perceptive and that not letting her know about the Pixies would be hampering her ability to help them in the future. She requested "Gwendaleir, could you and the others let Cassmetra see you?" The Pixies looked a little startled but did as she asked and winked into existence.

Cassmetra drew a long loud breath and exclaimed "Pixies! I thought they were nothing but myths! And so many of them." She gazed at the six Pixies with wonder, examining them critically with a pleased, stunned smile on her face.

"There are actually thirty of them now" Thelwyn said a trifle dryly. "I brought in four of these and fourteen others earlier when I rejoined you. Unless I ask them to hide themselves from you once more, you will be seeing all of them. Are you okay with that?"

The Pixies had surrounded Cassmetra somewhat as they watched her to see what her reaction to them was going to be. She gazed at each of them in turn as she took in their differences. "Oh, I'd love to be able to see them constantly" she replied as she smiled at the group of them. "What are they capable of?"

Thelwyn took some time to explain what the Pixies could help them with and why they were gathering such a large group of them to take them to Barcless with them. Cassmetra asked a number of questions about them and was quite amazed that Gwendaleir considered herself to be Thelwyn's personal Pixie. She remarked that it was likely that the six Pixies with them now considered themselves in the same way. Thelwyn thought about it and agreed with her although she didn't voice that opinion in fear that it might upset Gwendaleir. She would have been surprised to know that Gwendaleir thought of the five new Pixies as Thelwyn's as well even though she considered herself the first and most important of them.

They headed back to get their food, having taken longer than they had originally intended and Thelwyn asked to speak with Princess Aurolla, Lady Windlington, Lady Ashmont and Lagalaise after she'd eaten. The five of them wandered over towards the edge of the forest away from where people were washing up themselves and dishes in the stream. Thelwyn let them know that she'd let Cassmetra in on the existence of the Pixies and suggested that Annilee, and probably the Princess's two maids already were aware of them in some way. She expressed her belief that they should be fully informed about the Pixies. Princess Aurolla sat back and observed the others to determine what their opinions were on the matter; she knew what she thought. Lady Ashmont was ambivalent about the problem and held back to let Lady Windlington object if she wished to do so. The Sorceress thought about the issue for a few moments as she weighed the pros and cons of letting so many more people know about the Pixies. She was aware that Annilee and Cassmetra had to have seen them interacting with the Pixies and the fact that they hadn't brought up the fact that there was something going on reflected on how circumspect they could be. Plus they had the trust of all of them because of their protection of the Princess in regards to the assassination attempt. She stated "I think that you are probably right, Thelwyn. They do deserve to know the full information about the Pixies; they undoubtedly already suspect something of their nature." Princess Aurolla and Lady Ashmont nodded in agreement so they called Bettinka, Dezadillia and Annilee over to them and let them in on the secret. The three women were amazed even though they had been aware that something was going on.

Then they settled in for the night. Lagalaise woke up a few hours before dawn with a sense of unease and lay there listening carefully to try to determine what had woken her. She looked out with her magic and found four instances that appeared to be headed their way. They were moving quite fast and she estimated that they would arrive within a couple of hours. She couldn't define what they were by their signatures but didn't think that they were in any way natural. She left her bed to wake her mother so that they could plan how they were going to handle this new threat. It was apparent that their magical enemy was trying something and hoped to catch them unawares. Her mother woke with a start but became quickly aware of the situation as Lagalaise explained it to her.

"It will probably be a good thing if we meet this threat as far from the camp as we can. I suspect that our enemy might have some surprises embedded in his creatures and I'd rather not risk anyone we don't have to. Wake up Thelwyn and then go wake up Lady Ashmont" Lady Windlington quietly ordered her daughter.

"I'm already awake" Thelwyn said as she crawled out of her blankets. "I woke up when Lagalaise started moving about. I overheard what she told you and agree that we should go meet them rather than wait here for them." She got dressed and grabbed her weapons as she noticed that Princess Aurolla and her maids continued to sleep. There was no sense in waking them, she thought as she and Lady Windlington slipped out of the tent to where Lady Ashmont and Lagalaise were waiting for them. The Sorceress explained her preliminary thinking to Lady Ashmont and the swordswoman woke ten of her people to accompany them.

Since Thelwyn had the best night sight, she and Lagalaise led them in the direction that they could intercept the incoming threat. The six Pixies that had pledged themselves to Thelwyn accompanied them and spread out in front of the group. They probably wouldn't be too much help in a fight, Thelwyn thought, but they could detect magic and had night sight that was almost as good as hers so they could warn of more mundane threats as well. The group was quiet as they moved through the trees having decided to save their breath for the confrontation. Lady Ashmont couldn't give any orders in how to deal with the approaching threat until they had some idea about what they were facing. Lagalaise kept examining the approaching danger to see if she could puzzle out exactly what it was. It seemed to be somewhat close to the beast that they had taken care of in the mountains but there was something different about it. That is what concerned Lagalaise as she kept it under observation.

About forty minutes out of the camp, they came to a fairly fast moving river; the threat was about ten minutes away by Lagalaise's estimate. Lady Ashmont decided that the river might be the best place to surprise the oncoming threat. They would attack as whatever was approaching was navigating the problem of the river; Lagalaise was under the impression that whatever was oncoming didn't detect them and they would be able to accomplish surprise. It was too dark for her people to see in order to use bow and arrows but Thelwyn had assured her that she could see perfectly fine in the dark woods and she was the best archer anyways. So she gave instructions to her people to group near Lady Windlington and Lagalaise and protect them if anything made it across the river. She cautioned them not to get into the way of the two sorceresses until they absolutely had to so they wouldn't get in the way. They were positioned to the left of the sorceresses and Thelwyn was to their right, close enough to them so that they could work together as much as possible. Lady Ashmont stood a little further to Thelwyn's right to protect that side of them. Lady Ashmont wondered if there were any non-magical troops with the oncoming threat as well as what Lagalaise detected. She had informed everyone to be careful in case there was since Lagalaise acknowledged that she wouldn't spot them if there were.

Since there were four incoming threats, Lagalaise contemplated attacking them as soon as they were positioned but then reasoned that she might need Thelwyn to physically kill whatever was there once she removed the magic from it. Plus if she waited, she would get a better idea of what they might be before she launched her attack. And so, they all waited for whatever came at them, tense but unafraid.

A few minutes later, they heard a crashing sound as the creatures coming at them shouldered their way through the trees. Thelwyn caught the impression of large, hairy beasts as they came into her view at the bank of the river. Lagalaise lifted the magic off of the first creature, which was also the largest as it began to enter the water. Thelwyn was surprised when her sight revealed a large black bear that had been the animal that someone enchanted. She'd been ready for something like that, remembering the incident with the wolverine. She'd stuck a dozen arrows in the ground around her so that she could handle them faster than trying to draw them from a quiver. She launched her first arrow and grabbed a second, sending it on its way in a couple of heartbeats. She'd aimed at the heart of the bear and both arrows sunk into that area. The bear grunted and died, slipping into the shallow water along the edge of the river. Lagalaise had been wrestling with the magic she'd removed from the bear as it seemed to struggle to get loose. She was relieved that the magic broke up and dissipated when the bear died. It was apparent that the magic was somehow linked to the life force of the animal. That was a weakness that she could exploit she thought with satisfaction. She called out to Thelwyn "They are mortal once I remove their magic and the magic disappears when they die. I will start lifting their protection from left to right and will call out as I do each one. Can you see all three of them right now?"

"Yes I can" Thelwyn called back. Then Lagalaise called out the first one and Thelwyn sent two arrows at the target. It was still slightly back in the trees as the creatures had hesitated for a bit because of the river and the death of the leader. It died and Lagalaise moved onto the third one, calling out to Thelwyn who shot at it. It also died quickly. The final one tried to retreat but Thelwyn managed to shoot at it when Lagalaise lifted its magic. Since it had been turning, Thelwyn only wounded it initially and shot a second set of arrows at it once she recognized that she hadn't managed to kill it. It too died. They watched to see if anything else was going to appear or happen but nothing did.

After a moment or two, Lagalaise stated "That almost seemed too easy."

"Yes, I suspect it was simply a test" her mother said in reply. "This magic seemed to be very similar to that as on the wolverine but it was of a simpler nature. These beasts only seemed more ferocious since they already were of a fair size but these ones seemed rushed and incomplete. Whereas the magic on the wolverine was more complex and tougher to counteract. I think that the same sorcerer was involved with both of them but that he rushed his spells on these creatures. I think that he wanted to find out more about us. He couldn't be sure of our magic since you had if masked for most of the trip except for lately when you uncovered yourself so Gwendaleir could find us for Thelwyn. Now he may be aware that we can counteract magic and detect it from a distance if he is able to discover that we did this a distance from the camp. And if he knows about when it happened he may think that night attacks won't work any better than day attacks. We may have given him more information about us than we have gained on him."

They all thought about Lady Windington's words for a few minutes, turning them over in their minds to see if they had anything important to add. Lagalaise ventured slowly "Maybe we shouldn't have handled this like we did, then?" Both Thelwyn and Lady Ashmont shook their heads, disagreeing with that thought.

"No" Lady Windlington conceded. "We had to come see what these creatures were and we needed to make sure we did it away from the others in case it was something new. I'm just saying don't expect it to be as easy the next time and that there will be a next time. We have to remain alert for anything from now on. I think we should get Chesmyse, Charlymi and Pellaynu scanning ahead of us for any magic we might run into. They can take it in turns and that will leave Lagalaise and me rested in case we have to act." She looked at Thelwyn and asked "Do you need to retrieve your arrows?"

"No, there's nothing special about them and we have plenty more back at camp" Thelwyn replied.

"Then we might as well go back. We'll still need you to lead us on our way, Thelwyn" Lady Windlington said quietly. They started their walk back to the camp and reached there shortly after dawn. Once there they ate, helped pack up the camp and were on their way once more. Lady Windlington filled in Princess Aurolla and Chesmyse about what had happened and arranged for Chesmyse to schedule herself and her two magic users to keep a constant watch on where they were headed.

SPENDING THE NIGHT IN ZAKGREBKI

Two days later, in the late afternoon, they arrived at the town of Zagrebki where the bard and caravan had spent the night they had told the Princess and her party about. It was almost big enough to be classed as a city and had a wall protecting the inner area even though most of it sprawled outside of that protection. They hadn't been attacked in more than a hundred years and people got sloppy about these things. There were two functionaries with the city guards watching the road into the town and they stopped the Princess and her party. They were very polite as they insisted that they had to break up such a large party in order to house it for the night. Lady Ashmont had sent a rider on ahead to warn the mayor and council that the Princess was arriving.

Chesmyse had warned that the mayor and council would probably insist that the Princess join them for a celebratory dinner and be accommodated overnight in one of the better inns in the inner town. There wouldn't be room for all of the party in that inn she thought and the rest of them would probably be put up in the outer area that would generally be used for travelling caravans. Lady Ashmont had been in favour of just riding through the town and camping somewhere on the other side of it.

Lady Ashmont had met with Princess Aurolla, Chesmyse, Lady Windlington and Thelwyn to discuss how they wanted to proceed with the problem they were likely to find at Zagrebki. She professed her preference for just riding through the town without stopping but was met by frowns from everyone else but Thelwyn. Chesmyse stated "That would be most rude, Lady Ashmont. I realize that it would be optimal from a security standpoint but it would be a diplomatic nightmare. If Princess Aurolla doesn't attend a feast in her honour, the mayor and his council will take offense and probably start causing some troubles for our caravans that have to travel through this area. The people of the town are also quite good customers of ours and we would like to keep them happy."

Princess Aurolla said "I think that we can arrange adequate protection for me and our people in the town. We would probably be more vulnerable camping on the road. I agree with Chesmyse that we need to do this to keep our relations as warm as possible. I know that you feel exposed by having to split our party up but I have confidence in your abilities to handle that." Lady Ashmont looked to Lady Windlington and Thelwyn for support but neither of them did anything more than give her a small sympathetic smile. They knew that Princess Aurolla and Chesmyse were going to win the argument. But Lady Ashsmont had tried to continue her argument by pointing out some other objections which the Princess smiled at and simply overrode them. She was looking forward to the dinner in her honour with quite a bit of anticipation. Chesmyse wisely stayed out of the rest of the argument, knowing that she would get the solution that she was in favour of anyway.

So now these two smiling petty officials were directing her as to how they wished her to split up her party, Lady Ashmont thought gloomily; she was tempted to insist that she needed to be with the bulk of her people in order to ensure that they had no problems. But she was also the Princess's public bodyguard and needed to be with her so she had no choice in the matter. She'd instructed her lieutenant as to how she wanted him to handle affairs and he was prepared to do that. She knew that he was a good man for the job and she had complete confidence in him but she wasn't pleased about the situation and knew it. She tried to shake off her funk and do her job, same as she expected any of her people to do. She joined the Princess and the others to ride to the better inn. Along with the more important members of the party, they were taking along eight of her guard and the two bodyguards for Chesmyse and Charlymi. The functionaries had tried to argue that even that small number was too high but Lady Ashmont had put her foot down, insisting that she was not prepared to reduce it any further. The slightly more impressively dressed man led them through the town and on to the inn while his compatriot took the rest of the group to where they would spend the night. The man guiding them was pointing out the sights of the town as they rode through it to the Princess and her maids. He rode too close to the Princess for Lady Ashmont's liking but she decided not to make an issue of it. The Princess probably wasn't in any danger from him except for maybe being bored to death, she thought a little viciously. Nevertheless, she maintained a position behind them so that she could intervene if she needed to do so.

They arrived at the inn and the whole staff was out and beaming smiles at the incoming Princess. They quickly took control of the party's horses and handled the luggage while the innkeeper and his wife led the party inside to show them their rooms. The innkeeper was disappointed that the Princess wouldn't be dining with them since there was that dinner for her and was determined to do as much for her as he could so that he could claim the prestige of her approval. He'd arranged for hot water to be available for the group so that they could wash up for the celebration and as soon as the Princess was settled in her room the hot water began arriving.

These people were too civilized to have things like bathhouses like in Darkcloud; they used small tubs in the rooms. The Princess enjoyed completely washing the dust of the road off of her with the warm water; Bettinka helped her wash and comb out her long blonde hair. She settled down for a short nap before the celebration and the rest of her group all made sure that they were also cleaned up. Thelwyn wasn't above enjoying using warm water to wash up in rather than cold streams like she had been doing on the road and felt very refreshed once she had her bath. She also enjoyed the happy chatter of Bettinka, Dezadillia and Annilee even though they kept the volume low so as not to disturb Princess Aurolla. She and Cassmetra didn't contribute too much to the discussion but the other three had no problem filling the air with their talk.

Soon it was time to wake the Princess and to get ready for the meal. They all dressed in their best clothes, happy that the inn had taken off the rest of their items to wash overnight and return in the morning. They arrived and were seated. Thelwyn noted that she, Annilee and Cassmetra were all seated at the end of the farthest table from the head table where the Princess was but she'd kind of expected that. The Princess had looked at her when she was led from the group that went towards the head table but Thelwyn had shook her head to stifle her protest. Bettinka and Dezadillia were also not seated at the head table, having ben led to a table two down from it. Thelwyn relished the rich, spicy food and there was a great deal of it and had to keep from eating too much of it so people wouldn't ask how a girl as small as she could consume so much. The meal went well but Thelwyn was bored with all of the festivities. She could tell that Annilee was having fun looking at all of the ladies and lords in their finery but she wasn't that impressed by them. She wasn't sure what Cassmetra was thinking but had a stray thought that she might be appraising their jewels for what she might be able to get for them.

They made their way back to the inn without any incident. The Princess reported that not all of the townspeople were happy with her arrival and she had been warned that there might be some problems by one of the councillors. The woman had suggested that one of the major merchants might be behind the unrest and warned the Princess to keep a close watch during the night. The Princess thought that the threat was credible and she directed Thelwyn to maintain top security for the night. Thelwyn nodded at her instruction and didn't bother to inform the Princess that she had intended to do that anyway. She was in agreement with Lady Ashmont that the Princess could face more danger in the inn than on the road but had known that the Princess wouldn't have listened to her any more than the swordswoman if she'd agreed with her. Finally they all settled into bed and Thelwyn settled herself in a chair watching the shuttered windows. She felt that would be the more likely place of attack rather than the guarded door but she could also keep an eye on it from her position. She was somewhat surprised when Cassmetra joined her in her watch rather than settle into her shared bed but made no comment.

The hours passed but Thelwyn maintained her vigilance; Cassmetra appeared to doze somewhat but Thelwyn thought that she was still ready for any action. She heard a small sound coming from outside the window and made to get up and investigate when Cassmetra put her hand on her arm to restrain her. The thief was watching as a slim knife slipped in through the gap and began moving the restraining bar holding them closed. Cassmetra signalled Thelwyn to take one side of the window while she took the other. Thelwyn armed herself with a knife in her left hand and a chunk of wood in right; she wanted to take the intruder alive if she could in order to determine who had sent him but would kill him if she had to in order to protect the Princess.

The dark figure slipped in the open window stealthily and started across the floor; Thelwyn aimed a hit at the back of his head but somehow the intruder sensed the strike and hunched so that the blow landed on his shoulder than the back of his head. The figure immediately produced a pair of knives and started to attack Thelwyn. She smacked the knife out of his left hand and stabbed him in his right shoulder to disable him enough that she could then overpower and take him. The intruder grabbed his remaining knife with his left hand and tried a strike at Thelwyn. Cassmetra made her presence known by stabbing the figure in the lower back. The figure grunted in pain and tried to spin to face her exposing himself to Thelwyn. She decided that he was unlikely to give in without being killed and he could potentially wound her or Cassmetra. So she stuck her knife into his throat and opened it up; the figure sighed slowly and collapsed in a heap. She went over and lit a candle so that they could get a closer look at the intruder. When she brought the light over, she recognized that she had made the right decision because the figure was dressed in an outfit that left little doubt that he was here to try to assassinate the Princess. He wore a harness with a number of knives and garrotes on it. There was also some armour over his more vital spots and she had chosen one of the few places where he was immediately vulnerable. He was also hooded and when Thelwyn pulled the hood off she was surprised when a fall of long brown hair fell out. The assassin was a woman.

Both Cassmetra and Thelwyn examined the face for a moment but neither of them could recall seeing her before. Princess Aurolla was woken by the light and got up and joined them quietly, also looking at the intruder. Cassmetra frowned at the weaponry on the fallen figure and began carefully to remove it from the body; she was very careful not to touch any of the items with her hands because she was worried that they might have poison on them. "Don't touch the knives" she warned and the other two recognized her concern. Thelwyn went over to get some cloth to handle them and a sack to put the weapons into so that the Sorceress could examine them in the morning. They took over a dozen weapons off of the body and then Cassmetra started searching to find if the woman was carrying any item that might identify her employer. By this time, the others had woken up and Thelwyn sent Bettinka off to warn the guard and to send for Lady Ashmont. She knew that the swordswoman would want to know about the attempt right away. Cassmetra found three more items of deadly nature along with a vial she suspected would be poison but nothing else. Thelwyn wrapped the vial in cloth before placing it in the bag.

Lady Ashmont arrived at the door and was admitted by Bettinka; she left the guards outside, knowing that Thelwyn would have brought them inside if she felt the need for them. She went over and looked at the body. She asked Thelwyn "There was no chance to take her without killing her, I presume?"

Thelwyn showed her the bag with the weapons in it and replied "Not with all of these things that she was carrying. Cassmetra and I tried to take her without deadly force but she was determined to escape or die trying. Cassmetra thinks that her knives are poisoned so it is good that we took her out before she could land a strike." Lady Ashmont nodded, accepting the facts and didn't bother to say anymore for a moment as she looked over the body again.

Then she looked over at Thelwyn and asked "Is there anything more we can learn from the body?" When Thelwyn shook her head negatively, Lady Ashmont called in the guard and had them take the body outside. She'd woken the rest of her people so the Princess was adequately protected. Their movement had woken the innkeeper and he directed the guards to take the body into the stable so that the town guard could examine and take it. He sent off a young boy to alert them. He wanted to apologize to the Princess for the intrusion but the guard prevented him from approaching her to do so. When he caused a bit of commotion about that, Lady Ashmont went out and spoke to him; she promised to pass on his regrets to the Princess. Then she went back inside and suggested that everyone go back to try to sleep so that they could be ready to leave early in the morning; she would feel better once they were underway again. She replaced the guard, not because she blamed them for not foiling the attack, but so that fresher people could handle the problem and placed another guard outside of the inn to watch the windows.

Thelwyn had a discussion with Cassmetra and she left the inn to go reconnoiter the merchant who was their main suspect in the town. She would go in and see if she could find any incriminating information if she felt that she could do it. Thelwyn told her not to take any chances because it wasn't worth the risk. Thelwyn kept guard at the window for the rest of the night but nothing further happened. She was aware that the others took a long time to drift back to sleep but they remained as quiet as they could in case any of the others found the chance to drift off.

Early in the morning, they gathered their items and started getting everything ready to move on. Cassmetra showed up once she noticed activity happening in the room and reported that she'd entered the merchant's premises but found nothing of interest in them. Then she'd spent the rest of the night in the stable so she wouldn't disturb them with her return. The captain of the city guard had shown up about a half hour after the incident had occurred and had wanted to talk with the Princess and Lady Ashmont but the guards had refused to disturb them. They informed the man that he could return in the morning and talk to them when they were awake. The man had left reluctantly and in an ill temper. He now returned and Lady Ashmont was dealing with him.

He insisted on talking to the Princess and whomever had killed the intruder but Lady Ashmont was tired and decided not to put up with his demands. She told him that the Princess was busy getting ready to depart after a disturbed night and she wasn't going to bother her simply so that the guard captain could question her. She suggested that if he had a problem with that he could get his own mayor here to argue the fact with her. The guard captain relented on the Princess but tried to insist on talking with whomever had killed the intruder. Lady Ashmont debated whether it was worth producing one of her guards as the killer because she wasn't going to expose Thelwyn, no matter what, but decided she wasn't going to bother. She continued to refuse his demands. Lady Windlington arrived while she was arguing with the man because she wanted to let the swordswoman know that she found little of interest amongst the weapons she'd examined. There had been a lingering trace of magic but it was too faint to identify. When she ascertained what the disagreement was about, she leant her support to Lady Ashmont. Faced with the pair of them, the guard captain decided to try to find a graceful way out of his predicament.

By this time, the mayor had arrived and ordered his guard captain to stand down and let the Princess and her party depart as they wished to do. The guard captain looked to be about to argue the point but then he stood down, recognizing that this was his out, and the mayor apologized to Lady Ashmont for the trouble. She rather ungraciously accepted it and moved off to hurry her people up; she wanted to get moving away from the town as soon as possible in case someone else tried something. While the maids had been packing and Lady Ashmont had been occupied by the guard captain, Thelwyn and Cassmetra had discussed the attack more with the Princess. They felt that this latest attack was unlikely to have been orchestrated by anyone involved in the other attempts; it had more of a feel of a local effort by someone who might or might not be aligned with someone else interested in removing the Princess. The main problem was that there were too many reasons people had for trying to assassinate her. Thelwyn was aware that those reasons were why the Queen had wanted her to protect Princess Aurolla and she was starting to recognize the scope of that job. Princess Aurolla was shaken by the news and the thought that so many people wanted her dead but she managed to put on a brave face about the matter. She realized that going to pieces because she was scared wouldn't help anyone and might actually hinder her protection. Thelwyn gave her a hug to reassure her and Cassmetra patted her on the arm in admiration of her courage. Strangely, those gestures helped the Princess to bury her fears deeper as she didn't want to disappoint them.

Soon they were once more on their way and they all felt relief about leaving Zagrebki behind them.

A MAGICAL ATTACK ON THE ROAD

They travelled along the road and Lady Ashmont called three practices that day; her troops performed fairly well but she was critical of them and let them know it. Everyone knew that she was just showing her tiredness and worry so they didn't take offense at her criticism but just tried to do better the next time. After the third practice, she recognized that she wasn't really helping with her actions and spent the rest of the day talking with her people and encouraging them. Her people were grateful that she'd reverted back to her usual form and talked easily with her, drawing courage from her example. The Princess was somewhat amazed at the display of comradery that was occurring around her and she was very pleased and content about it. She also drew bravery from the feeling of professional confidence around her and that also heartened the people protecting her. They stopped for the night and set up camp. Lady Ashmont knew that the people she'd used to protect the Princess had slept less than the rest of her troops because of the incident so she made sure that they got the chance to rest more than the others. She also recognized her own tiredness and the effect it was having on her performance and judgement and went to sleep as soon as possible. It was a little tough because of her worries but she knew it was necessary.

Thelwyn had managed to sleep while travelling in the carriage during the day and she'd assured Lady Ashmont that she would keep watch over the security of the party while the swordswoman slept. She wasn't officially in charge because that responsibility had been left to Lady Ashmont's lieutenant but Lady Ashmont felt better knowing that Thelwyn was available to help. The rest of the people who had been awaken during the night all drifted off into a slightly disturbed sleep. They awoke in the morning feeling more refreshed and started their day off. Lady Ashmont spent the morning riding around and bolstering her people' confidence and courage. She was pleased with how they responded to her actions and felt better about her own demeanor as well.

They approached the border between Zobreski and Anscluse, which was the last kingdom that they would travel through before reaching the kingdom of Barcless.

There were no troops at the border, just a cairn of rocks that designated where the border was. There would be a few smaller towns along the road but this road had been built and was maintained more for military traffic than civilian. Some caravans used it but most of the towns and traffic used the roads that were more to the eastern area of the kingdoms they were travelling through. Zagrebki was the largest town along this route and they had already passed through it. Thelwyn was impressed with the condition of the roadway that they had been travelling across but there had been some areas that had required some more tricky negotiations to pass through.

They travelled for the rest of the afternoon and then picked a good spot to stay the night. Everyone was in a fairly good mood, even though they maintained an ardent watch against attack. They knew their journey was winding down but also that they were coming into an area where their foes would have more resources to mount any attacks against them. Now came the more dangerous portion of their trip as far as they were concerned. But once again they spent a fairly restful night. There was a light rain falling when they woke up in the morning and it looked like there might be worse weather waiting for them as they headed further north. That put a damper on their morning start but didn't really cause them any problems.

Lady Ashmont cautioned her outriders to keep a good watch on the areas about them as they rode because the heavy weather created some fog and made a good situation to launch an attack if one was to come. They rode on for most of the morning before the weather started to clear off and were relieved that no attack had come. The outriders did report that they saw some figures in the distance and that they suspected that they were being tracked by some opposing force. Lagalaise tried to scan the area to see if there were any magical items around them and she saw too many such items to be able to pinpoint specific targets. She was getting back more than a hundred signatures in the areas around them and the sheer magnitude of them gave her a splitting headache. She discussed the problem with her mother but they couldn't come up with a solution that would assist them. When Lady Ashmont was informed of the situation, she sympathized with Lagalaise but was more concerned that what she saw probably precluded an attack. She began scanning the area around the road to see if there might be a more defensive position that they might stop in for the night. She worried that the enemy most likely knew the area better than they did and might have chosen a place where they could be more successful with an attack.

She found an area which wasn't perfect but was what she thought would be the best that they would find so she called back the lead riders and directed the party to set up camp. She changed the layout from their usual setup so that she could provide slightly more protection to the Princess's tent from the direction that she assumed the attack might come from. She was worried about mounted men so the tent was closer to the trees than the road. She checked with Lagalaise to see what the enemy might be doing. Lagalaise stated that there were still too many magical signatures around to determine exactly which ones would signify a particular threat but she didn't think that the enemy was in position to attack them right away. She got the impression that they were hoping to ambush them further up the road and that Lady Ashmont's early stop upset those plans. The swordswoman spent some time with her troops as she designated what areas they would be responsible for if there was an attack.

Then she came back and instructed the Princess and her maids in how she wanted them to spend the night. They would have to be ready to move away from any assault and into areas of higher protection. They were not to involve themselves in trying to repel any enemy troops but to save themselves and let the troops fight the intruders. Then she took Thelwyn aside and suggested to her that she might want to inspect the woods around them and either report about any formation by the enemy or try to disrupt it if she could. Thelwyn thought about the fact that Lagalaise was being overwhelmed by magic and decided that most of the enemy must be wearing magical charms of some sort. She didn't know what those charms might be capable of so she would have to be very careful. But if she took Gwendaleir with her, the Pixie might be able to let her know if there was any group of the enemy about.

She prepared her small pack that she would carry in her mouth. She wanted as many knives as she could take and had a cloth bandolier that could carry six. She filled its slots with her favourite knives and folded it into the pack. That didn't leave any room for any clothing but she wasn't overly worried about that; she would fight in the nude and hoped that the fact that she did would possibly distract whomever she was battling. Purple Cedar, Blue Fox, Orange Moon, Red Creek and Striped Hawk who were the five Pixies besides Gwendaleir who had pledged themselves to her all insisted that they were determined to accompany her. She tried to convince them that they might get in the way but they couldn't be dissuaded. She pleaded with Gwendaleir to speak with them and get them to remain behind but Gwendaleir refused to get involved. She tried to order them to remain in the camp but quickly found the major problem with dealing with stubborn Pixies; namely that they wouldn't listen to orders that they didn't want to hear. She mentally cursed the tenacious little beings but realized that she was just wasting her breath in trying to induce them to stay; they would follow her as best they could if she didn't take them with her. So she gave in, it would be better for them if they were with her, she concluded, and she was quite fond of them.

Lagalaise accompanied her out into the woods to bring back her clothing once she'd changed. She didn't remark on the fact that the six Pixies were flying excitedly about Thelwyn, chattering happily about getting another wolf back ride. She'd overheard Thelwyn arguing with them and sympathized with her but recognized the futility of persuading a Pixie to do something she didn't want to do. She was impressed by how much Gwendaleir actually listened to Thelwyn and even though she was the most obedient Pixie, she could be quite obstinate about doing some things. Thelwyn put her pack down on the ground and slipped out of her dress. She changed into her wolf form and picked up the pack while the Pixies speedily found positions on her back. Gwendaleir and Purple Cedar took the positions of honour on each side of her neck where they could talk with her and give her directions as to where they detected enemy magical items. Thelwyn quickly trotted off in a wide circle of the camp before bearing mostly north.

As Lagalaise re-entered the camp, the darkness of the night began to close in on them. In the gloom of the evening, she could see the troops that Lady Ashmont had positioned around the camp and hoped that they wouldn't actually be attacked during the night, even though she didn't really believe it. She went over to check with her mother to see if she had any advice as to how they wanted to handle any threats. She and Lady Windlington talked for a while about how to possibly deal with magic without interfering too much with the non-magical troops protecting them. They concluded that there were too many magical items facing them for them to try to negate any small number of them that they might be able to do. So there best strategy was to deal with whatever bigger, closer incidents of magic as best they could. Lady Windlington had some suggestions about how to do this but told Lagalaise that she would have to trust her instincts because things would likely happen too fast for them to confer with each other once the battle began. She had trust in her daughter to perform well. She'd talked a bit with Chesmyse, Charlymi and Pellaynu while Lagalaise was busy with Thelwyn and they knew what was expected of them.

Lady Ashmont had settled at the fire to eat a quick meal. She would only worry her people if she wandered amongst them now that they were set up and she didn't want them distracted by her while they were keyed up about their duties. Lady Windlington and Lagalaise went over to speak with her so that she could inform them of her plans. Princess Aurolla and Chesmyse also joined them but stayed out of the conversation so as not to obstruct the people in charge of their protection. Lady Ashmont was appreciative that the Princess trusted her judgement in the matter and that she kept out of the way while arrangements were made. She knew that Princess Aurolla had a good mind and was forceful enough to speak her thoughts about things. The fact that she wasn't being vocal about anything meant that she recognized that Lady Ashmont had much more experience and knowledge about this than she did. It made her respect the young woman even more than she had previously. She could tell that the Princess was worried about the outcome, they all were, but that she wasn't letting it consume her.

When their brief conference was done, the Princess asked Lady Ashmont if she, her maids, Annilee and Cassmetra could take hot drinks out to the people who were situated to guard them. Lady Ashmont considered the idea for a while, recognizing that the Princess wanted to keep herself and her people busy so that they wouldn't just be worrying about the attack likely to come. She knew that her people would appreciate the hot drinks but was loathe to risk anyone she was charged with protecting. She told the Princess that she was to remain by the fire. The Princess could prepare the drinks if she wanted to do so and her maids and Annilee could take them to the nearer people. She wanted Cassmetra to be the only one to take drinks to any troops near the outside of their protection, trusting that the thief was the one who would be able to handle herself the best if an attack happened while she was near the edge of the safety. Princess Aurolla agreed to the restrictions readily and went off to organize her people. Nothing happened for a few hours as the night got darker.

Thelwyn trotted through the woods using her nose to try to scent out any enemy. She did catch a distant scent of some horses and thought about going to investigate that scent but she had the impression of a fairly large number of the big beasts and recognized that she wouldn't be very effective against more than six or eight men mounted. She would frighten horses but well trained mounts would be brought back under control of experienced men and would turn back to face her. Her speed and agility wouldn't help her too much if she was being assaulted by an overwhelming number who were mounted and eventually she would lose the battle. She thought about whether finding them and reporting them to Lady Ashmont would be of any use but determined that she wouldn't be able to provide the swordswoman with enough information to make any difference in any battle. It wouldn't really make any difference to Lady Ashmont to know the size of the opposing force because she couldn't do anything about it. It was not like she had the option of retreating and avoiding the battle. The enemy was going to attack them no matter what, Thelwyn thought. She decided that she would do better against a smaller group and prowled around to see if she could find any.

About fifteen minutes later, Gwendaleir reported a group of magical items ahead of them; she detected around a dozen magical signatures but warned that the number of people could be more. Thelwyn caught the scent of their horses first and then the men. She trotted close as she contemplated what this group might be involved in. A dozen men or so wasn't too many to try to attack the camp so she didn't think that they would be involved in a frontal assault. She wondered if they might be sorcerers since Gwendaleir said that they all had magical signatures but considered that if the enemy had that many magical allies then the Princess and her party were extremely unlikely to survive. She appreciated the strength and usefulness of Lady Windlington and Lagalaise but they wouldn't be able to defeat that many opponents that had similar talents as they did. She figured that if these men were sorcerers, she would attempt to kill or disable as many of them as she could before they destroyed her. She was content with the fact that she might be giving her life to give the Princess a slightly better chance of survival. Still, if the enemy had that many sorcerers, why was there a large number of horsemen not too far away. Wouldn't it have made more sense to keep the horsemen away from the battle so that they wouldn't get in the way of the sorcerers, she wondered.

When she got close, she dropped down and crawled up on her belly, intent on detecting any sentries before they noticed her. She thought she would probably have the advantage over them no matter the fact that they had magic to help them. If their magic was so advantageous, they should have detected her by now and she wouldn't be able to get any closer. She didn't detect any movement around her with people trying to surround her so she dismissed the usefulness of their magic against the likes of her. She reached a position where she could see what the men looked like and was surprised. Archers! These men were lightly armoured in leather and carried bows with them. They were creeping up to an edge of the woods that bordered the road and would give them the ability for a clear field of fire towards the Princess's camp. Thelwyn was behind them. She wondered about why these men would be able to shoot in the dark. There was only a small fire in the camp and that wouldn't give these men enough vision to hit too many targets, Thelwyn thought furiously. Then she had an epiphany. The magical charms that these men carried must give them some ability to see in the dark and allow them to see what they were shooting at. The fact that these men were all concentrating on what was in front of them as they began to move into their shooting positions and that their charms didn't appear to give them any help in detecting her meant that she could surprise them. There were only a dozen of them, they were lightly armoured and she felt that she could defeat them with little risk to herself. She grinned wolfishly and lolled her tongue as she thought about it. She twitched her back and neck muscles to alert the Pixies that she wanted them off of her. They quickly flew from her back, she dropped her pack from her mouth and changed into her human form. She pulled the bandolier out and strapped it onto her naked body. She was ready.

She slipped out from behind the tree that she'd stopped at and hurried forward, pulling out a knife with both hands. She had to hurry because the first of the archers looked to be in position and were preparing themselves to shoot. It looked like they wanted to make the first volley to include all of them rather than just shooting when ready so they were holding off from firing. She attacked the back of the man closest to her and sunk her longest blade into it. She pierced his heart and he went down with a soft sigh that no one else noticed. She pulled her knife out as soon as it hit as deep as it could and scurried to the next man. The nearest two men were close enough together in front of her that she felt that she could take them both without taxing herself too much. Since she was predominately right handed, even though she was fairly ambidextrous in handling weapons, she swapped her knives in her hands. This meant that her left hand held the long knife and she would stab the man on her left in his back while she tried to cut the throat of the man on her right. The trickier movement would occur with her right hand. She managed both attacks with good accomplishment but they made some noise as they died. This caused three of the nine remaining men to turn to look in her direction. They were amazed that a small, nude girl was attacking them.

While they were still immobilized by their surprise, Thelwyn closed the ground on them and stabbed the nearest man in the chest. Her knife sank into his heart and she twisted it slightly to cause maximum damage before she pulled it back out. The man collapsed as his life force left him. Thelwyn noticed that the Pixies had followed her and were trying to see if they could distract the men but she couldn't see that they were having any effect. Still she was encouraged that they supported her so much. She bared her teeth and snarled as she launched herself at the two men facing her. One man drew back in shock but the other moved forward to attack, not having been dissuaded by her grimace and noise. She quickly aimed a kick between his legs and felt her foot connect with his manhood. He grunted hard and started to slump over from the surprise and pain of her kick. She flashed out her right hand and stabbed him in the throat area. Since he was falling, she missed making a clean kill of him but she did open up his jugular vein and he bled out messily. Some of his blood splashed onto her but she ignored it as she attacked the other man.

The other six men heard the gurgling and moaning of the dying man and spun to assess the situation behind them. They were amazed that five of their number were already down and the only attacker appeared to be a small girl who was unarmoured. They paused to look at each other as Thelwyn once more attacked the nearest man. He managed to aim a blow at her with his belt knife and she used the long knife in her left hand to block and deflect it. She slashed out at his belly with her right hand knife and cut the leather with the sharp implement. She hadn't penetrated too far and just managed a shallow cut across his skin. He flinched and tried to move backwards giving her the opportunity to press her attack forward. She stabbed him in the upper chest area with her long knife. He wasn't dead but did go down. She ignored him and rushed forward once more.

Two of the six remaining archers tried to fire their arrows at her but she just grinned at them, quite pleased by their attempt. She was much too close and fast for them to be effective and she was happy they were wasting their time. The three furthest archers decided that they needed to fire like they had originally intended; namely towards the camp. They hoped that their comrades could kill this intruder while they turned and fired their arrows at the Princess's camp. This arrow volley was a signal to the sorcerer in charge of their attack to launch his armoured riders at the camp. Thelwyn closed the remaining distance to the two bowmen in a shifty zigzag motion, preventing them from being able to target her. She slashed at the face of the first man as she spun by him and hurled herself at the second bowman facing her. She knocked his cocked bow aside as she hit him and his arrow flew off and struck a tree. She stuck both her knives into his upper chest and he screamed in pain. She snarled in frustration as her long knife in her left hand caught on his leather armour and spun out of her hand as she tried to draw it out of him. She slashed his exposed throat with her other knife as he continued to howl in pain. She grabbed another knife out of her bandolier and pushed off of the dying man back towards the one who's face she'd slashed. He was still trying to clear his blood from his eyes as she slid in close and stabbed upwards into his heart. Her knife was too short to fully penetrate his heart but she knew she did enough damage to him to render him useless enough while she took care of the remaining archers. The three archers who'd been firing at the camp recognized that they had to take care of her instead of doing as they had been instructed to do. They had only gotten off ten arrows and they hadn't been the best aimed shafts either.

Three of the four bowmen facing her realized that their bows were useless to them and they dropped them and drew their belt knives. The fourth one wasn't too good with his knife so he stubbornly held on to his bow. The four of them faced Thelwyn in a half circle with the two men at the ends having knives. Thelwyn did a quick assessment of the four men to determine what her strategy was going to be. She snarled and let out a quick howl. The men were astounded by her howl. She recognized that the man to her left was more frightened than the one to her right so she made a quick feint at him. He flinched and threw himself back from her. But she'd guessed that the braver man on her right would take the opportunity of her attack to the left to launch an attack at her. The man would try to stab her while she was occupied. But she hadn't actually moved to her left very much at all and she spun and faced the man's attack. She could see the utter surprise in the man's eyes as she stabbed his upraised forearm with her left hand knife and pushed her body into him to cut his throat with her right hand knife. He couldn't prevent himself from moving into her because he'd committed himself to his attack. Thelwyn bounced away from the impact of his body and risked a glance at the knifeman to her left. He was still kind of stumbling away from her so she attacked the second man on the right side of the group.

This was the bowman and as she moved at him he abandoned his arrow and tried to hit her with the bow to slow her down. She laughed gleefully and eerily as she did this. She let him hit her in the left side of her ribs with the bow and clamped her arm down to trap it. He stared quite stupidly at her as she drove a knife up into his brain. Now there were only two men left. The two men shared a frightened glance and then took off running in different directions. They didn't know what sort of demon the sorceress they were facing had called up but they did know that they didn't want to face it. Thelwyn was somewhat amused by their flight. It was the worst thing that they could do and she felt a strong instinct to pursue. She knew that came from the wolf side of her makeup. Fleeing prey was vulnerable prey. She ran after the man on her right since he was heading towards where they'd left their horses. She caught him before he'd gone five feet and jumped on his back, plunging her knives into the base of his neck. She thought that she'd killed him but if she hadn't she'd damaged him enough to ignore him for a bit. She went off and ran down the second man, about twenty-five or thirty feet from the site of the attack. She dispatched him with relish, knowing that she'd saved her friends from some peril.

The Sorcerer had sent his mounted armoured men forward when the ensorcelled arrows that he'd provided the archers with started flying. He was concerned that he could spot only a few arrows and wondered if the archers had forgotten that they were to use those special arrows at the beginning of the attack. He wasn't able to see the regular arrows that the archers might be shooting. The mounted men rushed past Thelwyn's position as she was dealing with the final archer and soon were attacking the Princess's party. They were ensured that the archery attack would demoralize and reduce the group that they were fighting and were very surprised to find that wasn't the case at all. Only one of Lady Ashmont's people had even been wounded by an arrow and that was a flesh wound that Lady Windlington was handling. Because they had been waiting and were prepared for the mounted attack, the guards of the Princess's party were able to get on their horses so that they weren't at the disadvantage that the mounted attackers expected.

It soon became apparent that although Lady Ashmont's people were outnumbered almost two to one, they were better trained and more proficient. The attackers were used to splitting off and fighting one on one away from the main group but Lady Ashmont had ensured that her people stayed together to protect one another more. This meant that the attacker faced two swords rather than the expected one and the ones not at the front of the group simply milled around behind their front people. Because Lady Ashmont had halted them in an area where they could use natural formations to protect them, the attackers couldn't use their numbers to simply surround the camp. One of the attackers was a large powerful man with a long sword that he was swinging over his head. He attacked the guards in front of him with relish and knocked the sword out of the hands of the man directly in front of him, breaking that man's hand. He thought that he'd won the battle until the woman beside that man simply stuck her rather ordinary sword forward into him and spilled his guts out. The light went out of his eyes and he slumped forward and rolled off of his horse. The man with the broken hand moved his horse backwards and the rest of the guard closed ranks once more. The attackers had paused to allow their champion to attack so that they could admire him. They were shocked that he could be defeated so easily.

But the attackers knew that they had the numbers that should allow them to win and they had a sorcerer behind them that wouldn't hesitate to punish them if they balked. So they moved forward as best they could and swords started clashing all along the line. Two of the attackers tried to emulate what they saw of the defenders and work together but they hadn't ever practiced doing that and one of them grazed the other with his swinging sword. In fact, they so hampered one another that the defending group managed to kill both of them easily. But that didn't mean that the defenders were always successful. Some of the attackers were able to wound or kill their opponents but the defenders kept closing up their ranks so there was no breach. Since they were used to working together, Lady Ashmont's guards were able to assist each other even if their usual partner was disabled. Lady Ashmont had wanted to lead her people from the front but she knew that her duties to the Princess meant that she had to stay by her because Thelwyn wasn't there. She was able to watch the fight and direct her people as best she could as the fight wore on.

Thelwyn ran over to where the archers who'd managed to shoot some arrows had been standing and picked up one of their bows. She tested the weight of it but wasn't happy with it so she threw it aside. She grabbed another one but wasn't happy with its grip so she sent it flying as well. The third bow felt okay in her hands and she grabbed some quivers of arrows and began shooting into the rear of the attackers. Since she had wonderful night sight because of her abilities, she was able to see her targets well and was able to score some critical hits. It took a while for the attackers to notice that they were the targets of the arrows not the Princess's party like had been planned. They wondered why suddenly their archers were shooting them and not the enemy. Four men broke from the rear of the group and headed toward the archers shooting at them but Thelwyn easily shot them out of their saddles before they covered too much of the distance between them. Soon the attackers who weren't currently engaged in the front fighting began to recognize that there was someone behind them killing and wounding them. This began to make them feel quite demoralized. Nothing was going the way that the sorcerer had told them it would.

The sorcerer had seen some of his special arrows flying when he assumed his mounted men would have reached the defenders and frowned about that. Why would his archers be shooting when their own men obstructed the path of the arrows, he wondered. They would be more likely to hit their colleagues than the enemy. He decided that he should send one of the three Pixies he had with him to check on what was happening. So the lone Pixie flew towards the area. The Pixie flew into the slight clearing and saw that the archers were down and a lone, nude girl was doing the shooting. She was about to turn and fly back to report to the sorcerer when six other Pixies swooped at her and began to attack. Gwendaleir and her group had noticed the oncoming Pixie and ambushed her. The Pixie couldn't detect them because they were still being masked by Langalaise. Gwendaleir knew that she couldn't let the enemy Pixie report back to her commander what she had seen. She had considered demanding the Pixie surrender to them but decided that was an unlikely outcome to happen. She engaged the Pixie with her steel sword and was getting the best of her when Blue Fox skewered her in the back, killing her. The Pixies weren't enthused about having to kill one of their own but they recognized the necessity of doing it. They understood that war had consequences.

When his Pixie didn't return, the sorcerer became quite concerned. Something was happening and he didn't have adequate information to work out what it was. He knew that all battles were fought without the commanders of the opposing forces being able to control all aspects of the fight. Therefore unexpected things occurred and they could turn the tide of any fight. He was beginning to think that his men weren't going to be able to wipe out the Princess's group like he had planned. He couldn't understand what might have prevented his rather elegant plan from working. He knew that he had planned to launch his attack from an area further north and Lady Ashmont had foiled that by stopping early but that shouldn't have made too much of a difference. He began to worry about the results of the attack and started to think of what he should do. He decided that he needed to use his magic to make sure that the Princess and her party were wiped out. He began to gather his magic in him and released a large fireball at the Princess's camp.

Lagalaise became aware that the enemy sorcerer was gathering magic and wondered what sort of spell he was going to launch. She detected the fireball as soon as it left the sorcerer and searched her mind for a spell to oppose it. The only thing that came to mind was to create a magic shield to deflect the fireball. That was a dangerous option because the opposing magical forces were likely to create backlash. But there was nothing else she could do and she was running out of time so she created the shield. As soon as the fireball came in contact with it, Lagalaise felt her mind light up as her magic rebounded on her and she fell forward unconscious. Lady Windlington had seen the two magics being worked and was very concerned when her daughter fell. She knew the danger of what Lagalaise had done. The deflected fireball fell into the rear of the mounted attackers killing a dozen of them with a blast of eerie green fire. This broke the spirit of the attackers and they disengaged and fled as quickly as they could. They decided that it might be better to face that wrath of their sorcerer than continue trying to fight an enemy who appeared to have all of the advantages when they had assumed the opposite.

Thelwyn saw the fireball erupt in the rear of the attackers and wondered what had happened. She recognized that it must be magic but didn't think that it could have been the result of actions by Lady Windlington or Lagalaise because they would have used that ability earlier if they could do that. She could see that the attackers were now starting to flee and decided that she would continue to shoot at them as long as they were in range. She wanted them as demoralized as she could get them. If she didn't break them here, there was the possibility that they might regroup and attack further up the road. She wanted them to run all the way back to where they were from if she could achieve it. She had no qualms about killing or wounding a fleeing foe. Anyone she could take out of the opposing force now would be one less that she might have to face in the future. She knew that the romantic notion that fighting could be chivalrous was complete garbage and it was better to win than risk losing.

The attackers had worried about the wrath of their own sorcerer but they needn't have worried. The backlash of his fireball contacting Lagalaise's shield had caused him to be wreathed in green fire and he screamed out in agony from the burns before he fell unconscious. His assistants were stunned by the sudden happening but they soon tried to smother the fire covering their boss. They managed finally to put the fire out and recognized that the sorcerer would be out of commission for a fair while. They realized that this battle was lost and they needed to get out of there before they were discovered and attacked. They loaded the still smouldering sorcerer into a wagon and fled along the road as fast as they could. They were quickly followed by the retreating mounted men.

Thelwyn finished shooting at the retreating horsemen as they got out of her range and stalked angrily back to where the archer's bodies lay. She was holding in her anger somewhat, only letting it even surface because she could now allow it to happen. She knew she had to remain in tight control of her emotions when she was in action in order to perform to her best abilities. She only let her anger, fear and disgust show when she was coming down from her adrenaline high and she tried not to do it in front of other people. She walked up to start searching the archers to see what she could discover about them. As she was squatting down to search the nearest body, she glanced around and noticed the body of the Pixie lying on the ground. "What happened?" she asked, curious, when Gwendaleir buzzed up to check on her.

"We had to take care of an enemy on our own" Gwendaleir replied, making it clear that she really didn't want to talk about it. Thelwyn sympathized with the small creature understanding the myriad of feelings that the Pixie must be feeling, having endured them herself. She bent to her task and searched all of the bodies, not finding too much of interest. She had only taken a few minutes to do that because she was anxious to get back to check on the Princess and the rest of the people. She decided that they could look further at the bodies in the morning when there was more light to do that. She packed her knives up, changed to a wolf, took up her pack and trotted off. The Pixies quickly sat on her back as she was picking up her pack.

She didn't enter the camp, knowing that the sentries wouldn't understand about her, but rather angled off to a wooded area not too far away. She changed into her human form and asked Gwendaleir to go talk to Lagalaise so that she would bring out Thelwyn's clothes for her. The Pixie flew off to do that. When she arrived in the camp, she saw that Lagalaise was lying down unconscious still but wrapped in warm blankets. She looked around for Lady Windlington, found her and flew up to attract her attention. Lady Windlington had taken care of the more serious injuries already and was just wrapping up the broken hand of the man who'd first been injured in the melee. She saw Gwendaleir buzzing about and realized that Thelwyn must be waiting nearby for her clothes. She considered the matter; if she took the clothes out, people would notice and wonder about her actions. Lagalaise was able to do it because most of the people who didn't know about Thelwyn also didn't realize her importance either. When her daughter had collapsed, most of the guards thought she'd fainted because of her fear from the attack. Lady Windlington went over to where Cassmetra was sitting, having nothing much to do as the guards all put the camp back in order, and asked her quietly to take Thelwyn's clothes out to her. Cassmetra nodded and went to do that, following Gwendaleir out into the woods.

Thelwyn was concerned and surprised when Cassmetra arrived with her clothing rather than Lagalaise and the thief filled her in on what had happened in the camp during the attack as she got dressed. They made their way back into the camp and Thelwyn immediately went up to Lady Windlington to check on Lagalaise. Lady Windlington said that she was hopeful that her daughter would recover fully but they wouldn't know anything until she regained consciousness. She also let Thelwyn know that three guards had died and there were over a dozen with injuries, two of them quite serious. Thelwyn nodded her understanding and sympathy; both of them knew that things could have been much worse for them. The Princess came up and told Thelwyn firmly to eat some food so that she could recover her vitality; they would have a conference with Lady Ashmont and Lady Windlington when she'd eaten. Thelwyn understood that the Princess was concerned for her and grateful to her so she meekly went off to find some food. Cassmetra had already fixed a bowl of stew for her and brought it up to her. She rapidly ate it, thought for a few seconds and then got a second helping. She knew she would probably need the energy in the next few days. She shared her second bowl with the six Pixies that had accompanied her. When she was finished, she went back over to join the Sorceress and Princess where they sat by Lagalaise. Lady Ashmont came over a few minutes later and they quietly talked about the battle. Thelwyn filled them in on her actions and Lady Ashmont relayed the situation with her and Chesmyse's troops. Lady Windlington expressed some concern that they were now exposed to the enemy sorcerer now that

Lagalaise was no longer masking them. She didn't think that the sorcerer who'd attacked them was the one who had sent the previous magical attacks. This latest sorcery had a different feel to it and might be an associate. She and the other three magic users would try to keep a close watch. They didn't spend too long discussing matters because all of them were quite depressed and tired. They quickly went to bed to try to sleep so that they could function the next morning. Lady Ashmont had set a heavy guard but insisted that the remainder of her troops try to get as much rest as they could.

THE NEXT MORNING

Thelwyn woke at first light the next morning, since she had fantastic recuperative powers, she was close to being back to normal. That could not be said by anyone else. They were all feeling the after effects of being threatened and hurt with little chance to recover. None of them got too much in the way of sleep whereas Thelwyn had slept almost the same as usual because she knew that she had to sleep well when she could. She could nap easily right after being in a fight where she had killed someone. It was not that she didn't have feelings it was that she knew that if she let them rule her, she couldn't do her job. She went over to see if she could prepare some food because she was still extremely hungry, having used her reserves quite heavily the previous night. She was pleased to find that the sentries had made some oatmeal and it was bubbling by the fire. She helped herself to a fairly large bowl and sat cross-legged by the fire to eat it. Lady Ashmont came over, looking slightly haggard, and took a small bowl of the food. She nodded at Thelwyn but didn't say anything as she ate. They both finished about the same time and Thelwyn went to get up so she could wash both bowls. She was surprised when Cassmetra took the bowl from her hands and retrieved the one Lady Ashmont had used. Thelwyn watched the thief take them down to the stream to clean them. She looked back at Lady Ashmont to see what she was thinking but couldn't make anything out from the other woman. Lady Windlington joined them after looking in on Lagalaise. Lady Ashmont gestured to the pot of porridge but the Sorceress declined by holding up her hand. "Lagalaise is awake but she has a splitting headache. I told her to rest up and not to try any magic for a while until her head returns to normal. I think that she will probably recover fully. Shall we go and look at our enemy to see what we can find out about them?"

Thelwyn replied softly "I'd like to wait until Cassmetra is back so she can go with us. She's proven to be very observant and helpful in the past."

Lady Ashmont nodded in agreement and said "It will also be helpful if Chesmyse goes with us. She might be able to identify if these men come from one of the kingdoms that they are at war with. Such a large group is unlikely to be simply mercenaries." She struggled to her feet and said "I'll go get her." Thelwyn nodded, knowing that Chesmyse and her people were more likely to respond to the older woman than her, especially if she was still sleeping.

Chesmyse had anticipated that they would want to look at the enemy dead in the morning so she had instructed her people to wake her as soon as they saw someone stirring from the leaders of the Princess's party. She was prepared to join them if they headed out to look at them and insist that she could be of help to them. Therefore when Lady Ashmont came over to collect her, she was ready; she was extremely pleased that they had come to the conclusion that she would be of assistance without her having to point the fact out to them. She accompanied Lady Ashmont back towards the fire to collect the others. When they arrived at the fire, Cassmetra had returned from her cleanup duties and Thelwyn had told her that she would be coming with them. Princess Aurolla and Dezadillia were also by the fire with the Princess looking wan and tired. She enquired of Lady Ashmont "Would it be helpful if I came out with you to look over the dead?"

Lady Ashmont knew that the Princess and her maids had tended to the wounded for most of the night so that their protectors could get as much rest as possible. She was proud of the young woman but knew that she really couldn't help them too much with what they were going to do. Plus she would need some people to protect her in case there were any enemy around. There was no sense in having lost people in ensuring her safety only to let her expose herself the next morning. So she replied softly "I think it would be best for you to remain here, Princess. You're not likely to contribute too much in the way of information that the rest of us wouldn't. And there is no need to expose you to any possible attack." She didn't mention that she also didn't want the Princess to see all of the dead but knew that saying so would offend the Princess. She respected the young woman's bravery but didn't want her to see the awful aftermath of such an attack. "I know you were up most of the night seeing to the wounded and would appreciate you helping to get them ready to be moved." The Princess nodded and left.

"She's quite a brave young woman" Chesmyse said, slightly in wonder.

"She's not only brave but kind and generous as well" Thelwyn stated stoutly. No one else said anything but they all started to walk to where the enemy dead lay. The guards had moved the closest bodies a little ways from the camp but hadn't done anything else with them in the night. The group each looked over a number of bodies and each of them did a quick search to see if they were carrying any important information on them. After a number of minutes they gathered back together to discuss their findings.

"These troopers are all wearing armour from Darglype" Chesmyse stated. It was a kingdom to the northeast of Barcless. Chesmyse was slightly surprised about the fact since the kingdom didn't actually border Barcless. She knew that it was one of the kingdoms that her king had suspected of being aligned with the enemy but it wasn't the most suspect of them. "I don't think that this many troops could be down here, quite a ways from their homeland, without the knowledge of their king.

They were not the ones that we thought were acting as our enemies. My King will be surprised. I didn't find too much else on them though." They all displayed what they had found so that each of them could see the total of what they had found. Lady Ashmont had looked over the area with her commander's eyes and marveled slightly at the fact that they had managed to survive the attack with so light of deaths and injuries as they had. She estimated that the mounted attack had included about a hundred troops against her just over forty. She thought that less than twenty-five had managed to escape. She knew her people and Chesmyse's had fought well but there were a large number of enemy in the back of the attack that had arrows sticking out of them. She once again appreciated the fact that Thelwyn had proven herself to be such a deadly killer. If the young girl hadn't been able to both reduce and demoralize the enemy during their attack, she didn't think that they would have been able to repel it.

Cassmetra had looked over the collection of items that they had gathered and picked out nearly a dozen coins. She showed them to Chesmyse and asked "These appear to be from the same kingdom but not like the majority of the ones they were carrying. Can you identify what kingdom they are from?"

Chesmyse frowned as she handled the coins. She knew exactly where they were from and contemplated the significance of their existence here. "They are coins of Murgald which does border Barcless and makes more sense that it would be the aggressor" she replied. "Are you thinking that Murgald may be paying Darglype to perform this attack for them?"

Cassmetra shrugged her shoulders slightly and replied "It may be more complicated than that. The two kingdoms might be working together to accomplish something. If Darglype is helping Murgald to disrupt and take over Barcless, Murgald might then help Darglype to achieve something that they want. I agree with you that the king of Darglype wouldn't have let these troops come down here to attack us without being involved in something but from what you have been saying and what I know about them, Darglype wouldn't gain too much from having Barcless eliminated." The others wondered about the fact that it might be a coalition of countries that were involved. That would mean that things suddenly could be seen as much more dangerous than they had been thinking. Cassmetra tempered her statements by saying "Of course, it could be just a coincidence. There aren't that many coins and there isn't anything else that points that way." The others nodded but thought she was probably right in her original assessment.

"Well, we should head out and look at those archers that Thelwyn wiped out" Lady Ashmont said. "There may be something else there that might lend its support to Cassmetra's theory." They headed up towards the area where the archers had been. Lady Ashmont noted at least fifteen bodies on the way and thought that

Thelwyn had shot at them as they attacked her. Thelwyn had only killed about half of them that way; she'd shot the rest as they were running away.

They did a quick search of the area but didn't turn up anything of interest except for the dead Pixie. "I'm surprised that you managed to kill a Pixie" Lady Ashmont said quietly to Thelwyn. "They're so small and fast."

"I didn't" Thelwyn said firmly as she nodded at the six Pixies around her. "Gwendaleir and the others killed her." Lady Windlington looked slightly surprised at that statement. Even though she was gathering Pixies to offset the enemy's use of them, she hadn't really expected them to kill each other. She'd assumed that they would both rather sit out what they would think of as the big people's war rather than kill each other. That certainly put a different spin on matters, she thought.

"Thank you for helping us" Lady Ashmont told the six Pixies. She appreciated the fact that they were willing to go so far as to help them with their conflicts. The Pixies just nodded to acknowledge her thanks without saying anything. They all wore serious looks on their tiny faces, knowing what they had associated themselves with.

They made their way back to the camp where the group was now just about ready to depart. Some of the guards had cleared the road of its debris so that the carriage and wagon could make use of them. They started off slowly, trying to give the wounded as easy a ride as they could. Lady Ashmont was concerned about the fact that they were now travelling slower than they had but was determined not to aggravate her injured people's wounds any more than she had to do. Her troops appreciate her concern and worked hard to make sure that they were prepared for any occurrence. As they travelled down the road, Lady Windlington became aware of the area where the sorcerer had stood the night before; she could sense the magical resonance of where he'd been. She called out to the nearby guard who went up and alerted Lady Ashmont. Lady Ashmont directed the group to move back to where Lady Windlington was indicating. It took a bit of maneuvering to get the party turned back but the Sorceress was convinced that it would be worth it.

The group that had looked over the dead bodies now looked over the area where the sorcerer had been. They could see the scorched area where the sorcerer had burst into flames. All but Lady Windlington wondered about what had happened; the Sorceress knew what had occurred and was inspecting the area closely to gain as much as she could from it. The others could see evidence that the party had departed the area in a hurry. They spent a few quiet minutes watching as Lady Windlington examined the scorched area with her powers. Finally she looked at Lady Ashmont and stated "I don't think that we will have to worry too much about another magical attack on our way. There might be some more magic at work when we get to our destination." Lady Ashmont frowned but nodded, accepting the pronouncement, as Lady Windlington pointed to the scorched area. "There was a sorcerer here who threw that fireball last night. He suffered more than Lagalaise did when their magic collided. She just collapsed. He burst into flames from the backlash of his power. I can tell that he was dreadfully injured. I believe that his helpers probably hauled him off as quickly as they could. If they had possessed any significant magic on their own, they would have helped him in the attack. Since they didn't, I don't think that we will be facing much opposing magic for a while." The group accepted Lady Windlington's assessment and made their way back to continue with their journey. Lady Ashmont set out the sentries as she had always done; she knew that even though there might not be a magical attack coming, there might be another physical attack.

The party continued to move forward at a slow pace so that the injured people could recover more easily. Lagalaise had managed to eat some porridge and drink some tea even though her head was still throbbing; she knew that she wouldn't be performing too much magic in the next few days. Thelwyn just cleaned and sharpened her weapons as they traveled knowing that she would be using them once more.

ARRIVAL AT BLACKWOODS ESTATE

The journey that would have taken them slightly more than a day and a half took them over three days to complete at their slow pace. They arrived at the home of Chesmyse and Charlymi's parents lived just after midmorning. A small group of riders had joined them shortly after they started off in the morning demonstrating to Lady Ashmont that they had been keeping a watch for them. Chesmyse reacted with surprise at one of the riders, thereby drawing Lady Ashmont's attention to him; she saw the slight movement of his hand as he warned her not to give him away. Lady Ashmont kept an eye on him while trying to appear not to be watching him as they rode toward the walled estate houses. She didn't think that the man represented a threat to the Princess but rather was a member of the king's intelligence corps. She looked forward to being properly introduced to him to see how he would handle his introduction. They continued toward the houses at a slow pace.

Lagalaise had recovered and proven that she could still use her magic but wasn't up to too much feeling quite tired much of the time still. The rest of the wounded were also recovering slowly but one of the more serious cases had passed away as they travelled and they had stopped to bury his body. Nonetheless the party was quite happy to be arriving at the termination of their journey and were looking forward to hot baths and food not prepared over a campfire. Chesmyse's mother, father and older siblings were standing outside the walls to greet them because there really wasn't room for all of their party to fit in the open space in between the walls. Princess Aurolla hadn't realized that Chesmyse wasn't the heir to her father's estates but had three older brothers and one older sister as well as some younger ones of both sexes. She'd assumed that since Chesmyse had been the one that had made the trip to ask her to come to Barcless that she had a significant interest in preserving her father's land and position. Then she recognized that probably Chesmyse was one of the few of the family that would have been able to assess what magical help Darkcloud could provide and that would have been why she was the one sent. There was a brief ceremony welcoming her and her party but the family wanted their guests to be able to get as comfortable as they could as soon as they could and kept it quite short. They were especially concerned since some of the party had what were serious injuries and they didn't want to bother them with rather meaningless actions. They knew that they would be able to talk with the Princess and her advisors quite extensively at a later time. Princess Aurolla recognized their benevolence and smiled her appreciation at it, stating "Thank you for welcoming us and we look forward to working with you in the near future once we have time to settle in a bit. I look forward to sitting down with you to discuss our cooperative strategies in the near future." Then she let herself be guided off to the rooms that had been set aside for her use. Everyone enjoyed a hot bath and meal. Thelwyn had been amused by the six Pixies that had bathed with her. Gwendaleir hadn't really shown much interest in sharing a bath with her previously but when Purple Cedar and Blue Fox decided to try it, all of them had become more interested in the process. The Pixies enjoyed falling off the edge of the wooden tub into the water before flying up, shaking water from their wings. Thelwyn recognized that she was now never going to enjoy a solo bath in the future; the Pixies would always want to be with her as she cleaned herself up. She wasn't upset by that prospect as she found that she really did enjoy their happy chatter. She knew that they had been upset by having to make the choice that they had but now were starting to resolve their feelings.

The next morning, Chesmyse came by and invited the Princess and her immediate party to join her older sister, her and her three younger sisters for breakfast in one of the smaller rooms that could be used for dining. She informed the Princess that her parents were interested in meeting with her and her advisors for a late lunch. She stated that this breakfast wasn't intended as any sort of diplomatic event but rather just more of a family meeting to get to know the Princess better. Princess Aurolla was impressed by Chesmyse's attempt to ease her into her duties, giving her a chance to meet the family that she would be allying herself with if she agreed with them. They made their way into the room and the young women in there came up and led them to their places. The Princess realized that her people were scattered amongst the family members and those young women were chatting easily with them. She sat with Chesmyse on one side of her and her older sister, Chytressa, on the other. She felt herself calming somewhat as the young women all chatted and discussed more everyday matters rather than the trip or what was happening at the estate. She started to feel tension and fear leeching out of her as she discussed fashions and jewelry with them. Thelwyn could see the Princess losing her tenseness and her drawn face seemed to fill back in somewhat. She could tell that this informal discussion was a balm for her soul and when she looked over at Chesmyse, she felt that this breakfast had been organized to do just that for the Princess. Thelwyn nodded her head in respect for the other woman, who gave her a slight smile back. They spent nearly two hours at breakfast and left feeling quite refreshed, almost as good as a couple of nights uninterrupted sleep.

In the afternoon, they all met in the largest dining room which was the only place big enough to contain them. The man who Lady Ashmont had marked as one to keep an eye on was with them and introduced himself. "You may call me Lieutenant Archer" he stated with a twinkle in his eye. "That is not my real name but it would be better for all if you didn't know my real name. That way nothing can be said of it to the enemy. It's not that I don't trust you but it is safer for all this way. I am a lesser member of the royalty." Lady Ashmont didn't need for him to tell her this information, she'd already come to the conclusion that he must be part of the royalty because of the two large troopers who accompanied him. They were very obviously bodyguards. She thought that his little subterfuge probably didn't fool the enemy at all but if he wanted to play his little game, it wasn't up to her to wreck his plans. She simply smiled at the handsome man and nodded her head. He continued "I have the confidence of the King and am able to have some contact with him so if you need anything from him along the way, please feel free to talk with me." He then brought them up to date on the situation, taking almost fifteen minutes to do so. He was quite thorough so Lady Ashmont only asked a few questions when he was done. But he hadn't addressed the magical interference very much so Lady Windlington asked questions about that.

She asked "Chesmyse has told us that you are being plagued by Pixies. I don't see any evidence of them right now. Have they left?"

Chesmyse's mother, Chaklyme, answered "They only seem to bother us when there is a need to do a lot of work in a short amount of time or have a large gathering. There is a feast day coming in eight days celebrating our King and his family. It is likely that this might be a time that they will show up. Perhaps you can help us come up with some way to counter them." She gave them a broad, friendly smile.

"Have you had any other magical occurrences that Chesmyse might not have known about?" the Sorceress asked. Chaklyme relayed attacks by some magical beasts that had happened when Chesmyse and her party had been making their way to Darkcloud and back. She also mentioned some suspicious fires that appeared magical in nature. She told them that some winds had blown down some far buildings but that they were unsure if that was natural or magical.

Lady Windlington nodded and then asked "What made you decide to send to Darkcloud for Princess Aurolla? I would have thought that you could have gotten magical help closer at hand."

Chaklyme smiled brightly over at the Princess and replied "I don't have very much magic but I do have some. Some of my children are more accomplished than I am and have helped us to identify that we were under magical assault." She nodded towards Chesmyse and Charlymi as she said this. "I can not see the Pixies like they can but I have a gift of foretelling. It doesn't provide me with too much in the way of information but has been quite useful in allowing me to know when people I meet might assist me in the future. One of the people that I saw in my dreams was Princess Aurolla. She is striking enough that I recognized who she was from descriptions that I heard of her. The other person who seemed to be involved was someone that I really couldn't identify. That person was constantly shadowed in my dreams but I got the impression that Princess Aurolla would bring her along if we sent and asked her for help. That person appeared to be small, dark-haired and fierce." Chaklyme rested her eyes on Thelwyn, who was sitting in behind the Princess, in her shadow at this point. "I don't know what you can do for us but I have the feeling that if you help us we will be successful." Lady Windlington saw where Chaklyme was looking and nodded her head in understanding. She discussed some other matters with Chaklyme but didn't turn up too much more in the way of information. They spent some more time discussing what strategies had been used and what might be used before breaking up the meeting to get ready for dinner for the night.

The next week was a busy one for Thelwyn. While Lady Ashmont worked with Lieutenant Archer and his troops and Lady Windlington and Lagalaise examined the area for magical traps and items, Thelwyn explored the area in her wolf form. She did it to feel more comfortable about the land that they might have to fight over and because Lagalaise detected a fair Pixie population in the area. Lagalaise had asked her to go out and approach the local Pixies to see if they were involved with the enemy sorcerer and if they weren't, if they would be interested in helping to defend their land from the incursion of the invading group of Pixies. Lady Windlington and her daughter suspected that the sorcerer was bringing his own Pixies with him, rather than using the local ones. Thelwyn quickly found out that they were correct in that assumption. The local Pixies that she came into contact with were aware of the invading Pixies but were at a loss about what to do about it. The six Pixies that associated closely to Thelwyn were very persuasive in talking the Pixies into joining with them. The local Pixies were very interested in the gifts that they were being offered as well as the chance to make sure they kept control over their areas. Thelwyn had gathered over sixty Pixies to join with them before the week was over. Lady Windlington, with the help of Lady Ashmont, had started training the Pixies to rudimentary work as an organized group as Thelwyn explored and brought new ones in. If Chaklyme was correct, the next day would be when the enemy Pixies would attack and they were as prepared for that as much as they could.

THE PIXIE ATTACK ON BLACKWOODS MANOR

Lagalaise reported that she saw a massing of magical signatures along the eastern border of the estate; she'd been attempting to make sure that she wasn't overwhelmed by the sheer number of magical contacts as she had been previously. She stated that the contacts seemed to be Pixie sized so that was probably the attack that they were expecting. Once she gave directions to Gwendaleir, who would act as commander of the Pixies to her pleasure, Lagalaise worked to block their signatures from her mind. She searched the other areas to see if there might be some other magic approaching them in a surprise attack. The Pixies moved out to an area where they could intercept the approaching hoard; Lagalaise had estimated over two hundred Pixies in the oncoming group. That meant that the oncoming group outmatched the defenders by slightly more than two to one. A troop of the local guard with Lieutenant Archer in command went with them in case there was anything larger coming with the enemy Pixies. They were also there to protect Lady Windlington and Thelwyn who were headed nearby in the carriage to provide whatever help they could to Gwendaleir and her group. Lady Windlington was unsure what she could do magically against such a large number of small magical creatures but she would do what she could. Thelwyn was there mainly to determine if she might have the same effect on the enemy Pixies as she'd had on the Pixies that had joined them. The local Pixies were as impressed by the fact that she was a Wolf Princess as the ones that had joined them on the trip. She would also try to act as Gwendaleir's strategist for the upcoming battle.

Since the Princess's Pixies were being masked by Lagalaise, the oncoming Pixies weren't aware of the opposition that they were headed toward. Lagalaise thought that the enemy sorcerer hadn't recognized that the local Pixies had been disappearing from his magical sight for the last week and wouldn't have recognized the significance of that fact. Therefore she thought that the oncoming Pixies wouldn't be prepared to be challenged. Thelwyn hoped that she was right but agreed that it made sense. They would find out shortly, she thought.

They arrived at the area where they were going to ambush the enemy Pixies, Gwendaleir set out her troops in the pattern that Lady Ashmont and Thelwyn had suggested to her. She was using the five Pixies pledged to Thelwyn and the three that had come with them from the castle as her squad commanders because she was the most familiar with them and them with her. All of her followers were wearing bright blue armbands so that they would be able to identify friend from foe easily in the heat of battle. She had proven to be the best swordfighter of them all and was very proud of that fact. When she watched Lady Ashmont teach Thelwyn how to use the sword better, she practiced the moves; flipping and rolling through the air as she emulated Thelwyn.   Since Thelwyn practiced her craft for hours each day, Gwendaleir got very accomplished at mimicking the moves the small girl made. She felt that her expertise made her more like her idol, Thelwyn. She would lead her small army from the front like Lady Ashmont had suggested, knowing that the Pixies weren't trained enough to perform well on their own. They would need to see someone demonstrating how they should act when fighting. She intended to challenge the leader of the enemy to single battle in hopes that she could convince the other enemy Pixies to join her once she won the fight.

Soon the enemy came into the area where Gwendaleir and her small army waited; they were extremely surprised to see what waited for them since they couldn't sense the other Pixies. They were led by a Pixie who was quite tall and wide for a member of that group. The enemy Pixies came to a halt as they assessed the intent of their opposition. Their leader scowled as she surveyed the number of Pixies in front of her group. This turned into a sneer on her somewhat plain face as Gwendaleir flew up to a point five feet in front of the defenders. "What do you have in mind, tiny one?" the leader asked even though she wasn't really that much bigger than Gwendaleir. "How come I can't see your magic? Do you think that will protect you from my wrath somehow?" She hoped to see the defenders start to worry about the numbers that they faced but was unhappy to see that they seemed to be unaffected. She decided to see how resolute Gwendaleir was by continuing to try to insult her. "You look to be too young to throw your life away, tiny one? What does this land mean to you?" She had examined how Gwendaleir was dressed and come to the correct conclusion that she wasn't a local. "Your body will feed the birds when I am done with you" she threatened. Gwendaleir remained silent throughout her speech, having been told by Lady Ashmont that doing so would intimidate her opponent. She just hovered in her spot with her thumbs hooked in her swordbelt, looking as confident as she could. She was fairly sure that she would win this fight.

Finally she said in an even voice "I challenge you to a fight. Your Pixies will leave if I beat you. Mine will leave if you happen to win. Do you agree to this?" The Pixie leader thought for a moment. She knew that the sorcerer that had sent them would never agree to such a demand and the Pixies were all scared of what he could do to them. The Pixies were committed to attacking no matter what happened. But this small creature in front of her offered a way to do that with a minimum of fuss. She was quite sure that she could overpower Gwendaleir and she thought that the defending Pixies would probably be stupidly honourable enough to respect the agreement.

She called her lieutenant over and whispered to her "We attack no matter what." The lieutenant nodded and moved back to her place in the mob. Lady Windlington and Thelwyn crept quietly closer so that they could observe what was happening; the Pixies were too intent on each other's group to have noticed. They had left Lieutenant Archer and his troops behind, guarding a possible approach by human antagonists; they wouldn't have been able to see the Pixies anyways. The leader of the attackers said to Gwendaleir "I accept your offer. Prepare to die!" She drew her bone sword and flew forward, trying to surprise Gwendaleir with her sudden attack. Gwendaleir had been expecting something like that and she pulled her steel needle from its small scabbard while she shifted to her left to avoid the attack. She was under no illusion that the enemy Pixies wouldn't attack no matter who won the fight since the leader had made the quite obvious move of giving instructions to her lieutenant before launching her attack. The sudden rush also showed the dishonourable manner of the Pixie. But she wouldn't worry about that. She concentrated on watching her opponent to see if she could pick out a weakness to exploit like Lady Ashmont had shown Thelwyn to do. She knew that her steel needle didn't have an edge to it and was therefore more of a thrusting implement but that was the type of fighting that Lady Ashmont had taught. Her steel blade could be used to block any slashes by her opponent though she knew.

The leader tried to slash at Gwendaleir as she flew by where Gwendaleir had been but missed her by quite a margin. Gwendaleir turned to face her opponent as the leader flew up at a more measured pace and made another slash at Gwendaleir. Gwendaleir parried the blow, forcing it off to her right. She felt a brief stinging in her arm as she did this indicating the force of the blow. She decided that she had speed on her side and would undoubtedly succeed the best if she let her opponent tire herself out so she didn't attempt to counterattack right then. The two Pixies circled one another with the leader of the enemy Pixies continually slashing hard at Gwendaleir while she just parried the blows. Gwendaleir could see that soon she would have the opportunity to parry a blow and then thrust into her opponent's shoulder, wounding her and most likely ending the fight. Her opponent was tiring and leaving that opening more open with each attempt. Lady Windlington wasn't overly familiar with sword fighting and was worried because Gwendaleir wasn't attacking only defending. Thelwyn wasn't concerned at all because she recognized what the Pixie was doing and approved; she was somewhat surprised that Gwendaleir had learned to do that so well though.

The leader made a slightly wild slash with her tiring arm. Gwendaleir decided that she left a large enough opening for her to perform her maneuver and slid her needle forward so the point went deep into her opponent's shoulder. The leader groaned in pain as she dropped her sword and grabbed at her injury. Gwendaleir lifted her sword in front of her and asked "Do you yield?" She didn't want to have to kill if she didn't have to do so. The leader snarled at her, grabbed a knife from her belt and charged. Gwendaleir had somewhat expected that and put the point of her sword into the chest of the other Pixie, allowing her own charge to impale her deeply. The leader of the enemy Pixies sputtered as the sword pierced her heart and then died, falling to the ground. Gwendaleir held onto her sword as her opponent collapsed to the ground and her sword slid out of the dead body.

All of the Pixies watched the end of the battle in shock that it had ended so suddenly when it appeared that Gwendaleir might be losing. They thought that Gwendaleir was hesitant to attack because she was afraid to do so. But then the whole field erupted in battle as they began to square off against each other. The defenders tried to fight in pairs as much as they could, standing slightly at an angle to each other so that they could provide as much protection to their partner's back as they could without compromising their own defence. The first few attackers that attempted to assault this formation on their own found out how perilous that was. A number of them went down, dead or injured. One enemy Pixie looked to be gaining when she attacked the left hand Pixie of a pair and that Pixie fell back somewhat from her partner. The enemy pushed the attack thinking that she had the advantage but the pair was only baiting her. Once she came close enough and was fully intent on her immediate opponent the right hand Pixie launched a series of thrusts at the enemy. She managed to wound the enemy Pixie enough that the enemy fell injured to the ground, her wings folding up on her. Lady Windlington was checking on as many Pixies on the ground as she could, ignoring if they were defenders or attackers and trying to help any injured ones she found. She regretted that the fight had to come to this; the poor little creatures shouldn't really be involved in disputes that didn't really benefit them. She was aware of her part in it and would defend her own position against anyone who thought she was being a hypocrite about it. Thelwyn saw what Lady Windlington was doing and began to help her since she really couldn't do anything to help the defending Pixies.

Purple Cedar had moved forward to partner Gwendaleir when her battle with the leader of the enemy Pixies was complete. The two of them moved forward, attacking vigorously and downing quite a number of the enemy. They had been practicing their moves for quite a while and had become very good at anticipating what the other might attempt. Purple Cedar moved too far forward in her fight with an enemy and exposed herself to attack but Gwendaleir quickly swooped up closer and fought off the Pixie that was attempting to take advantage. She blocked the sword of the enemy and then thrust through her fragile wings, hampering her ability to fly. The enemy Pixie fluttered to the ground. Both of them were shouting back and forth encouraging and trying to warn each other. They were excited but weren't happy about what they were doing. They had some regrets about hurting their own kind but knew that they were really doing the correct thing. Various fights ended in different ways but it became apparent to the attackers that they were ending up on the losing end more often than not. Their numerical superiority was being whittled down with each passing moment. One of the attacking Pixies began to shout "Retreat" to her comrades as she began to make her way back to where they had started their journey. She felt that they had to regroup if they were going to have any hope of possibly winning the battle. The attackers began moving backwards as quickly as they could. They fled the battle ground and some of the defending Pixies pursued them, attempting to keep the fight going.

Thelwyn quickly ran up to Gwendaleir, who hadn't joined the chase of the enemy, and told her "Quick, Gwendaleir, call them back. They can't try to follow them. They could become quickly outnumbered and killed. Go after them and call them back."

So Gwendaleir flew after them calling "Blackwoods Farm Pixies to me!" She did this a number of times as loud as she could; her lieutenants also took up the cry. The pursuing Pixies heard, stopped and began to return back to where the battle had taken place. The defending Pixies began cheering and congratulating one another for haven won. They were dancing through the skies and doing flips of happiness.

Once more, Thelwyn sought out Gwendaleir where she was almost crowing with glee. "Yes, you did very well, Gwendaleir" she said soothingly, hoping to calm down the enthusiastic Pixie. "I'm very proud of you and what you accomplished. You were a wonderful commander and your army succeeded. But this is only a battle. The war has yet to be won. I need you to calm your group down. They should eat, drink and rest because we most likely will see a return of those Pixies. You need to be in as good a shape as you can be because they still outnumber you and you will have to fight them again." She made calming motions with her hands as she said this and was relieved that Gwendaleir seemed to be calming down and listening to her. Soon they were both going around instructing the Pixies to settle down and rest; Thelwyn had brought a large basket of food for the Pixies and began doling it out. Lady Windlington was tending to the injured Pixies from both sides and didn't participate in what Thelwyn and Gwendaleir were doing.

After she had made sure that the Pixie army was resting and recuperating in case they had to fight another battle, Thelwyn went over to where the injured Pixies were. She called to the injured enemy Pixies "I am a Wolf Princess and I want you to stop fighting us and join us. I promise you that we will take care of you the best that we can." She took off her clothes and changed into her wolf form for a moment to demonstrate what she was before changing back. She assumed that the enemy Pixies would all want to join them now.

She was quite stunned when the enemy Pixies only looked at her with slightly blank looks; they weren't overly impressed by the fact that she was able to change into a wolf at all. One of them said "That's a nice trick but it really doesn't mean anything to us. We are forced to work for a sorcerer who has no hesitation to kill us if we don't do as he commands. Becoming a wolf isn't going to do too much against him. He has a great deal of power at his command." Thelwyn quickly realized that these Pixies didn't have the same stories about Wolf Princesses that the local ones and the ones she met on their trip had. She had thought that she could convince these injured Pixies to persuade their friends to stop the war but now it seemed like that wouldn't happen. She cursed under her breath a bit in frustration as she considered what they should do next. She had been so sure that the Pixies would automatically follow her once she revealed what she was.

She went over to Lady Windlington and said in dismay "These Pixies don't seem to be in awe of me like the recent ones we met."

"Well, dear, you can't expect all Pixies to be like that. Gwendaleir and the castle Pixies hadn't really heard about your reputation either before we met these newer ones" Lady Ashmont stated as she looked intently at Thelwyn. "You aren't upset about the fact are you?" she asked softly.

"Well I hoped that maybe I could've been able to shorten the battle and save some of the Pixies. If they would've all agreed to follow me, they wouldn't have to fight one another" Thelwyn replied sadly. Lady Windlington could see that it was her concern for the Pixies that was motivating her and not her own notoriety. She felt a brief burst of pride for the young woman but decided it was best not to say too much. They did what they could for the injured Pixies before taking a brief rest to eat. Thelwyn had to go back to Lieutenant Archer to ask for him to send for more food and to get Lagalaise to come out to them if she could. Lagalaise arrived and the three of them discussed what they were going to do. They decided that the best plan would be to hide the magical signatures of the injured enemy Pixies so that the opposing sorcerer wouldn't know about them. So Lagalaise did that.

The enemy sorcerer was very displeased that his Pixies came rushing back with tales of being ambushed by an army of their own kind. He couldn't detect any such thing out there and was inclined to disbelieve them. But then he recognized that the Pixies were too frightened of him to try to make up such a story. He got as much information from the excited Pixies as he could and then took some time to think about the matter. He knew that there were some magic users opposing him. He knew that his acolyte who had been involved in the attack on the Princess's party had run afoul of something that caused his magic to backlash on him but he wasn't sure if that was the actions of a person or an item. Then he could no longer find the magical signatures of his Pixies that had been where the battle had occurred. It was becoming more apparent that it must be a person. That person seemed to have the ability to mask his ally's magical signatures from him, he thought. He wondered if he was facing more than just one new person. He was already aware of Chesmyse, Charlymi and Pellaynu and knew that they didn't have the ability to do what was now occurring. That made things more dangerous he thought but decided that he had to continue to try to advance the planning that had been put in place. It still might be successful, he thought hopefully. Once he decided that, he went back and harangued his Pixies, commanding them to attack once more and that they had better be winners this time.

So, once more, the Pixies headed back to attack the defenders; Lady Windlington saw them as they headed their way and warned Gwendaleir and the defenders to be ready. The remaining enemy Pixies came on slowly and cautiously; they weren't looking forward to the upcoming fight and it reflected in their reluctance. Gwendaleir kept her troops from moving forward, making the enemy cover the ground rather than her own people. This ensured that her troops maintained their formations. She could tell that her Pixies were nervous and wanted to get on with the battle but they understood why she wanted them to keep where they were and they strived to do that. Still, there were a couple that broke forward once the enemy were close. Gwendaleir shouted for everyone to keep their position when this happened so they weren't all put at risk. Of the seven that had broken ranks, only two rushed all the way up to the enemy and were quickly overwhelmed. The other five Pixies brought themselves back under control and returned to their spots with their faces burning with shame.

The enemy Pixies paused as they observed the situation; they still outnumbered the defenders but were no longer confident in their superiority. They also had less discipline and a number of them rushed ahead of the pack to get started fighting. Gwendaleir's better trained troops quickly started knocking them from the sky. The new leader of the attackers signalled for all of them to attack and the sky was once more covered with scattered fights. The defenders were once again getting the better of the attackers but the attackers knew that they had nothing to return to and were fighting desperately. Lady Windlington was feeling terrible anguish about the number of Pixies falling to the earth and she cried out "Stop! Enough! Everyone stop!" She used her magic to project her cries over the fighting Pixies.

The attacking Pixies were amazed and stopped so the defenders courteously didn't press their sudden advantage. The Pixies hovered facing one another as some of the attacking Pixies started crying "She's a sorceress. They have a sorceress. Is she more powerful than our sorcerer? Maybe she can save us from our sorcerer."

Lady Windlington realized that she could take advantage of this situation and stated "If you cease with your attack, I will protect and reward you." She used her powers to help her to reach all of them and waved her hands toward the injured Pixies. "I have tended to your wounded to the best of my abilities and will do the same for you. Please stop this fighting at once."

The leader of the attacking Pixies flew forward and asked "Can you defeat our sorcerer? If he gets his hands on us we will all perish. We need your guarantee that you will be successful against him. He has quite a bit of power."

Lagalaise was still with them and she recognized what she had to do. She dropped her mask from everyone. The Pixies gaped as they suddenly saw the power of the young girl, her mother and Thelwyn. They were also shocked to see that they could once again see their comrades as well as the defenders. At their camp, the enemy sorcerer saw the massive light up of magical sources at the site of the battle and wondered about it. Since he was at a distance and there were so many instances of it, he couldn't tell how strong any individual was. Lagalaise once more masked everyone on the battlefield. "Do I appear to be strong enough to defeat your sorcerer?" she challenged.

"Yes, you do" a number of the attackers replied, in awe. Their leader cried out "Please protect us then, sorceresses. We will surrender to you." All of the attacking Pixies then began dropping their weapons. Lady Windlington directed them to come forward to an area where she could look them over to see how injured they might be. They meekly followed her orders. Thelwyn started giving them the leftover food and Lagalaise went off to arrange for more food to be brought forward. The Pixie battle was over.

THE FINAL BATTLE

For nearly a week after the end of the Pixie battle, nothing much happened. The two sides sent out scouts and caught sight of each other but didn't engage in any fighting. Lagalaise couldn't detect any magic being performed and even lost track of the enemy sorcerer. When they all gathered to discuss the matter, she stated that she thought that the enemy sorcerer had left the area shortly after losing his control over his Pixies. She didn't think that he had given up the fight but rather went off to ready whatever other magic he might be planning. Questioning the Pixies that had just joined them didn't lead them to discovering what that magic might be; the Pixies would eagerly have told Lady Windlington or Lagalaise but they had no knowledge of what he'd been doing. But a number of injured Pixies did manage to regain their health during the respite. Gwendaleir and most of the six who pledged themselves to Thelwyn had only slight injuries but Red Creek had been slashed in the wings and couldn't fly. Thelwyn and the Pixies all worried about her and tried to help her as much as possible and it looked as though she would recover fully. There had been numerous discussions about what to do with all of the Pixies. Chesmyse's family had no problems with agreeing to take care of the local Pixies after this war had ended but they didn't want the enemy sorcerer's army to remain. Princess Aurolla discussed the matter with Lady Windlington, Lagalaise and Thelwyn and didn't need much persuasion to agree to take them back to Darkcloud with them. Since the enemy sorcerer no longer had any Pixies and the captured ones stated that they didn't think he could recruit any more very quickly, Chesmyse questioned what the Pixies could do to help them in the expected battle. Lady Windlington and Thelwyn quickly stated that the Pixies could do quite a bit for them by just following their natural instincts of being pests. Thelwyn stated that the Pixies could harass enemy human troops by hiding equipment, cutting bowstrings or undoing saddle girths. Chesmyse became more satisfied that they could indeed help if they were willing to do things like that.

Lady Ashmont spent quite a bit of time with Lieutenant Archer devising strategies for whatever attacks the enemy launched at them. She found that he was starting to grow on her and spent some nights together with him in his rooms. She understood that they were facing danger and knew that such situations tended to arouse feelings in her. The lieutenant was someone that she didn't think that she would be with for a long time so he was perfect for relieving those itches. She still made sure that she was focused on the job at hand and handled the strategy meetings with her usual efficiency. She and Lieutenant Archer spent a long time going over the lay of the land with Thelwyn. Lieutenant Archer was surprised at the amount of knowledge that Thelwyn was supplying regarding the local area; it was almost as though she had travelled over it but that was impossible he thought. Neither Thelwyn or Lady Ashmont bothered to inform him about how Thelwyn knew what she did. Thelwyn had spent a fair amount of time as a wolf looking over the eastern side of the kingdom since they expected the attack to be launched from the kingdom over on that side. The kingdom was Purkusse. Lieutenant Archer didn't think that the royal family of Purkusse was involved in the attack on Barcless because it was in a total disarray as they tried to determine their succession. The king had died and his four sons were all trying to attain the throne. They had most of their people tied up in their internal battle which was occurring mostly on the eastern side of their kingdom and away from Barcless. He felt that if Darglype and Murgald were the enemy, and there was no reason to think that they weren't, they would attack Blackwoods Manor through Purkusse, since there wouldn't be much opposition there. Lady Ashmont had agreed with his thinking once he had explained the situation to her. So they were making their plans based on that rationale. Lady Windlington and Lagalaise contributed by outlining what they might be able to do in a magic sense but didn't contribute too much to what was planned for the troops. Thelwyn suggested the placement of some of the troops but deferred to the two more experienced leaders for most of the planning. So while there was this respite, they were making the most of it.

Lagalaise kept watch over the eastern border so that she could warn them if there was anything magical approaching it; there were also a fair number of scouts out there as well since she couldn't detect anything non-magical. On the morning of the ninth day after the Pixie battle, she detected a number of magical signals headed toward that area. She thought that they were larger than Pixies but couldn't tell anymore about their size. She also noted that there were a good deal of smaller signatures behind them. When she discussed this with her mother and the others, she ventured that these might be troops with charms of some sort rather than Pixies. This belief was based on the feeling of the captured Pixies that the enemy sorcerer wouldn't be able to recruit more Pixies. She had already seen the enemy sorcerer's associate using charms for his attacking troops so this wasn't just speculation on her part. One thing that she had noted with these sorcerers was that they tended to link their charms to the life force of the soldiers wearing them. She knew that this could be done but it tended to shorten the life of those soldiers. She wondered if the soldiers knew what was being done to them and suspected that they didn't.

The different groups of defenders were already in place so Lieutenant Archer only had to send messengers to them warning that it appeared like the enemy was on the move. Lady Ashmont and her small group were near the centre of the defenders with the main mounted troop. Princess Aurolla was barricaded in the manor with Chesmyse's family and their personal protectors. There were six troopers with her and her maids to provide personal security for her. Three of the six were wounded enough so that they couldn't ride but were fit enough to provide protection for the Princess. The other three had been drawn by lots from the group that Lady Ashmont felt she could spare from defending the attack. Lady Ashmont had impressed on them that they shouldn't consider their duty as any sort of diminishment but as being supremely important, protecting their Princess. She had made that arrangement so that Thelwyn could be freed up to help out in the attack; knowing that the wolf girl's talents could prove to be extremely useful as the battle waged on. Lady Ashmont knew that if they lost the battle, Princess Aurolla would be in peril but she also knew that the Princess wasn't the target of this fight and should be all right where she was providing they won the battle.

Thelwyn was scouting the area in her wolf form with five Pixies since Red Creek was still recovering and unable to fly for very long. The Pixies would warn her if they saw any magic ahead and she could go out and see what she could do about it. She knew that she couldn't take on the probable magical creatures the sorcerer might be sending against them; that would be the job of Lagalaise and her mother. But she could disrupt small groups of troops and the fact that they were in small groups could signify their rarity and importance. She found herself grinning wolfishly as she recalled how well she had done against the archers during the ambush on the journey. She wasn't bloodthirsty but did enjoy doing a task well. She scented a bunch of horses and worked her way downwind of them so that they wouldn't spook as she crept to a place that she could observe them. When she caught a glimpse of the group, it looked like there were about two hundred of them that were working their way through the woods to try to flank the defenders. She knew that Lady Ashmont had foreseen such an attempt and had set some defenders that should be able to intercept a group like this. Thelwyn hoped that they would be able to hold them up long enough for Lady Ashmont to reinforce them and drive the attackers away. It was an awful lot of troops. But she knew that she really couldn't do anything much about these attackers and made her way carefully past them looking for better targets for her.

Lady Ashmont was quite concerned. The number of targets that Lagalaise was reporting seeing worried her. She knew that she would be outnumbered but was troubled by how high that number was appearing to be. She had set Lieutenant Archer and most of his people at where she thought the center of the battle would be. She was glad that he'd agreed to let her command the fight and devise the strategy.

He'd been initially reluctant to do that but she demonstrated what her thinking was and he'd come around to the conclusion that she really did know what she was talking about. She was on a small hill overlooking the farms that she'd chosen to be the area that they would face any oncomers. The cleared area would allow her to see the attacking troops so that she could determine the best way to counteract them. She had sent off some of her people with each of the groups so that they could relay her orders to the troops. Her people were familiar with the signals that she may be sending. She knew that some of the defenders would get caught up in the battle and ignore her instructions but she hoped that only a few would do that. More than one battle had been lost by troops being so intent on pursuing an enemy that they overreached their protection and were wiped out. She hadn't had enough time to work with the local troops to ensure that such an action wouldn't happen. She knew that troops in Darkcloud were constantly being trained so that they wouldn't do that but having talked to Lieutenant Archer, found that his troops didn't really concern themselves with such training. She scanned the area to see if she could spot where the attackers would be coming from even though she had scouts out to warn her and Lagalaise was also tracking any magical signature.

She looked over to where Lagalaise and Lady Windlington had been positioned and saw that they were gone, having moved off towards the western edge of the surrounding woods. She frowned as she thought about what that suggested; Lagalaise most likely detected some of the magical animals that the sorcerer seemed fond of creating and moved off to intercept them. The young sorceress and her mother were really the only defense that they had against such attackers. Lady Ashmont had sent her best archers and some of the local troops with her so that they might be able to defeat such an attack. She hoped that they would be enough but was apprehensive that they wouldn't be.

She spotted movement over to the left and realized that her scouts had spotted a flanking movement setting up and the troops she had placed over in that area to prevent such a maneuver were readying to attack that group. Thelwyn had suggested that from her scouting, that area might be where such an attack might occur and that she perceived that it had been scouted by the enemy because of the scents she detected in the area. Lady Ashmont once more thanked the gods that had sent a treasure such as Thelwyn to them. She was worth her weight in gold, the swordswoman thought. She watched what was happening over there anxiously while trying to keep an eye on the area in front of them in case the enemy launched their main attack. She was pretty sure that her people had spotted the flankers earlier than the enemy had hoped and thus had disrupted the timing of the attackers but wondered if the enemy would be flexible enough to speed up their actions. She watched the fight from afar; it appeared to her that her smaller group had taken advantage of their surprise appearance to the enemy and had evened up the odds quite a bit. Lady Ashmont saw that the flanking movement chose to retreat after a few minutes of fighting; she wasn't too surprised by this retreat because the group had lost their purpose once they had been detected early. It made more sense for the flankers to return back to their main army than try to hold an untenable position. The group she had over there didn't bother pursuing the attackers through the woods back to where they would join with their main group. Their job had been to make sure that the flankers didn't establish themselves in an area where they could threaten the defenders main army at a later time in the battle and they had achieved their purpose. Lady Ashmont could see some of the group that had been positioned over there moving back to support the main line of defence and knew that her orders were being followed. It was unlikely that the enemy would send another group through that area so only a token force would be stationed there.

Lady Ashmont had most of the Pixies with her and they would be sent to plague the enemy once she determined where their main force was; they would be like invisible spirits to most of the troopers who wouldn't be able to see them. She wanted to keep them away from any of the enemy who could do magic in case they had figured out a way to combat the small creatures. She didn't want to have to put the Pixies at too great a risk. Thelwyn and Gwendaleir had argued for quite some time about the deployment of the Pixies. Thelwyn thought that they needed Gwendaleir to be their commander in order to make the most use of them and Gwendaleir insisted that she had to be with Thelwyn to help her as much as possible. The tiny creature refused to be moved on the matter. She knew that Thelwyn would have to put herself at quite a bit of risk and she was determined to be there in order to do what she could to lessen it. None of the other four able Pixies that had pledged themselves to Thelwyn would take over the command either so Lady Ashmont had Petunia, from the castle, as her commander. Petunia had seen the tactics that Gwendaleir had been using all through the trip so she would be an adequate commander for the Pixie army. Lady Ashmont understood Gwendaleir and the other's devotion to Thelwyn and sympathized with them.

So the five Pixies were currently riding on Thelwyn's back as she curved over to the east so that she could check on an area where she thought the enemy might set up a specialty squad. Hopefully she could disrupt them in what they were doing. She came to a small hill and started running up it when she caught a scent that was both familiar and unexpected. She slowed down as she thought furiously about what it meant. Suddenly she was surrounded by nine larger shapes. Wolves, she thought with some dismay. She dropped into a submissive posture and stated in her best wolfish "I beg your pardon for intruding on your range. I am a stranger and have no wishes to stay on your land. I am involved in something for the two-legs right now and can't spend a lot of time explaining matters to you. Please let me pass." One of the young males of the pack snickered at her accent but the others just stood watching her.

"We know that you aren't a true wolf" the leader said as he stared hard at her. "We know that you are involved with the two-legs and that you can turn into one of them. You also associate with these small creatures and let them ride on your back." His nose flicked up to indicate the Pixies who'd taken to the air around Thelwyn. "We have been watching you for the past few days doing most peculiar things. Are you interested in a bunch of two-legs that have set up in an area you have checked for the last two days?"

"Yes, I am" Thelwyn replied cautiously with the hope that the wolves were going to let her pass without any bother. She didn't want to hurt them if she could help it.

"There is a bunch there with a female two-leg directing them" the wolf leader said. "We will take you to them and help you dispatch them."

Thelwyn was shocked by the wolf's offer of help. Wolves didn't involve themselves in the affairs of humans, she knew. What had changed, she wondered but was polite enough not to ask. "Thank you. I appreciate that" she said simply and the pack began to move through the woods with her following.

Lagalaise had detected a dozen magical signatures that were heading in from the east and assumed that these were probably some of the massive animal creatures that the enemy sorcerer seemed to favour. She directed the troop assigned to help her over to where they seemed to be headed. It looked like they would be coming out of a wooded area over there. There was no way that they could get the carriage close to that area so she discussed the matter briefly with her mother. They had known that this might happen and had a plan of how they were going to respond to such a happening. Since Lady Windlington couldn't ride a horse but Lagalaise could, they would split up with Lagalaise going on with the troopers to deal with the magical creatures. Lady Windlington would remain with her carriage and keep watch for any other sorcerous attacks. Lady Windlington was concerned for her young daughter but was extremely proud of her and confident that she would be successful. She knew her daughter had more power available to her than herself and should be able to defeat the attack. So Lagalaise mounted her horse and guided the troop of soldiers to where they could intercede with the attack.

Lagalaise set up her group with the help of their leader and started examining the oncoming magical signatures. These creatures weren't the same as the hastily devised ones that she and Thelwyn had defeated so easily on their trip north. They appeared to be better constructed to her than those ones and she felt a brief touch of worry. She tried to examine their spells as best that she could from the distance but didn't see the weakness that she had been able to exploit in that earlier encounter. It also seemed that these new creatures didn't have the weakness of the wolverine either. She thought that she could probably overpower the other sorcerer's spell with sheer might but that would take a great deal of effort and some time and she had to deal with a dozen of them. She wouldn't be able to wrest the magic from all of them before they were on top of her, she thought with dismay. She didn't like the fact that some of the troops protecting her were likely to die as they tried to keep those magical creatures off of her so that she could deal with them. Still, she thought as she squared her shoulders in determination, I will do the best that I can. A dozen archers moved forward at her signal as she grabbed the spell of the lead creature and started to tear it away. She concentrated hard as the spell fought its removal and after a moment managed to lift it enough that the archers could kill the creature enveloped in it. She signalled to the leader beside her and he relayed the signal to the archers. They started shooting at the animal. She hoped that the spell was linked with the life force of the animal like the others had been and would dissipate once the animal was dead. She felt the animal start to die and felt the magic beginning to fade away. She felt some elation but recognized that the creatures were now very close. She wasn't going to be able to handle them all before they overran her and her protectors. She considered telling the leader to call his troops back so that they could retreat but that would mean letting these creatures attack the flank of the main army of the defenders which would likely lose them the battle. She decided that she would sell her and her protector's lives as dearly as she could.

Meanwhile Thelwyn had followed the wolf pack to a small hill just off a trail; she had scented some activity in this area as well. The pack stopped a distance from where a group of about twenty humans had gathered. The woman sitting cross-legged in the center of them was obviously the sorceress, Thelwyn thought. Her eyes roamed the group as she considered her options to attack them. She was going to have to expose herself to a magical attack she thought with consternation; even though she was quite fast, there was no way she could cover that amount of ground before the sorceress became aware of her. She hoped that she would be able to dodge such an attack knowing that she couldn't leave this sorceress here. She took a deep breath to steady her nerves and said to the wolf leader "Thank you for bringing me here. I don't want to put you in danger. Please just go with my thanks." She bowed her head to him in respect.

The wolf leader snorted and said slightly derisively "You aren't getting rid of us that easily. We said that we would help you and we will. I assume that you are most interested in the female two-leg sitting there in the center. We will attack those around her so that you can deal with her."

Thelwyn looked at him in wonder, thinking that wolves didn't fight for humans; they avoided any such conflicts as much as they could. But these wolves were quite determined to help her however they could, at much danger to their own lives. Once again, she simply said "Thank you." She dropped her pack and changed into her human form. She dug out her bandolier and put it on as the wolf pack watched her with interest. She didn't feel any more self-conscious about being nude in front of them than she had in her wolf form. The five Pixies buzzed around her as they displayed their agitation about the upcoming battle. The wolves slipped through the woods so that they could attack from different directions and cause as much havoc as they could; Thelwyn approved of their tactics.

She waited a few minutes to let her allies get into position and then burst out of the woods to signal to them to begin. She ran as fast as she could towards the sorceress as the enemy started trying to react to her sudden appearance. Then the wolves came erupting out of the woods around them and ran through their camp, snapping and biting at them. Thelwyn was about half way across the small clearing when the sorceress turned her attention towards her. Thelwyn felt a small shiver of fear run up her spine as she contemplated what might happen. The sorceress smiled evilly and cast a burst of power towards her in a dismissive manner. She expected the power to consume the small nude girl who for some strange reason was attacking her and her protectors. She began to turn her attention back to her creations that were heading towards the main defending army and were in battle with the defending sorcerer.

Gwendaleir saw the spark of power heading towards Thelwyn and rapidly made the decision to sacrifice herself to save her idol. She sped forward to intercept the spark. She hoped that it would dissipate by consuming her small form and spare the Wolf Princess. Thelwyn watched with utter dismay as Gwendaleir attempted to intercept the spell; she was totally distraught that the Pixie would sacrifice her own life to save her. No, she thought wildly as she concentrated her mind on the spark of power. Just before it reached Gwendaleir, the spark veered off and crashed into the woods, knocking over ten or so trees as it impacted. Thelwyn was confused as to what had happened but ecstatic that Gwendaleir still survived. She drove all such thoughts from her mind as she launched herself at the dumbfounded sorceress, driving her knives into that woman's chest. The sorceress gurgled and tried to talk but Thelwyn quickly slashed through her throat, ending her life. She spun to face the protectors ready to attack them. They stood looking at her like she was something out of their worst nightmare with open mouths. She started towards them and they quickly began scrambling for their mounts; the wolves harassed them as they tried to get away and brought down a couple more of them to join the half dozen they'd already killed.

Lagalaise had destroyed four of the evil creations and was battling with the fifth as some of her troop had to move out against the other seven creatures since they were now close enough to threaten the whole group. Lagalaise was distraught to see a female trooper being hauled off her horse and slammed against against a tree by one of the nearer creatures that was probably based on a bear. She drove her feelings from her mind as she sought to wrest the magic from the creature she was fighting. It would do no one any good if she gave into her despair, she needed to destroy or damage these creatures to the best of her ability before she died, she thought. She contemplated trying to use a burning magic against them. She'd discussed that action with her mother and they had come to the conclusion that it was liable to be as dangerous to her and her protectors as it was to the creations. But she knew that she was being left with no choice. She would rather destroy everyone and everything over here than let the monsters proceed against her friends and allies. She managed with the help of her archers to kill the fifth creature and was sucking in a breath to start the spell that would undoubtedly annihilate them all when something suddenly changed. She was at a loss momentarily to determine what it was but then she realized that the gigantic creatures had all shrunk back to their original forms. These creatures were now staggering slightly in a daze but might still be dangerous so she encouraged the troopers to kill them all. While they were doing that, she searched with her magic to discover what had changed. She realized that she no longer felt the sorcerous presence to the north of her. What had occurred, she wondered with awe. Then it struck her. Thelwyn must have found the sorcerer and had managed to kill him. That was really the only logical explanation, she thought. She hoped that the wolf girl was all right but didn't really have much time to think about her as she scrambled to help the injured members of her party before any of them succumbed to their wounds.

Thelwyn surveyed the scene as the eight uninjured wolves chased away the remaining humans, running them as far away as they could before giving up and returning. One young female wolf was down and whining piteously, a large gash bleeding on her left shoulder. Thelwyn rushed over and slid in beside her, putting pressure to prevent too much blood loss with her right hand. With her left hand she tore the tunic from one of the dead nearby soldiers and wadded it up to stuff into the wound. She held it there and watched as the bleeding slowed down. She awkwardly gathered some more cloth and fashioned it around the bandage. She tied it as tightly as she could. She was somewhat amazed that the hurt wolf hadn't tried to avoid her or to bite at her. She looked into its eyes and saw the understanding and gratitude that the wolf felt towards her. She stroked it soothingly and said calmly as she could "You should be all right now. You'll be hurt for quite a while but you should recover. You should rest here. When this fight is over I will come back and move you somewhere where you can be better protected and recover. I will make sure that you are fed." She hadn't realized that the wolf pack had returned as she'd started saying this and were sitting silently in a half circle watching her and the wolf.

Suddenly she became aware of them and turned to face them. The leader of the pack said "You honour the young one, Wolf Princess. We thank you for caring for her and making your promise to her. We will do our utmost to ensure that you are on the winning side of your war. She'll have plenty of food to sustain her while she waits." Thelwyn felt a brief moment of shame that she'd involved these magnificent creatures in the war but then shook it off. She needed to get her mind focused back on what she could do to help the rest of her friends, she thought.

Gwendaleir had been quiet while Thelwyn was occupied with saving the wolf, respecting her need to concentrate on what she'd been doing. But now that the crisis had passed, she crowed excitedly "Did you see what I did? I threw myself at that burst of power and it veered away. I must be magic resistant. I am invincible to sorcerers and sorceresses." She flew about performing backflips in the air and all other sorts of stunts. Thelwyn watched her with some amusement as she thought about what had occurred. She didn't think that Gwendaleir was magic resistant as she thought. She knew that it wasn't much use in trying to talk to the ecstatic Pixie at the moment because she wouldn't listen anyway. She wondered why that burst of power had veered like that. She remembered being very worried for Gwendaleir just before it happened but wasn't sure if she had done anything either. She gathered her items together as she prepared to move on to see what else she could accomplish. She did attempt to calm Gwendaleir somewhat but the Pixie refused to be calmed as she rode her adrenaline high.

Purple Cedar buzzed over and said a little breathlessly "I think there is another sorcerer. I see a powerful magical signature over to the northwest. It is on the limit of my ability to detect it and has been fading in and out. Should we head over there to see what it really is?" Thelwyn nodded and they all got ready to depart.

The head sorcerer was at the headquarters for the attacking army with the leaders and staff of both the Darglype and Murgald contingents. The mounted men in the army were about sixty/forty from those two kingdoms. The army leaders had sent forth their large group to attack the much smaller group of defenders. They felt that this battle would be a walkover and were strutting about in their confidence of the results. The sorcerer had noted the cessation of his assistant and was concerned somewhat about what may have happened. He had sent her over there to tie up and possibly eliminate the strong defending sorceress while he worked with the main attack. He didn't think that his sorceress had been overcome with magic because he hadn't sensed any disturbance that an action like that would have created. But he wasn't positive that he could see something like that given the fact that the defending sorceress could mask powers from him. He wondered if she could cover her sorcerous attacks like that. But he pushed all that from his mind as he tried to deal with the pompous fools leading the army. He had nothing but contempt for anyone who couldn't use magic to bend things to their will.

Lady Ashmont had chosen the area of the battle quite well. There wasn't a great deal of open area where the attackers could build up their speed in an attack but rather a fairly rough number of farm fields that would threaten to break horse's legs.

That meant that the attackers wouldn't be able to sweep in and overcome the defenders but would have to approach fairly cautiously instead. She also had the advantage of having a large number of archers who could shoot at the enemy as they approached. The attacking army only had a few mounted archers since waiting for men walking would have delayed their approach. Lady Ashmont knew that this made the attackers more vulnerable but recognized that they were confident of the sheer number of troops that they could put on the field versus what the defenders could muster. She experienced a sinking feeling as she surveyed the numbers of attackers moving into view. There were more than she had been hoping would appear.

Lagalaise left some people to attend to the wounded and moved with the others to rejoin her mother. She quickly filled in her mother on what she thought had happened. Lady Windlington had also observed what had occurred and agreed with her daughter's suppositions. They moved over to rejoin Lady Ashmont to see what they could possibly do to help.

Lady Ashmont decided that it was time to send the Pixies to do what they could against the enemy horde. They obediently flew off to cause as much havoc as they could manage. Lady Ashmont sent out a signal and her hidden troop of mounted archers opened up from the left flank of the slowly moving enemy. They managed to score a number of hits before the enemy organized itself enough to send out some troops to drive them out of their spot. Lady Ashmont was heartened to see that her archers held their ground long enough to reduce down the oncoming mounted men before they made their way back to safety. She wondered if the enemy troops would try to continue to pursue her smaller group and thereby weaken the main attack a bit. She was happy to see that it appeared that they were prepared to do exactly that. She heard the enemy horns apparently signalling the troops to return to the main group but it didn't look like they were obeying the signals. She smiled slightly. These attackers didn't have iron discipline that she hoped her borrowed troops would exhibit.

Signals started being blown from the headquarters directing the field leader pf the attackers to start his attack. He ignored them for a couple of minutes as he tried to sort out his line of attack. The hidden archers had disrupted his original line and he was moving some men to cover for the ones that were off chasing those archers. He began to worry that the carefully planned battle wasn't going to proceed like they'd discussed. Lady Ashmont would have told him to ignore the small defect that the archers had created and simply move forward with his attack. He had sufficient numbers to overcome that small issue and should have proceeded with as much speed as he could before his large army became tangled up in itself. But he didn't have the experience and training that Lady Ashmont possessed.

Thelwyn and the wolves were racing through the trees of the forest with Purple Cedar guiding her to where they were going. Gwendaleir was still too giddy from her brave action to be of too much help. Thelwyn didn't begrudge the Pixie her actions, knowing that the Pixie was still marvelling that she was still alive after having expected to die. The lead wolf barked a quick warning and dove into the heavy underbrush. Thelwyn and the other wolves followed suit as a troop of horses went roaring by in front of them. Thelwyn watched their progress with extreme interest. These weren't the enemy that were passing by; they were troops of the King of Barcless and it didn't look like they were ones that Lady Ashmont was now commanding. So, she thought with some glee, reinforcements have arrived. I hope that there are more than just these and that there is a large group headed towards where Lady Ashmont would be fighting the main battle. She jumped up to follow and filled the wolves in on what was happening as they continued their journey. Now they wouldn't be the only ones attacking the headquarters of the army, she thought. Maybe we can slip in and cause some chaos amongst the leaders of the enemy and I can do what I can to disrupt the sorcerer.

Lagalaise felt some unease as she suspected that the enemy sorcerer once more had an ace up his sleeve and she wondered what that could be. At the far range of her senses, she detected something stirring and wondered what it could be. She'd learned to be very wary of this sorcerer; he seemed to have access to a great deal of power and little compunction about using it. She looked over the battle field to see how it was shaping up; she had been present while Lady Ashmont detailed to her officers what she expected to happen. She was surprised to see an fairly open area in the enemy's attack to the east. Why would the attackers be avoiding that area, she wondered, curious. Lady Ashmont had troops stationed over on that area so she must be expecting the enemy to attack there but there were no enemy troops over on that side. As she was wondering about that, a large group of horsemen came rushing in from that direction and she was dismayed that the enemy had that many more troops. Then she realized that these weren't attacking troops but were men of the King of Barcless; they were allies here to help them. She was gladdened to see them and they caused a major disruption in the attack as they assaulted the flank of the attackers. But that didn't explain why that hole was there and allowed them to take advantage of it, Lagalaise thought.

The enemy field commander was trying to turn the troops on his eastern flank so that they could face the enemy but was having a great deal of problems in accomplishing that. One of the Murgald squads over there had panicked and their retreat was hampering the squads around them as they tried to face the assault from the King's troops. The field commander was grateful that the new troops didn't include any archers in their midst, the same as he didn't. Of course, Lady Ashmont was quick to realize the opportunity that this surprise attack was creating on the enemy and was moving her unmounted archers forward to try to take advantage of it. She instructed most of the mounted troops to advance towards the enemy to protect the more vulnerable archers.

The leaders of the attackers in the headquarters camp were concerned by the sudden presence of the new defending army that was relayed to them by signals from their field commander and approached the sorcerer with their concerns. They hadn't understood why the sorcerer had insisted that they leave that space in their attacking army and it looked to them that they were now going to pay the price for listening to him. He listened to their arguments with ill grace and sneered at them, telling them to wait and watch. He insisted that he would take care of this new group of defenders.

As they were moving forward, Lagalaise began to perceive what the enemy sorcerer was sending at them. She detected more monstrous creatures headed their way and was sickened to recognize that these new creations were based on human men. She could sense that the sorcerer was having to control these creatures quite closely but as she examined his spells she couldn't find any weakness to them. The monstrous men stomped closer to the defending army. Lagalaise started to detect that there were a number of dangerous spells wrapped up in the spells that created the monstrous creatures and worried about what might happen if they managed to destroy any of them. She hurried her people forward so that she could get as close as possible as her mind whirled with thoughts about how she was going to deal with this danger. The mounted men were so intent on fighting one another that they didn't even notice her and her people or the oncoming threat.

Thelwyn and the wolves had followed the King's men as fast as they could with Thelwyn urging them on; she suspected that the sorcerer might make short work of them if they attacked before she was in position to try to take him on. They arrived shortly after the troop attacked the headquarters, panting from their effort. When the King's men had attacked, the troop from Murgald was closest to them and were taking the brunt of the attack; the sorcerer was aware of their attack but he was occupied with keeping control of his creations, so he ignored them. He felt that the troops protecting him and the headquarters could handle them for a while as he destroyed the larger group on the battlefield. Once he was satisfied that the destruction was happening, he would take care of the minor irritant close to hand. Thelwyn quickly changed forms and dug out her bandolier, putting it on as she ran forward. She burst out of the trees a fair distance from the sorcerer, moving forward quickly; there were only a half dozen dismounted men between them.

The sorcerer's monstrous creations came crashing through the woods and into the open. All the fighters stopped momentarily to stare at them in wonderment. Lagalaise tried a spell against them but felt it fail as it struck them. She tried to find an area where she could try to rip the spell from them but couldn't find a place to grasp. The huge men creatures moved forward towards the King's main army, mindlessly grinding anything in their way under their feet. Lagalaise tried harder, knowing that if they reached the mounted men that they would create total havoc among them. Lagalaise felt despair as she recognized that she wasn't even slowing down the advance of those creatures. The lead monster reached the edge of the mounted men and picked up a horse with rider and began smashing the horse against the other mounted men, knocking a half dozen men from their mounts with each swing. The attackers rallied somewhat as they recognized that the monsters were all headed towards the defenders and resumed their fighting against the beleaguered troops.

Now that it looked like his flank was going to rally and protect themselves and the rest of his army, the enemy field leader encouraged his men to respond to Lady Ashmont's group in front of them. Her archers had caused a fair amount of damage to his army and now was the time to take care of that problem. Lady Ashmont directed her archers to abandon their attack and retreat while the mounted troops covered their actions. Her people fought hard to make sure that the lightly armoured, slower archers made their way back to the area of protection they had moved up from. A number of her troops were injured and killed as they kept the enemy away from the archers. Lady Ashmont knew that the tide of battle had turned again and that they were in danger of losing that fight but she encouraged her troops to fight as hard as they could manage. Her smaller group was making things difficult for the attackers but were being pressed back onto the people they were protecting. Lady Ashmont started to think that they would only survive if there was some sort of miracle.

The enemy sorcerer watched with interest as Thelwyn came running out of the trees; he almost laughed with derision as he wondered what sort of hope this young, nude girl possessed to pit herself against trained armoured men. He dismissed her from his mind as he exhorted his monstrous creations to continue their attack. He saw Thelwyn attack the first man in the corner of his eye and was amazed when she made short work of him. Thelwyn launched herself against the first man. He wasn't prepared for the speed or ferocity of her attack and wasn't able to defend himself at all. Thelwyn's knives quickly plunged into his neck area and he went down from his fatal wounds. The remaining five men gaped in surprise as she speedily took down the second man in her way. The remaining four men recognized that they had to defend themselves quickly or she would easily wipe them all out. They moved closer together to protect one another from her attack as she snarled at them and stalked closer. The enemy sorcerer realized that he'd made a mistake in dismissing her so quickly and he paused to flick a burst of power towards her.

Once again, Gwendaleir launched herself with suicidal intent at the spark of power. Thelwyn cursed as she worried for her tiny friend; she concentrated in her mind in hopes of doing something to protect the Pixie as she threatened the four men in front of her. Again, the spark of power deflected away and crashed into the trees to her left. The four men were distracted when the trees burst apart and began to burn. Thelwyn didn't let them recover and attacked them, killing three of them before the fourth one managed to even put up any defense. The sorcerer looked at her with concern as he wondered how his throw of power had gone so awry. He didn't think that this young girl had deflected it with a shield of power because he didn't feel any backlash from the interaction of their powers. He carefully examined the girl as she fought and killed the final man between them. He saw some sort of magic permeating her but couldn't really identify it. He sent another burst of power at her as she pulled her knives from the dead body of the man she'd been fighting. The blasted little Pixie once again threw herself forward at it and it went curving into the woods once more. He didn't think that the Pixie had caused the deflection but couldn't understand why his magic wasn't working on the little girl.

Thelwyn went rushing at the sorcerer, surprised when he didn't seem to try to avoid her attack. Instead he stood there and sneered at her, saying "I'm not worried about you, little girl. You may have been able to kill those men fairly easily but I have enchanted my skin so that only magical knives will penetrate it and I can tell that your knives are just ordinary blades. Try to do your worst. You're just wasting your time." Thelwyn worried a bit about his confidence that she couldn't hurt him but he didn't seem to be able to stop her either. She launched herself at him and thrust the blade in her right hand towards his chest. She prepared herself for some sort of negative reaction as his magic protected him like he'd stated.

Lagalaise found herself trying to fight the monstrous man advancing towards her while attempting to move backwards so she wouldn't be overwhelmed. Her protectors were still trying to overcome the monster but weren't having too much success; they could only seem to slow its advance, not stop it or kill it. She despaired as each of her people lost their lives in an attempt to give her the time to end the enormous creation but she wasn't able to find a way to do that. She gave some thought to just creating a massive magical explosion that would consume her and everything around her but she didn't believe that she could take out all of the creatures that were attacking and if she did that, she would leave the survivors with little to protect them. She racked her brains as she tried to come up with a method to overcome these monsters.

Lady Ashmont and her riders had been pressed back far enough that they were starting to overrun their own retreating archers. They were being pressed hard by the huge number of mounted men that the enemy field commander could muster against them because the monstrous men were tying up the King's troops. Lady Ashmont ordered her people to hold their positions at all costs, knowing that they were losing the battle. She briefly wondered what Thelwyn was currently doing.

Thelwyn's blade struck the sorcerer's skin. She felt a tremendous buzz echo through her mind and was blinded by a flash of brilliant purple light. But the blade sunk into the sorcerer's rather skinny chest. He looked at her incredulously and gurgled "How?" He began to choke on his own blood. She wasted no time but struck him with both of her knives about a half dozen times each. The sorcerer sank down to the ground and she fought to maintain contact with him to ensure that he did indeed die. She paused in her attack and examined him quickly before cutting his throat to ensure that he was indeed dead. She looked around for her next target as she hoped that she'd been in time eliminating the sorcerer for her friends to have survived. She knew that the battle wasn't over and was moving to help the small remaining group that were fighting the enemy mounted contingent protecting the headquarters.

The general of the Murgald army had been under tremendous pressure as his people were the main ones fighting the troop of the Barcless King's army attacking the headquarters. He'd lost almost a third of his fighters in the battle while the Darglype fighters provided little support to him. He was not happy about what was happening as he felt that his counterpart from Darglype was taking advantage of him. He saw the nude little girl emerge from the forest and attack and destroy armed men on her way towards the sorcerer that he had been designated to protect by his king. He couldn't believe what his eyes were seeing. Then she attacked the sorcerer and he quickly went down. As far as he was concerned, that was the straw that broke the horse's back; he no longer had a sorcerer to protect and there was no reason to continue this battle. He summoned his signaller and informed him to sound a full retreat before shouting orders to his men to cease their fighting and withdraw. The Darglype general was astounded as the shield of mounted men dissolved in front of him and suddenly his troops were fighting for their lives. The whole headquarter group from Murgald hastened away from the battle as quickly as they could manage. The King's fighters recognized that they were retreating and began to ignore them as they concentrated on the attackers from Darglype.

Lagalaise felt a tremendous surge of joy as she saw the monsters in front of her begin to shrink back to their normal size. Somehow Thelwyn must have managed to kill the enemy sorcerer and now she could take care of his still dangerous creatures. She knew that the spells that had enchanted the men were extremely toxic and still dangerous. She shouted to her people to stay as far from the enchanted men as possible and kill them from afar. One of the King of Barcless's fighters didn't pay any attention to her and attacked the nearest creature. As his blade bit into it, it exploded in a burst of green sorcerous fire that consumed him and three of the people around him. That explosion caused some consternation on the part of the defenders but now that they weren't being threatened by the enchanted monsters the King's army could once again fight the attacking army. They rushed to relieve the pressure on Lady Ashmont's remaining people. They were aided by the fact that the Murgald general had sounded retreat. Fully a third of the remaining attacking army was now streaming away and the odds were now fairly even. The King's army now hit the flank of the attackers and began to roll it up.

Lady Ashmont was on the east flank of her people, fighting hard against an opponent. She was concentrating on what she was doing because she was being hard pressed. She was exhausted from the fighting that she'd been doing and was concerned that she was going to fail soon. She was shocked when her opponent grunted and fell from his saddle as one of the King's troopers stabbed him in the back as he rode by on his way towards the attacker's field leader. She looked around quickly to see what was happening and recognized that the monsters were now being dealt with, having shrunk back to normal size. She knew that that meant that Thelwyn had found the enemy sorcerer and dealt with him. She felt a surge of joy as she urged her people to continue to fight any attackers. She saw that a great deal of the attacking army was retreating.

Thelwyn saw that she wouldn't be able to do too much to help the Barcless troops fighting the remaining attackers at the headquarters site. She really couldn't take on the mounted men very efficiently and the shock of the sorcerer's death seemed to have ended the agreement between Darglype and Murgald. It looked to her as though the defenders would be able to take care of the rest of the battle without her and the wolves so she howled orders of retreat to the wolves. The wolves reluctantly ceased their worrying of the attackers and bounded back towards her. She quickly thanked them and told them that she would come back to see to any of their wounds and to arrange for treatment of the injured once she had time to check on her friends. She changed to her wolf form, allowed the Pixies to mount her back and ran as fast as she could towards the main battlefield so that she could see what had happened to her friends.

Thank you for reading this book.

Please rate this book. I would like to remind you that all independent authors rely on you as the reader to help them to spread the word about their works and you can help them continue to publish by letting your friends know about them or rating them on the different websites. If you want to read about further adventures of Thelwyn and Princess Aurolla, rating this story so that others also enjoy it will help that happen. If you wish to contact me, you may send an email to sjarcwyk@mail.com or look me up on GoodReads.

You may also like

Adventures In Princess Aurolla's Castle

www.ingramcontent.com/pod-product-compliance
Lightning Source LLC
Chambersburg PA
CBHW021958190626
46808CB00017B/2437